T0332145

Praise for *Dreadful Young Ladies and Other Stories*

"[A] playful, witchy collection of addictive tales."

—*O, The Oprah Magazine*

"Finds the author at her most poignant and surprising."

—*Entertainment Weekly*

"Haunting and beautifully told . . . Each story is written in intensely poetic language that can exult or disturb, sometimes within the same sentence, and evokes a dreamlike, enchanted mood that lingers in the reader's mind. These tales are made to be reread and savored." —*Publishers Weekly*, starred review

"Barnhill's exquisite prose leads readers down many fantastical roads . . . The themes of love, grief, power, and hope tie the individual stories together in a masterly way."

—*Library Journal*, starred review

"Exquisite . . . Perfect for readers of the weird and fantastically wonderful." —*School Library Journal*

"Newbery medalist Barnhill dazzles in her short story collection for adults . . . Fantasy readers—especially fans of Neil Gaiman or even Kelly Link—will appreciate this spellbinding collection."

—*Booklist*

DREADFUL YOUNG LADIES

AND OTHER STORIES

DREADFUL YOUNG LADIES

AND OTHER STORIES

KELLY BARNHILL

ALGONQUIN BOOKS OF CHAPEL HILL
2019

Published by
Algonquin Books of Chapel Hill
Post Office Box 2225
Chapel Hill, North Carolina 27515-2225

a division of
Workman Publishing
225 Varick Street
New York, New York 10014

First paperback edition, Algonquin Books of Chapel Hill, March 2019.
Originally published in hardcover by Algonquin Books of Chapel Hill in February 2018.
Printed in the United States of America.
Published simultaneously in Canada by Thomas Allen & Son Limited.
Design by Carla Weise.

Grateful acknowledgment is made to the following, where these stories were first
published: to Tor.com for "Mrs. Sorensen and the Sasquatch"; to *Clockwork Phoenix*
(Mythic Delirium Books) for "Open the Door and the Light Pours Through"; to
Sybil's Garage (Senses Five Press) for "The Dead Boy's Last Poem"; to *Shimmer*
for "Dreadful Young Ladies"; to *Clarkesworld* for "The Taxidermist's Other
Wife"; to *Fast Ships, Black Sails* (Night Shade Books) for "Elegy to Gabrielle—
Patron Saint of Healers, Whores, and Righteous Thieves"; to *Fantasy* for "Notes
on the Untimely Death of Ronia Drake"; to *Lightspeed* for "The Insect and the
Astronomer: A Love Story"; and to PS Publishing for "The Unlicensed Magician."

Library of Congress Cataloging-in-Publication Data

Names: Barnhill, Kelly Regan, author.
Title: Dreadful young ladies and other stories / Kelly Barnhill.
Description: First edition. | Chapel Hill, North Carolina :
Algonquin Books of Chapel Hill, 2018.
Identifiers: LCCN 2017039839 (print) | LCCN 2017042621 (ebook) |
ISBN 9781616208301 (ebook) | ISBN 9781616207977 (hardcover : alk. paper)
Subjects: | LCGFT: Short stories. | Fantasy fiction.
Classification: LCC PS3602.A777134 (ebook) |
LCC PS3602.A777134 A6 2018 (print) | DDC 813/.6—dc23
LC record available at https://lccn.loc.gov/2017039839

ISBN 978-1-61620-924-7 (PB)

10 9 8 7 6 5 4 3 2 1

First Paperback Edition

To the Ladies of the Sewing Guild
(and you know who you are)
this volume is lovingly dedicated.

Table of Contents

DREADFUL YOUNG LADIES

AND OTHER STORIES

MRS. SORENSEN
and the
SASQUATCH

++++++|+||++

THE DAY SHE BURIED HER HUSBAND—A GOOD MAN, BY ALL
accounts, though shy, not given to drink or foolishness; not
one for speeding tickets or illegal parking or cheating on his taxes;
not one for carousing at the county fair, or tomcatting with the
other men from the glass factory; which is to say, he was utterly
unknown in town: a cipher; a cold, blank space—Agnes Sorensen
arrived at the front steps of Our Lady of the Snows. The priest was
waiting for her at the open door. The air was sweet and wet with
autumn rot, and though it had rained earlier, the day was starting
to brighten, and would surely be lovely in an hour or two. Mrs.
Sorensen greeted the priest with a sad smile. She wore a smart
black hat, sensible black shoes, and a black silk shirt belted into a
slim crepe skirt. Two little white mice peeked out of her left breast
pocket—two tiny shocks of fur with pink, quivering noses and
red, red tongues.

The priest, an old fellow by the name of Laurence, took her
hands and gave a gentle squeeze. He was surprised by the mice.
The mice, on the other hand, were not at all surprised to see *him*.
They inclined their noses a little farther over the lip of the shirt

pocket, to get a better look. Their whiskers were as pale and bright as sunbeams. They looked at one another and turned in unison toward the face of the old priest. And though he knew it was impossible, it seemed to Father Laurence that the mice were *smiling* at him. He swallowed.

"Mrs. Sorensen," he said, clearing his throat.

"Mmm?" she said, looking at her watch. She glanced over her shoulder and whistled. A very large dog rounded the tall hedge, followed by an almost-as-large raccoon and a perfectly tiny cat.

"We can't—" but his voice failed him.

"Have the flowers arrived, Father?" Mrs. Sorensen asked pleasantly as the three animals mounted the stairs and approached the door.

"Well, n-no . . ." the priest stammered. "I mean, yes, they have. Three very large boxes. But I must say, Mrs. Sorensen—"

"Marvelous. Pardon me." And she walked inside. "Hold the door open for my helpers, would you? Thank you, Father." Her voice was all brisk assurance. It was a voice that required a yes. She left a lingering scent of pine sap and lilac and woodland musk in her wake. Father Laurence felt dizzy.

"Of course," the priest said, as dog, raccoon, and cat passed him by, a sort of deliberation and gravitas about their bearing, as though they were part of a procession that the priest, himself, had rudely interrupted. He would have said something, of course he would have. But these animals had—well, he could hardly explain it. A sobriety of face and a propriety of demeanor. He let them by. He nodded his head to each one as they crossed the threshold of the church. It astonished him. He gave a quick glance up and down the quiet street to reassure himself that he remained unobserved. The last thing he needed was to have the Parish Council fussing at him again.

(This was a near-constant worry. The Parish Council consisted of a trio of widowed sisters who, since they no longer had their prominent-enough husbands' careers to manage, and whose grown children had all taken respectable jobs in far-off cities, now had little else to do all day than to fuss and preen over their beloved church. And woe indeed to anyone who got in their way. They worried after the building and squawked at parishioners and pecked and pecked at the priest's every move. It seemed to Father Laurence that their life's purpose now was to make him feel as though they were in the midst of slowly stoning him to death using only popcorn and lost buttons and bits of yarn. Three times that week he had found himself in the crosshairs of the sisters' ire—and it was only Wednesday.)

He was safe for now. He rubbed his ever-loosening jowls and cleared his throat. Seeing no one there (except for a family of rabbits that was, *en masse*, emerging from under the row of box elders), Father Laurence felt a sudden, inexplicable, and unbridled surge of joy—to which he responded with a quick clench of his fists and a swallowed yes. He nearly bounced.

"Are you coming?" Mrs. Sorensen called from inside the Sanctuary.

"Yes, yes," he said with a sputter. "Of course." But he paused anyway. A young buck came clipping down the road. Not uncommon in these parts, but the priest thought it odd that the animal came to a halt right in front of the church and turned his face upward as though he was regarding the stained-glass window. *Can deer see color?* Father Laurence didn't know. The deer didn't move. It was a young thing—its antlers were hardly bigger than German pretzels and its haunches were sleek, muscular and supple. It blinked its large, damp eyes and flared its nostrils. The priest paused, as though waiting for the buck to say something.

Deer don't speak, he told himself. *You're being ridiculous.* Two hawks fluttered down and perched on the handrail, while a—*dear God. Was that an otter?* Father Laurence shook his head, adjusted the flap of belly hanging uncomfortably over his belt, and slumped inside.

The mourners arrived two hours later and arranged themselves silently into their pews. It was a thin crowd. There was the required representative from the glass factory. A low-level supervisor. Mr. Sorensen was not important enough, apparently, to warrant a mourner from an upper-level managerial position, and was certainly not grand enough for the owner himself to drive up from Chicago and pay his respects.

The priest bristled at this. *The man died at work,* he thought. *Surely . . .*

He shook his head and busied himself with the last-minute preparations. The pretty widow walked with cool assurance from station to station, making sure everything was just so. The mourners, the priest noticed, were mostly men. This stood to reason as most of Mr. Sorensen's coworkers were men as well. Still, he noticed that several of them had removed their wedding rings, or had thought to insert a jaunty handkerchief in their coat pockets (in what could only be described as *non-funeral colors*), or had applied hair gel or mustache oil or aftershave. The whole church reeked of men on the prowl. Mrs. Sorensen didn't seem to notice, but that was beside the point. The priest folded his arms and gave a hard look at the backs of their heads.

Really, he thought. But then the widow walked into a brightly colored beam of stained-glass sunlight, and he felt his heart lift and his cheeks flush and his breathing quicken and thin. *There are people*, he thought, *who are easy to love. And that is that.*

Mrs. Sorensen had done a beautiful job with the flowers, creating arrangements at each window in perfect, dioramic scenes. In the window depicting the story of the child Jesus and the clay birds that he magicked into feathers and wings and flight, for example, her figure of Jesus was composed of corn husk, ivy, and dried rose petals. The clay birds she had made with homemade dough, and had affixed them to warbled bits of wire. The birds bobbed and weaved unsteadily, as though only just learning how to spread their wings. And her rendition of Daniel in the lion's den was so harrowing in its realism, so brutally *present*, that people had to avert their eyes. She even made a diorama of the day she and her husband met—a man with a broken leg at the bottom of a gully in the middle of a flowery forest; a woman with a broken heart wandering alone, happening by, and binding his wounds. And how real they were! The visceral pain on his face, the sorrow hanging over her body like a cloud. The quickening of the heart at that first, tender touch. This is how love can begin—an act of kindness.

7

The men in the congregation stared for a long time at that display. They shook their heads and muttered, "Lucky bastard."

Father Laurence, in his vestments, intoned the Mass with all of the feeling he could muster, his face weighted somberly with the loss of a man cut down too soon. (Though not, it should be noted, with any actual grief. After all, the priest hardly knew the man. No one did. Still, fifty-eight is too young to die. Assuming Mr. Sorensen was fifty-eight. In truth, the priest had no idea.) Mrs. Sorensen sat in the front row, straight backed, her delicate face composed, her head floating atop her neck as though it were being pulled upward by a string. She held her chin at a slight tilt to the left. She made eye contact with the priest and gave an encouraging smile.

It is difficult, he realized later, to give a homily when there is a raccoon in the church. And a very large dog. And a cat. Though he couldn't see them—they had made themselves scarce before the parishioners arrived—he still *knew they were there*. And it unnerved him.

The white mice squirmed in Mrs. Sorensen's pocket. They peeked and retreated again and again. Father Laurence tripped on his words. He forgot what he was going to say. He forgot Mr. Sorensen's name. He remembered the large, damp eyes of the buck outside. *Did he want to come in?* Father Laurence wondered. And then: *Don't be ridiculous. Deer don't go to church!* But neither, he reasoned with himself, did raccoons. *But there was one here somewhere, wasn't there?* So.

Father Laurence mumbled and wandered. He started singing the wrong song. The organist grumbled in his direction. The

Parish Council, who never missed a funeral if they could help it, sat in the back and twittered. They held their programs over their faces and peered over the rim of the paper with hard, glittering eyes. Father Laurence found himself singing "O God, Your Creatures Fill the Earth," though it was not on the program and the organist was unable to play the accompaniment.

"*Your creatures live in every land,*" he sang lustily. "*They fill the sky and sea. O Lord, you give us your command, to love them tenderly.*"

Mrs. Sorensen closed her eyes and smiled. And outside, a hawk opened its throat and screeched—the lingering note landing in harmony with the final bar.

That was October.

Father Laurence did not visit the widow right away. He'd wait. Let her grieve. The last thing she needed was an old duffer hanging around her kitchen. Besides, he knew that the insufferable sisters on the Parish Council and their allies on the Improvement League and the Quilters Alliance and the Friends of the Library and the Homebound Helpers would be, even now, fluttering toward that house, descending like a cloud.

In the meantime, the entire town buzzed with the news of the recent Sasquatch sightings—only here and there, and not entirely credible, but the fact of the sightings at all was significant. There hadn't been any in the entire county for the last thirty years—not since one was reported standing outside of the only hotel in town for hours and hours on a cold, November night.

People still talked about it.

The moon was full and the winds raged. The Sasquatch slipped in and out of shadow. It raised its long arms toward the topmost windows, tilted its head back, and opened its throat. The mournful sound it made—part howl, part moan, part long, sad song—was something that people in town still whispered about, now thirty years later. It was the longest time anyone could ever remember a Sasquatch standing in one place. Normally, they were slippery things. Elusive. A flash at the corner of the eye. But here it stood, bold as brass, spilling its guts to whoever would listen. Unfortunately, no one spoke Sasquatch.

It had been, if Father Laurence recalled correctly, Mr. and Mrs. Sorensen's wedding night. They were asleep in that same hotel.

Sasquatch sightings were fairly common back then, but they ceased after the hotel incident. No one mentioned it right away— it's not like the Sasquatch put a notice in the paper. But after a while people realized the Sasquatch were gone—just gone.

And now, apparently, they were back. Or, at least one was, anyway.

Barney Korman said he saw one picking its way across the north end of the bog, right outside the wildlife preserve. Ernesta Koonig said there was a huge, shaggy something helping itself to the best crop of Cortland apples that her orchard had ever produced. Bernie Larsen said he saw one running off with one of his lambs. There were stick structures on Cassandra Gordon's hunting land. And the ghostly sound of tree knocking at night.

Eimon Lomas stopped by and asked if there was an ecclesiastic precedent allowing for the baptism of a Bigfoot.

Father Laurence said no.

"Seems a shame, though, don't it?" asked Eimon, running his tongue over his remaining teeth.

"Never thought about it before," Father Laurence said. But that was a lie, and he knew it. Agnes Sorensen had asked him the exact same question, a little more than thirty years earlier.

And his answer made her cry.

On Halloween, in an effort to avoid the Parish Council and their incessant harping on the subject of holidays—godless or otherwise—and to avoid the flurry of phone calls and visits and Post-it notes and emails and faxes and, once, horrifyingly, an intervention ("Is it the costumes, Father," the eldest of the sisters asked pointedly, "or the unsupervised visits from children, that makes you so unwilling to take a stand on the effects of Satanism through Halloween-worship?" They folded their hands and waited. "Or perhaps," the youngest added, "it's a sugar addiction."), Father Laurence decided to pay Mrs. Sorensen a visit.

Three weeks had passed, after all, since the death of her husband, and the widow's freezer and pantry were surely stocked with the remains of the frozen casseroles, and lasagnas, and brown-up rolls, and mason jars filled with homemade chili and chicken soup and wild rice stew and beef consommé. Surely the bustling and cheeping flocks of women who descend upon houses of tragedy had by now migrated away, leaving the lovely Mrs. Sorensen alone, and quiet, and in need of company.

Besides. Wild rice stew (especially if it came from the Larsen home) didn't sound half bad on a cold Halloween night.

The Sorensen farm—once the largest tract in the county—was nothing more than a hobby farm now. Mr. Sorensen had neither the aptitude nor the inclination for farming, so his wife had convinced him to cede his birthright to the Nature Conservancy, retaining a small acreage to allow her to maintain a good-sized orchard and berry farm. Mrs. Sorensen ran a small business in which she made small-batch hard ciders, berry wines, and fine jams. Father Laurence couldn't imagine that her income could sustain her for long, but perhaps Mr. Sorensen had been well insured.

He knocked on the door.

The house erupted with animal sounds. Wet noses pressed at the window and sharp claws worried at the door. The house barked, screeched, groaned, hissed, snuffled, and whined. Father Laurence took a step backward. An owl peered through the transom window, its pale gold eyes unblinking. The priest cleared his throat.

"Mrs. Sorensen?"

A throaty gurgle from indoors.

"Agnes?"

Father Laurence had known Agnes Sorensen since her girlhood (her last name was Dryleesker then)—she was the little girl down the road, with a large, arthritic goose under one arm and a bull snake curled around the other. He would see her playing in front of her house at the end of the dead-end street when he came home for the summers during seminary.

"An odd family," his mother used to say, with a definitive shake of her head. "And that girl is the oddest of them all."

Laurence didn't think so then, and he certainly didn't think so now.

Agnes, in her knee socks and mary janes, in the A-line dresses her mother had made from old curtains, with her pigtails pale as stars, had an affinity with animals. In the old barn in their back-yard, she housed the creatures that she had found, as well as those who had traveled long distances to be near her. A hedgehog with a missing foot, a blind weasel, a six-legged frog, a neurotic wren, a dog whose eardrums had popped like balloons when he wandered too near a TNT explosion on his owner's farm. Agnes once came home with a wolf cub, but her father wouldn't allow her to keep it. She had animals waiting for her by the back door each morning, animals who would accompany her on her way to school, animals who helped her with her chores, animals who sat on her lap as she did her homework, and animals who curled up on her bed when she slept.

But then she got married. To Mr. Sorensen—a good man and kind. And he needed her. But he was allergic. So their house was empty.

Mr. Sorensen was also, Father Laurence learned from the con-fessional booth, infertile.

Agnes came to confession only once a year, and she rarely spoke during her time in the booth. Most of the time she would sit, sigh, and breathe in the dark. The booth was anonymous in theory, but Mrs. Sorensen had a smell about her—crushed herbs and apple cider and pine sap and grass—that Father Laurence could identify from across the room. Her silence was profound and nuanced. Like the silence of a pine forest on a windless summer day. It creaked and rustled. It warmed the blood. Father Laurence would find himself fingering his collar—now terribly tight—and mopping his brow with his hands.

He worried for Mrs. Sorensen. She was young and vibrant and terribly *alive*. And yet. She was in stasis somehow. She didn't seem to age. She had none of the spark she had had as a child. It was as though her soul was hibernating.

There was a time, maybe fifteen years ago, when Mrs. Sorensen closed the door of the booth behind her and sat for ten minutes in the dark while the priest waited. Finally, she spoke in the darkness. Not a prayer. Indeed, Father Laurence didn't know what it was.

"When a female wolverine is ready to breed," Mrs. Sorensen said in the faceless dark. "She spends weeks tracking down potential mates, and weeks separating the candidates. She stalks her unknowing suitors, monitoring their habits, assessing their skills as hunters and trackers. Evaluating their abilities in a fight—do they prefer the tooth or the claw? Are they brave to the point of stupidity? Do they run when danger is imminent? Do they push themselves to greatness?"

Father Laurence cleared his throat. "Have you forgotten the prayer, my child?" he said, his voice a timid whine.

Mrs. Sorensen ignored him. "She does not do this for protection or need. Her mate will be useful for all of two minutes. Then she will never see him again. He will not protect his brood or defend his lover. He will be chosen, hired, *used*. He will not be loved. His entire purpose is to produce an offspring that will eventually leave its mother; she needs a child that will *live*."

"*Bless me, Father, for I have sinned,*" prompted Father Laurence. "That's how people usually—"

"Now, in the case of a black bear, when the female becomes aware of the new life in her womb, she makes special consideration to the construction of the den. She is at risk, and she knows it. Pheromones announcing her condition leak from every pore. Her footsteps reek pregnant. Her urine blinks like road signs. Her fertility hangs around her body like a cloud."

"Agnes—"

"When she digs her den, she moves more than a ton of rock and soil. She designs the space specially to provide a small mouth that she can stopper up with her back if she needs to."

"Agnes—"

"She will grow in the dark, and birth in the dark, and suckle her babies in the feminine funk of that tiny space—smelling of mother and baby, and sweat and blood, and milk and breathing and warm earth—hiding under the thick protection of snow." Her voice caught. She hiccupped.

"Agnes—"

"I thought I was anonymous."

"And you are. I call all my confessionals Agnes."

She laughed in the dark.

"I am asleep, Father. I have been asleep for—ever so long. My arms are weak and my breasts are dry and there is a cold dark space within me that smells of nothing." She sat still for a moment or two. Then: "I love my husband."

"I know, child," he whispered.

"I love him desperately."

What she wanted to say, the priest knew, was "I love him, but . . ." But she didn't. She said nothing else. After another moment's silence, she opened the door, stepped into the light, and vanished.

Father Laurence had no doubt that Agnes Sorensen loved her husband, and that she missed him. They had been married for thirty years, after all. She cared for him and tended to him every day. His death was sudden. And certainly one must grieve in one's own way. Still, the sheer number of animals in the house was a cause for concern. The list of possible psychiatric disorders alone was nearly endless.

The priest walked out to the apple barn but no one was there. Just the impossibly sweet smell of cider. It nearly knocked Father Laurence to his knees. He closed his eyes, and remembered picking apples with one of the girls at school when he was a child—sticky fingers, sticky mouths, sticky necks, and sticky trousers. He remembered her long hair and her black eyes, and the way they fell from the lowest tree branch—a tangle of arms and legs and torsos. The crush of grass underneath. Her freckles next to his eyelashes, his front tooth chipping against hers (after all those years, the chip was still there), the smell of her breath like honey and wine and growing wheat. So strong was this memory, and so radically pleasant, that Father Laurence felt weak, and shivery. There was a cot in the barn—he didn't know what it was there for—and he lay upon it.

It smelled of woodland musk and pine. It was covered in hair. In his dream he was barefoot and lanky and young. He was on the prowl. He was hungry. He was longing for something he could not name. Something that had no words (or perhaps he had no words; or perhaps words no longer existed). He was watching Agnes Sorensen through a curtain of green, green leaves. She carried a heaping basket of apples. A checkered shirt. Apple-stained dungarees. A bandana covering her hair. Wellington boots up to her knees, each footfall sinking deep into the warm, sweet mud.

When Father Laurence woke, it was fully dark. (Was someone watching? *Surely not.*) He got up off the cot, brushed the hair from his coat and trousers. His body ached and he felt curiously empty—as though he had been somehow scooped out. He walked out into the moonlit yard. Mrs. Sorensen wasn't in the barn. She wasn't in the yard. She wasn't in the house, either. (Was that a shape in the bushes? Were those eyes? *Heavens, what am I thinking?*) The house had been emptied of its animal sounds, and emptied of its light and smell and being. It was quiet. He knocked. No one answered. He walked over to the car.

There were footprints, he saw, in the mud alongside the driveway. Wellington boots sunk deep into the mud and dried along the edges. And another set, just alongside. Bare feet—a man's, presumably. But very, very large.

For Agnes Sorensen, Thanksgiving passed with several invitations to take the celebratory meal with neighbors or former coworkers or friends, who all would have welcomed her with open arms, but these were all denied.

She said simply that she would enjoy the quiet. But surely that made no sense! There had been no one on earth quieter than Mr. Sorensen. The man had hardly spoken.

And so her neighbors carved their turkeys and their hams, they sliced pie and drank to one another's health, but their minds wandered to the pretty widow with hair like starlight, her straight back, her slim skirts and smart belts, and her crisp footsteps when she walked. People remembered her lingering smell—the forest and the blooming meadow and some kind of animal musk. Something that clung to the nose and pricked at the skin and set the mouth watering. And they masked their longing with another helping of yams.

(Only the three sisters on the Parish Council didn't see what the big fuss was about. They had always thought she was plain.)

Randall Jergen—not the worst drunkard in town, but well on his way to becoming so—claimed that, when he stumbled past the Sorensen house by mistake, he saw the widow seated at the head of the well-laid table, heaped to the point of breaking with boiled potatoes and candied squash and roasted vegetables of every type and description. Each chair was filled, not with relatives or friends or even acquaintances, but with animals. He reported two dogs, one raccoon, one porcupine, one lynx, and an odd-looking bear sitting opposite the pretty widow. A bear who grasped its wine goblet and held it aloft to the smiling Mrs. Sorensen, who raised her own glass in response.

The Insufferable Sisters investigated. They found no evidence of feasting. And while they *did* see the dogs, the tiny cat, the raccoon, the lynx, and the porcupine, they saw no sign of a wine-drinking bear. Which, they told themselves, they needed to know whether or not was true. Drunken bears, after all, were a community safety hazard. They reported to the stylists at the Clip 'n' Curl that Mr. Jergen was, as usual, full of hogwash. By evening, the whole town knew. And the matter was settled.

For a little while.

By Christmas, there had been no fewer than twenty-seven reports of Sasquatch sightings near, or around, or on the Sorensen farm. Two people claimed to have seen a Sasquatch wearing a seed cap with the glass factory's logo on it, and one swore that it was wearing Mr. Sorensen's old coat. The sheriff, two deputies, the game manager at the local private wildlife refuge, and three representatives from the Department of Natural Resources all paid the widow a visit. They all left the farm looking dejected. Mrs. Sorensen was not, apparently, available for drinks, or dinner, or dancing. She gave their questions crisp answers that could have meant anything. She watched them go with a vague smile on her pale lips.

The Insufferable Sisters investigated as well. They looked for footprints and boot prints. They looked for discarded hats and thrown-off coats. They hunted for evidence of possible suitors. They interviewed witnesses. They found nothing.

By late January, neighbors noticed that Mrs. Sorensen had begun to walk with a lightness—despite the parka and the heavy boots, despite the sheepskin mitts and the felted scarf, her feet floated atop the surface of the snow, and her skin sparkled, even on the most leaden of days.

Bachelors and widowers (and, if honesty prevails, several uncomfortably married men as well) still opened doors for the pretty widow, still tipped their hats in her direction, still offered to carry her groceries or see to her barn's roof, or check to make sure her pipes weren't in danger of freezing (this last one was often said suggestively, and almost always returned with a definitive slap). The Insufferable Sisters arrived, unannounced, at the Sorensen farm. They came laden with hotdish and ambrosia salad and bars of every type and description. They sat the poor widow down, put the kettle on, and tapped their long, red talons on the well-oiled wood of the ancient farm table.

"Well?" said Mrs. Ostergaard, the eldest of the sisters.

"Oh," said Mrs. Sorensen, her cheeks flushing to high color. "The tea is in the top drawer of the far right cabinet." Her eyes slid to the window, where the snowflakes fell in thick curtains, blurring the blanketed yard, and obscuring the dense thicket of scrub and saplings on the other side of the gully. The corners of her lips buzzed with—*something*. Mrs. Ostergaard couldn't tell. And it infuriated her.

Mrs. Lentz, the youngest of the sisters, and Mrs. Ferris, the middle, served the lunch, arranging the food in sensibly sized mounds, each one slick and glistening. They piled the bars on pretty plates and put real cream in the pitcher and steaming tea in the pot. They sat, sighed, smiled, and interrogated the pretty widow. She answered questions and nodded serenely, but every time there was a lull in the conversation (and there were many), her eyes would insinuate themselves toward the window again, and a deepening blush would spread down her throat and edge into the opening of her blouse.

The dogs lounged on the window seat and the raccoon picked at its bowl on the floor of the mudroom. Three cats snaked through the legs of the three sisters, with their backs an insistent arch, their rumps requiring a rub, and all the while an aggressive purr rattling the air around them.

"Nice kitty," Mrs. Ostergaard said, giving one cat a pat on the head.

The cat hissed.

The sisters left in the snow.

"Be careful," Mrs. Sorensen said as she stood in the doorway, straight backed and inscrutable as polished wood. "It's coming down all right." Her eyes flicked toward the back of the yard, a flushed smile on her lips. Mrs. Ostergaard whipped around and glared through the thick tangle of snow.

A figure.

Dark.

Fast.

And then it was gone. Snowflakes clung to her eyelashes and forehead. Cold drops of water crowded her eyes. She shook her head and peered into the chaos of white. Nothing was there.

The sisters piled into their Volvo and eased onto the road, a dense, blinding cloud swirling in their minds.

The next day they called a meeting with Father Laurence. Father Laurence withstood the indignities of their fussing in relative silence, the scent of apples, after all this time, still clinging sweetly in his nostrils.

The day after that, they called a second meeting, this time of the priest, the mayor, the physician, the dogcatcher, and a large-animal veterinarian. They were all men, these officials and professionals that the sisters assembled, and all were seated on folding chairs. The sisters stood over them like prison guards. The men hung on to their cold metal chairs for dear life. They said yes to everything.

Three days later, Arnold Fiske—teetotaler since the day he was born—nearly ran Mrs. Sorensen over with his Buick. It was a warm night for February, and the road was clear of any snow or ice. The sun had only just gone down and the sky was a livid orange. On either side of the road, the frozen bog stretched outward, as big as the world. Indeed, it was the bog that distracted Arnold Fiske from the primary task of driving. His eyes lingered on the dappled browns and grays and whites, on the slim torsos of the quaking aspens and river birches and Norway pines fluttering like flags on the occasional hillock. They rested on the fluctuations of color on the snow—orange dappling to pink fading to ashy blue. He returned his gaze to the road only just in time. He saw the face of Mrs. Sorensen (*that beautiful face!*) lit in the beam of his headlights. And something *else* too. A hulk of a figure. Like a man. But more than a man. And no face at all.

Arnold Fiske swerved. Mrs. Sorensen screamed. And from somewhere—the frozen bog, the fading sky, the aggressively straight road, or deep inside Arnold Fiske himself—came a ragged, primal howl. It shook the glass and sucked away the air and shattered his bones in his body. His car squealed and spun. Mrs. Sorensen was pulled out of the car's path by . . . well, by *something.* And then everything was quiet.

Arnold Fiske got out of the car, breathing heavily. His dyspepsia burned bright as road flares. He pressed his left hand to the bottom rim of his rib cage and grimaced. "Oh my god," he gasped. "Agnes? Agnes Sorensen! Are you all right?" He rounded the broad prow of the Buick, saw the horror on the other side of the car, and fell to his knees, scrambling backward with a strangled cry.

There was Agnes Sorensen—her long down coat bunched up around her middle, her hood thrown off, and her starlight-colored hair yanked free of its bun and rippling toward the ground. She was curled in the long arms of a man. A man covered in hair.

Not a man.

Her voice was calm. Her hands were on the man's face. No. Not a man's face. And not a face either. It was a thicket of fur and teeth and red, glowing eyes. Arnold Fiske's breath came in hot, sharp bursts.

"What is that thing?" he choked. He could barely breathe. His chest hurt. He pressed his hands to his heart to make sure it wasn't going out on him. The last thing he needed was to have a heart attack in the presence of a . . . *well.* He couldn't say. He couldn't even *think* it.

Mrs. Sorensen didn't notice.

Her voice was a smooth lilt, a lullaby, a gentle insistence. A lover's voice. "I'm all right," she soothed. "You see? I'm here. I'm not hurt. Everything is fine. Everything is *wonderful.*"

The man (*not a man*) bowed its head onto Agnes Sorensen's chest. It sighed and snuffled. It cradled her body in its great, shaggy arms and rocked her back and forth. It made a series of sounds—part rumble, part hiccup, part gulping sob.

My god, Arnold Fiske thought. *It's crying.*

He sat up. Then stood up and took a step away. Arnold shook his head. He tried to hold his breath, but small bursts still erupted, unbidden, from his throat, as though his soul and his fear and his sorrow were all escaping in sighs. He looked at the widow and her . . . *erm* . . . companion, feeling suddenly and inexplicably calm. And inert. As though he had been, without warning, suddenly hollowed out. Like a squash shell before it's shoved into the oven.

He cleared his throat. "Would you," he said. And faltered. He started again. "Would you and your, um, *friend* . . ." He paused again. Wrinkled his brow. Muscled through. "Need a ride?"

Mrs. Sorensen smiled and wrapped her arms around the Sasquatch's neck.

Because that, Arnold Fiske realized, *is what I'm seeing. A Sasquatch. After all these years. Well. My stars.*

"No, thank you, Mr. Fiske," Agnes Sorensen said, extricating herself from the Sasquatch's arms and helping it to its feet. "The night is still fine, and the stars are just coming out. And they say the auroras will be burning bright later on. I may stay out all night."

And with that, she and the Sasquatch walked away, hands held, as though it was the most normal thing in the world. And perhaps it was.

In any case, Arnold Fiske couldn't shut up about it.

By noon the next day, the whole town knew. And the whole town talked about it.

A Sasquatch. The widow and a Sasquatch. Ain't that just a kick in the pants.

Two days later, the pair had been spotted in public, walking along the railroad tracks.

And again, picking their way across the bog.

And again, standing in the back of the crowd, at a liquidation auction. The Sasquatch sometimes wore Mr. Sorensen's old seed hat and boots (he had cut out holes for his large, flexible toes), and sometimes wore the dead man's scarf. But never his pants. Not even some kind of shorts. Or, dear god, at least some swimming trunks. The Sasquatch was in possession, thankfully, of a bulbous thicket of fur, concealing the area of concern, but everyone knew *what was behind that fur*, and they knew it would only take a stiff breeze, or a sudden movement, or perhaps the presence of a female Sasquatch to cause a, how would you say—*a shaking of the bushes*, as it were. Or a parting of the weeds. People kept their eyes averted, just to be safe.

The sisters were enraged.

Mrs. Sorensen was spotted walking with a Sasquatch past the statues and artistic sculptures of Armistice Park.

("Children play at that park!" howled the sisters.)

They called Father Laurence at home nineteen times, and left nineteen messages with varying levels of vitriol. *Fool of a priest* was a phrase they used. And *useless*.

Father Laurence, for his part, went to the woods, alone. He walked the same paths he followed in his boyhood. He remembered the rustle of ravens' wings, and the silent pounce of an owl, and the snuffling of bears, and the howling of wolves, and the scamper of rabbits, and the slurping of moose. He remembered something else too. A large, dark figure in the densest places of the wood and the tangled thickets of the bog. A pair of bright eyes and sharp teeth and a long, loose-limbed, lumbering gait that went like a shot over the prairie.

He had been eleven years old when he last saw a Sasquatch. And now all he had to do was pick up the phone and invite Mrs. Sorensen over for dinner. *Huh*, he thought. *Imagine that.*

The meal, though quiet, was pleasant enough. The Sasquatch brought a bowl of wildflowers, which the priest ate. They were delicious.

Two weeks later, Mrs. Sorensen brought her Sasquatch to church. She brought her other animals too—her one-eyed hedgehog and her broken-winged hawk and her tiny cat and her raccoon and her three-legged dog and her infant cougar, curled up and fast asleep on her lap. The family arrived early, and sat in the front row, Mrs. Sorensen and the Sasquatch in the middle, and the rest of the brood stretching on either side. Each one sat as straight backed as was possible with the particulars of their physiology, and each one was silent and solemn. The Sasquatch wore nothing other than Mr. Sorensen's father's old fedora hat, which was perched at a bit of a saucy angle. It held

Mrs. Sorensen's hand in its great, left paw and closed its large, bright eyes.

Father Laurence did his pre-Mass preparations and ministrations with the sacristy door locked. The sisters hovered at the other side, pecking at the door and squawking their complaints. Father Laurence was oblivious. He was a great admirer of the inventor of earplugs, and made it a habit to stash an emergency set wherever he might find the need to surreptitiously insert a pair at a moment's notice—at his desk, at the podium, in his car, in the confessional, and in the sacristy.

"*A sacrilege!*" Mrs. Ostergaard hissed.

"*Do something!*" came Mrs. Lentz's strangled gasp.

"GET THAT DEER OUT OF THE CHURCH," Mrs. Ferris roared, followed by a chaos of hooves and snorting and the shouting of women and men, and the hooting of an owl and the cry of the peregrine and the snarl of—actually, Father Laurence wasn't sure if it was a coyote or a wolf.

Agnes Sorensen was too old to have children. Everyone knew that. But she had always wanted a family. And now she was so happy. Didn't she deserve to be happy? The sisters pecked and screeched. He imagined their fingers curling into talons, their imperious lips hardening to beaks. He imagined their appliquéd cardigans and their floral skirts rustling into feathers and wings. He imagined their bright beady eyes launching skyward with a wild, high *kee-yar* of a hawk on the hunt for something small and brown and wriggling.

The priest stood in the sacristy, his eyes closed. "*O God, your creatures fill the earth with wonder and delight,*" he sang.

"Doris," he heard Mrs. Ferris say. "Doris, do *not* approach that cougar. Doris, it isn't safe."

"And every living thing has worth and beauty in your sight."

"Oh, god. Not sheep. Anything but sheep. GET THOSE ANIMALS OUT OF HERE."

"So playful dolphins dance and swim; Your sheep bow down and graze."

"Father, get out here this minute. Six otters just came out of the bathroom. Six! And with rabies!"

"Your songbirds share a morning hymn, To offer you their praise."

There was a snarl, a screech, a cry of birds. A hiss and a bite and several rarely used swears from the mouths of the Parish Council. Father Laurence heard the clatter of their pastel heels and the *oof* of their round bottoms as they tripped on the stairs, and the howl of their voices as they ran down the street.

Several men waited at the mouth of the sanctuary, looking sadly at the pretty widow next to her hulking companion. The men reeked of mustache oil and pomade. Their shoulders slumped and their bellies bulged and their cheeks went slack.

"Eh, there, Father?" Ernie Jergen—Randall's sober brother—inclined his head toward the stoic family in the front row. "So that's it, then?" He cleared his throat. "She's . . . not single. She's *attached*, I mean."

Father Laurence clapped his hands on the shoulders of the men, sucked in his sagging belly as tight as he could.

"Yep," he said. "Seems so." Family is family, after all. The dead have buried the dead, and the living scramble and struggle as best they can. They press their shoulder against the rock and urge forward, even when all hope is lost. Agnes Sorensen was happy, and Agnes Sorensen was alive. *So be it.*

Father Laurence nodded at the organist to start the processional. The red-tailed hawk opened up its throat, and the young buck nosed the back of the priest's vestments. A pair of solemn eyes. A look of gravitas. Father Laurence wondered if he should step aside. If he was interrupting something. Two herons waited at the altar and a pine martin sat on the lectionary.

The organist sat under a pile of cats and made a valiant effort to pluck out the notes of the hymn. The congregation—both human and animal—opened their throats and began to sing, each in their own language, their own rhythm, their own time.

The song deepened and grew. It shook the walls and rattled the glass and set the light fixtures swinging. The congregation sang of the death of loved ones. A life eclipsed too soon. They sang of the waters of the bog and the creak of trees and of padded feet on soft forest trails. Of meals shared. And families built. Seeds in the ground. The screech of flight, the joy of a wriggling morsel in a sharp beak. The roar of pursuit and the gurgles of satiation. The murmur of nesting. The smell of a mate. The howl of birthing and the howl of loss, and howl and howl and howl.

Father Laurence processed in. Open-mouthed. A dark yodel tearing through his belly.

"*I am lost,*" he sang. "*And I am found. My body is naked in the muck. It has always been naked. I hope; I rage; I despair; I yearn; I long; I lust; I love. These strong hands that built, this strong back that carried, all must wither to dust. Indeed, I am dust already.*"

Mrs. Sorensen and her Sasquatch watched him process down

the aisle. They smiled at his song. He paused at their pew, let his hand linger on the rail. They reached out and touched the hem of his garment.

It was, people remarked later, the prettiest Mass they'd ever heard.

Mrs. Sorensen and her family left after Communion. They did not stay for rolls or coffee. They did not engage in conversation. They walked, together, into the bog. The tall grasses opened for a moment to allow them in and then closed like a curtain behind them. The world was birdsong and quaking mud and humming insects. The world was warm and wet and *green.*

They did not come back.

OPEN THE DOOR
AND THE
LIGHT POURS
THROUGH

++|+||+|||+||++

What he wrote:

My dearest Angela,

I have spent weeks dreading what we must do today, and even as I write this, I am not entirely convinced that it is right. We are, and have been, and will be for the foreseeable future, overrun with soldiers, which is to say, *our dear American guests*. (Which is worse, love, their public drunkenness, or their incessant leering?) Far better, my darling, that you should be far away from this nursery of convalescing men, and far from the multitudes of explosives that spin like vultures in the sky. London will be flattened before the year is up, if the rumors are true. How could we not be next?

My family, yes, are tiresome. The house, yes, is drafty and unpleasant. But the grounds are lovely. And if you cannot paint the sea, perhaps you could paint the wood. Or paint the sea from memory. Or paint me from memory. Or paint a memory of me. Dear god, my girl, but I shall miss you.

Ever yours,
John

What he did not:

John watched the train wait at the platform with Angela's pale, lovely, and petulant face framed by the greasy window. She would forgive him in time, of course. She always did. And the things that she did not know, she had no need to forgive.

The train shuddered, then rumbled, then slid out of sight. John stood still, watching the empty space where Angela's face had been, as though a shadow of his wife still hung in the air, like a ghost. Unaccountably, he shivered, and his skin was damp and icy cold. He breathed in, deeply, through his nose, luxuriating in the smell of oil and smoke, and faintly, he was certain, the smell of lavender and lilac that was ever his wife.

He missed her.

And yet, he did not.

Shivering again, he rubbed his arms briskly with his long, narrow hands. Hands that were meant to entertain; fingers that could coax music from reluctant instruments and moans from hesitant lovers. Hands that now produced documents—perfectly accurate, deadly quick—for his superiors in the RAF. His instruments lay untouched and abandoned in the music room. His lovers—well, that was a different story.

He turned and headed out of the station.

The day was fine again, the fifth in a string of fine days, with a warm sun set in a cool blue sky with a bracing wind coming up over the water. The promenade was inundated, as usual, with soldiers—big, strong-jawed Americans with their strange shimmer and stink, their arms weighted by simpering girls. There were English soldiers too, but by comparison, they were pale, worn, their edges fraying to dust and light. No spending money in their pockets. And they were without women.

He cut through the gardens into a street of row houses. A man stood framed between a doorway and a shuttered window, leaning against one of the houses. The door was red, the shutters green. The man was trim and pale and *clean*. He shimmered. John approached the man and leaned where he leaned. The man did not smell like lilacs or lavender. And yet. The bricks were warm and solid. They smelled of sun and oil and smoke. Without a word, the pair slipped inside the red door.

Later John would try to piece together the events of the day following his wife's departure, though for the life of him, he could not. He did not know how long he had leaned. He did not know how long he had been inside. A gentleman does not, after all, keep time in such circumstances. Nevertheless, over the course of the late morning and early afternoon, the wind increased and began to rattle at the windows and walls and door. Later, John heard moaning. And whether the moaning was the wind or the lover or something else entirely, he could never be sure.

Until he was. And by then, it was too late to do anything about it.

What she wrote:

Dear John,

It was a disaster, my love, and it was all your fault. When one travels, one should be rested and fresh, and I am neither (and I believe you know why, you naughty man). As you suggested, I had my sketchbook on my lap, and prepared myself to draw my last images of the sea before I was delivered to that den of stuffy rooms and tiresome conversation that is the place of your birth, but instead of a picture, all I have are the first intimations of wind before my hand drifted to the side of the page and I drifted to sleep. So the sketch is ruined, the painting is ruined, and you, dear husband, are dreadful.

To make it worse, I missed my stop at Westhoughton, as I was fast asleep, dreaming of you (my love, you wretch). The train stopped with a terrific jolt just outside of Bolton, in view of the station, though not pulled in. Whether it was a faulty engine, or that we simply ran out of fuel, I do not know. No one could say. In fact, no one spoke to me at all. The other passengers milled about outside of the train for some time, muttering, the lot of them, like idiots. I marched myself to the desk and attempted to ring the bell, which did not ring, and I immediately began to hate the war. Now in addition to sugar and jam and beef, we must, apparently, also give up bells.

And I the sea, and you your wife. What will be next?

The man did not turn away from his telephone as I tried to talk to him, and instead just jabbered endlessly about the train. What was there to say about the train? It didn't work, clearly, and it had, evidently, devoured my trunk.

A kindly man with a truck agreed to give me a lift, though he did not speak either, deaf and dumb, poor

man. But I listened as the station guard gave him directions to Westhoughton, and then repeated the directions,
not once but three times, to the poor, dear simpleton,
and then wrote them all out. So I sat next to him on the
cart as we drove. He never once glanced upon me—I
daresay he is little used to female companions, so I drew
his portrait for him and left it on the seat with a note. I
assume he liked it, because as I walked down the track to
your infernal mother's house, I could hear him weeping.
Weeping like a child.

As I wept *then*. On that terrible day. When we were
children. Do you remember? How strange that I should
think of that now!

Forever yours,

Angela

What she did not:

She should have been thinking of greetings and directions.
But as she walked down the well-trod track that led to the dark
hulk of her mother-in-law's family home, she barely noticed where
her feet touched the earth. For all she knew, they might not have
touched the earth at all. What she did notice was memory. A
memory so sharp it pricked her tongue. After a while, she tasted
blood. Or, she thought she did.

When Angela was a child, she and her parents and brother
spent their summers at John's family's home, as their parents were
all musicians and spent *their* summers playing endless adagios in
the garden. John, four years her senior, had little time for Angela

the child, and spent most waking hours in the company of her elder brother, James, a thin, pale, serious boy, often ill, who much later died of pneumonia while studying at Oxford.

During that summer in question, however, James had, yet again, taken ill with a fever and could be neither visited nor played with for two weeks. On one particularly fine day, Angela found John in the library, lounging in a pool of sunlight on the floor, and poring over a stack of books. Angela, then nine years old, sat next to John and patted him on the thigh. He didn't notice her at first. Or at least he pretended not to. She patted him again. John propped the book on his chest, uncurling and stretching his long limbs outward into the sunlight, like a cat.

"What are you doing?" she asked.

"Watching," he said, not looking up from the page.

"Watching what?" she asked.

"Ghosts," he said.

"What ghosts?"

"Well, it's an old house, isn't it? The older the house, the more spirits haunting it. Thought everybody knew that."

"I don't believe you," she said.

"Well, it's as true as I'm sitting here. Look around you. You can see 'em trapped in every window."

Angela looked up. She gasped. She saw them. *Saw them.* Each window held a face—pale, dark eyed, and livid. Each with a pink slash for a mouth. Each with seaweed hair and seafoam skin. Each moving softly, as though underwater. Angela screamed and covered her face with her hands. She wept for each face, each pink mouth. She wept for things lost and things she could not name.

John laughed loudly, with gusto, and slapped Angela hard on the back as though they were both men.

"Poor little idiot," John said both kindly and unkindly. "Poor little thing." He left the room, still laughing, and shut the door with a hollow click.

The ghosts remained in the windows for the rest of the day. Angela shut her eyes when she could and stared at the floor when she could not. Her parents thought she was ill like James, and sent her likewise to bed.

The next day, Angela started to paint—and she would continue to do so, daily, for the rest of her life, often for hours at a time. The day after that, John decided that she would one day be his wife. She was, he said, the only girl for him. It was mostly true.

What he wrote:

My darling,

I set out today, prepared to be cross. Deeply cross, if you must know. When the post arrived, I tore through the stack of envelopes looking for the clean, sure stroke of your most beloved hand and found it was nowhere to be seen. Is this, I asked, what a devoted husband should expect from his wayward wife?

In the meantime, Mrs. Wooten at the tea shop scolded me this morning for not sending my beautiful wife away from this unholy den of lusty soldiers.

"They pant after her like dogs, the poor little lamb," she said, smacking her wooden spoon upon the counter with a deafening crack.

"My dear lady," said I, "I sent her to my mother's house not two days ago." She did not believe me, of course, and insisted on calling me everything from a horse's ass to a fiend-of-a-man, unworthy of the angel who is my Angela. She insisted that she had seen you just that morning, sitting in your chair by the sea, painting a landscape of wind. She said that your hair was undone and you had a carpetbag at your feet.

And just as I was about to speak ill of you, my dear, I placed my hand in my pocket and withdrew your letter. How it came to be there, I'm sure I don't know, but I assume I must have slipped it in without even thinking. Oh, to see your lettering, my love! Oh, to hold the paper once held by your dear fingers. Perhaps this is what happens when we force the artist into the office instead of the studio—a weakened mind, my dear. I do hope you'll forgive me for it.

Mrs. Wooten, I'm glad to say, was pacified, my darling. And so am I.

Ever yours,

John

What he did not:

Although he had received offers of company the previous night, he opted to sleep alone. The wind continued to hiss at the windowpane and insinuate itself into the cracks. The brass bed beneath him creaked and whined each time he shivered. Eight times he attempted to sleep. Eight times he slept, though briefly and not well. Eight times he woke to a dream of Angela. Angela, seated by the sea, her hair undone and sailing like notes in an insistent breeze. Angela, whose long fingers were brought to her mouth as she puzzled over her paints. Angela, whose head was cocked curiously to the side, listening to a faraway sound of twisting metal and dying engines—the percussive slap of compressed explosives hurtling themselves into the sky. She listened as though hearing music. A smile played upon her pale pink lips. John woke in tears. He did not know why.

What she wrote:

Dearest John,

It is official. Your mother is not speaking to me. I do not know what I have done to offend her, but whatever it is, will you please inform her that it is your fault, and I, as usual, am blameless. I arrived last night in the dark and though I rang endlessly, the house was silent. So like a thief, I entered your mother's home unawares and settled into your old room. The next morning, at breakfast, I greeted your mother and sat down across from her. She ate her egg and sipped her tea—she hoards it you know, and buys it from the blackest of black markets from possibly German spies—and said nothing. I was dying for tea. *Dying* for it, darling. Yet no place was set, no breakfast called for. I was glad to see that dear old Charles was still in her employ, though he did not speak to me either—doubtless on his mistress's orders. Once I tilted my head in an utterly charming way and fluttered my fingers toward him. He looked at me then, managed to raise his eyebrows in hello before turning quite white and staring at the ground.

—Everything all right, Charles? your mother said with toast in her mouth.

—Fine, madam, Charles whispered. I wondered if he was trying not to laugh. And your mother said

—Would you be so kind as to ring my son, I'd like to speak to him.

—Speak to him, indeed, I shouted (yes, dear, I shouted. But honestly what would you have done?) but your mother ignored me.

—It is not possible, madam, Charles said. There was some amount of trouble last night and the lines are down.

Your mother asked what sort of trouble, and of course, Charles did not know. No one knows anything anymore, we just soldier on like good little Britons. You might know, of course.

Do you?

Ever yours,

Angela

What she did not:

The only room with decent light was the music room, so she carried her sketchbook and carpetbag to the third floor, stopping at the dumbwaiter to place a note which read, *Tea and sustenance to the music room at ten o'clock, if you please,* and send it on its way.

A large rectangle of sunlight brightened half the room and fell, like silk, to the ground. When Angela had visited as a child, she would sometimes position her body just so within the rect-angle and listen to the parents play, while enjoying the press and weight of light. She wondered if the light could somehow pen-etrate her small body, or perhaps radiate through it, if the outline of her hands and torso and spindly legs would somehow dissolve, leaving only heat and faded color behind.

The music room was quiet and dusty. She could sketch the room, of course. Perhaps she would. She stood upon the lit rect-angle and tilted her face toward the window. Normally, she would squint, but now she found that she had no need. She stared open-eyed at the sun, drinking it in. She looked at her hands. They were faded, translucent, lovely. This did not strike her as odd. She was an artist. She lived on light. She sat and sketched a woman fading into the sun. Then, she slept. She did not know for how long.

Later, Charles came in with tea. No one was there.

He saw a sketch on the table.

Go away, he whispered.

He didn't mention it to anyone else.

He didn't touch the sketchpad.

What he wrote:

My darling Angela,

I regret to tell you that I have, apparently, been sacked. Or not *sacked* per se, but temporarily relieved of my duties. Fortunately for the two of us, I will remain on the rolls, which is good, because I don't know how I would eat otherwise. I might have considered joining you in Westhoughton, but the rails are closed for the time being. Only military business now, and rarely that. It is oddly quiet without the regular churn of the engines. I never thought I would miss it, but I do.

I do not know what I have done to deserve the ire of my commander. He said they were overstaffed, but I know for a fact that is a lie. Every man in the office cowers under the stacks waiting on his desk. The commander was not, however, unkind. He told me to divert myself, that I would be back on my feet in no time, and to have a stiff upper lip and so forth, which was nonsense because I shall still be paid and shall apparently return after a suitable time. Suitable for what, they could not say.

But fortunately, after an unpleasant day, I came home and discovered that your letter was not in the post basket with everything else, but was resting prettily on the mantel, which means that our dear Andrew must have seen it and brought it in as a surprise. Don't worry about my mother. I'll write to her. Everything will be beautiful.

Yours,

John

What he did not:

He celebrated his newfound free time by enjoying a lovely afternoon with his shining American, accompanied by three liters of a lovely Côtes du Rhône from his jealously guarded prewar cache of wine, drunk directly from the bottles. The American spoke little, drank much, and was exquisitely, brutally beautiful.

The walls shook. The bed moaned. The American left at sunset, pausing, briefly, at the door, and slipping away without a word. While drinking what was left of the wine, John read and reread Angela's letter so many times, he began to recite it.

When he woke, he squinted at the slant of light penetrating his room. He rubbed his eyebrows and between his eyebrows and blinked. Then, he blinked again. A girl stood in the light, a pretty girl staring first at the sun, then at her hands. John cleared his throat. The girl turned to him, smiled, and vanished. John fell heavily back onto the pillows. The girl, of course, looked like Angela, and was Angela. But it could not have been, so it must not have been. He sat back up and the room was empty, as it should be.

He yawned and noticed the letter from Angela was now on her pillow. He had, apparently, resealed it, de-creased it, and placed it where her head should go. He laughed at himself, at what drink can do to a man. He wrapped himself in a robe and padded into the kitchen. The letter was there too, sealed and unopened. He opened it. It was the same letter.

Three letters leaned against one another in the fireplace, their edges now seared by the hot remains of yesterday's coal. Two letters floated in the sink. Six had been slipped between the door and the jamb and stuck out like nails waiting to be hammered in. And somewhere quite close, a girl was singing.

John gathered the letters in his hands and stood by the window. Bringing the paper to his nose, he closed his eyes and breathed them in. Lilac, of course. And lavender. He let them fall; they spun like dry leaves and scattered on the floor. He sat down and wrote to his mother.

What she wrote:

Dearest John,

Today I sang in your honor, and I found that I could not stop. All day I have been here, drawing portraits of light. Singing odes to light. I open my mouth and light hangs upon my mouth, drips from my tongue, spills down my front, and pools at my feet. Charles came in with tea. (Did I want tea? Do I even drink tea? It's strange, but I have only a vague notion of the *substance* of tea. I believe it is not unlike the consumption of light.) He is so pale, poor man. I took his hand. His skin was papery and cool. My hand slipped over it like graphite along the clean space of an empty sheet. He shivered. I could not feel him shiver—not with my hands, anyway. But I *felt* it all the same. Within. If you understand. *Do* you understand? You always did understand. There was a day when I learned to see. And learning to see, and making art, and loving you were bound inextricably together. Much now, my dear, is unbound, but those three remain.

Once, there were people in the window. Do you remember, my love? Their mouths were pink and open, and their hair floated like seaweed. It floats still. Charles told me to go away, but you would never tell me so.

Not you, John.

Never, ever you.

Angela

What she did not:

She knew to keep her distance from the windowpanes. The people inside were clearer to her now, clearer than they had ever been. She had always seen them, of course, ever since that day when she was a child. But never directly. They had hovered vaguely at the corners of her eyes, the glass clearing itself every time she stared straight on.

But now they sharpened; they defined themselves. They pressed their long fingers on the glass and called her name. Their cold, pink mouths were open, toothless, hungry—an uneven gash in a cold white space. Their eyes were blank and black—hollow pits where once there was a soul or a self or at least *something*, but now was not.

Her drawings littered the floor. Her letters too. How they reached their destination was a mystery, though she *knew* they did. Implicitly. She made something. She *was*. She would, she decided, remain so. Charles did not pick up the papers she scattered on the floor. He avoided the music room as much as he could. He averted his gaze when she wandered into his quarters at night. He shut his eyes at the seaweed float of her waterlogged hair. He clapped his hands over his ears when she opened her pink slash mouth.

Open the door when the light pours through, she sang.
Openthedoorwhenthelightpoursthrough

Openthedoorwhenthelightpoursthroughopenthedoorwhenthe lightpoursthrough

openthedooropenthedooropenthedooropenthedooropenthedoor,

she sang, and sang, and sang. After two days of her ceaseless song, he opened the door. She poured herself into the light, and she *was* light, and line, and space, and negative space, and thought, and the lack of thought, and being, and nonbeing. She *was*. She knew it.

What he wrote:

My darling,

Have you noticed any strange doors of late? Doors that, I don't know, darling. That, er, appear out of nowhere, perhaps. Doors that you might have a strong desire to open.

Or have you noticed, on the edges of your vision, well, a sort of *veil* or shimmering substance? A light, as it were.

I do not ask to cause you to feel alarm or to rush you into anything for which you may or may not be prepared. I only write this (my dear, my precious, my heart's sweet angel) on the chance that you may be—I mean to say—putting anything *off*, as it were. Lingering, you know? For my sake.

What I am trying to tell you, my love, is that if you should happen to, in some sense, *run into* (assuming, of course, that one does run in this, er, *condition*) anyone— a beloved person, for example—who has been, well, *gone* for some time, and you feel yourself wanting to, I mean to say, *go*—you know—*along* . . . please my darling, do not tarry on my account. Please do not. I cannot bear the thought that you may have found yourself stuck, and that it is my fault. I am fine. I will be fine, my love.

Your most Affectionate Husband,

John

What he did not:

He wondered who would be the one to meet his wife in her nebulous state, and who would be given the great privilege to grasp that delicate hand, and lead her . . . *there*.

Wherever *there* was.

Specifically, he wondered if it would be her brother, James— beautiful, sickly James. James of the downy hair. James of the willowy limbs. James of the seafoam skin. James of the irritable lungs. James of the bloody cough. James, red lipped, pale to the point of translucency, and dead in John's arms. James who loved him, but not *like that*. And who broke John's heart. John knew that if James came for *him*, he'd follow him through any door in the universe, and would not hesitate. Not for a moment.

Though he had guessed well enough on his own, someone at the office had thought to slip a copied report—classified, of course—detailing the known facts of the train crash. The number of souls aboard. Lost, all of them. All, all lost. And Angela—angel, angel Angela—who wasn't supposed to be there, but *was*, and now she *wasn't*.

And yet.

The letters massed in the corners. They smothered the fire

in the grate and mounded over the sink. They poured across the floor, particularly near the windows. They seemed to prefer light. Before he sat down to breakfast, John swept the letters into great heaps at odd intervals throughout the house, intending to burn them in the fireplace, but found he didn't have the heart for it. Instead, the heaps grew, and the letters multiplied. They kept John up all night. At ten o'clock the next morning the American opened the front door. He did not knock.

"What's with the letters?" he said.

"It's complicated," John replied. He tugged at the folds of his dressing gown. It could be cleaner, of course. Angela always saw to such things. His American was pressed, shaved, and clean. He shone brightly in the doorway. John squinted and gasped.

"I'm leaving," the American said, keeping his eyes slanted to the floor.

"When?" John asked. He also did not look up. Light poured in from all directions. It swirled across the floorboards. The letters rustled in their heaps, paper murmuring against paper.

"Tomorrow," he said, and before John could speak, he added, "and don't ask me where. I can't say."

"Of course." The light intensified. John shaded his eyes. He sweated and squinted.

"Are you—" The American cleared his throat. "I mean, have they found out—told you for sure. About your wife." He said the word *wife* as though pronouncing a word in a foreign tongue. "Is she—"

"Yes," John said while clearing his throat. "Which is to say. We assume. In all likelihood."

"Terrible thing," the American said, unstraightening, then straightening, his tie.

"Yes."

"If I don't—you know. If I don't see you again. I—"

"Of course, of course," John said, running his fingers through his hair, watching with growing panic how the letters spread like mold across the surface of the ottoman, stacked themselves higher on the desk, spilled down the edge of the table. The American didn't seem to notice. John wondered briefly if they should embrace, declare their love, plot an escape. He wondered if they should begin making plans to settle in the Lake District, raise lambs, live on milk and bread and young meat, live on wine and sex and song.

"Well then," the American said, and opened the door. The light poured in. John fell to his knees, raised his hands to the light, "Oh! God!" he said, but the American turned and departed without a word. He left the door open.

What she wrote:

Dearest,

Once there was a boy who loved a boy who did not love him back. Once there was a girl who loved a boy who loved a boy. Once there was a girl who loved a boy who loved her back. *Mostly.*

If love is light and food is light and life is light, are we always in day? Are we doomed to never sleep?

Ever yours,

Angela

Dear John,

I dream of your hands. I dream of fingers as they play along, across, and in. I dream how a moan becomes song and song becomes art and art becomes light. Your light enters me and I shine forever.

Ever yours,

Angela

Dear John,

Light

Art

Light

Song

Light

Light

Light

Do you understand me?

Ever yours—

Dear John,

adooropensawomanlovesalifeblendsintolightandlight andlight

ever yours

ever

ever

What she did not:

There are three things that seem important to her now:

First, light. Light is useful. Particularly when one has no form, but still has substance. Light is a vehicle, though unreliable, particularly given the climate.

Second, the body. Despite its fading, and dissolution into light, she still feels the opening of the mouth, the electric nerves of the fingertips, the hungry scoop between her thighs.

Third, doors. There are doors that remain impenetrable, doors that yield to the gentle insistence of her will, doors that lead her from place to place. There is a door that she needs to find. But what or where it is, and of what use, this is a mystery.

She slides through space and time. The moments of her life unfurl before her, an elegant geometry of angles and arcs and perfect reasoning. She sees a boy who showed her how to see ghosts—which is to say *death*—which is to say *art*—which is to say *infinity*. She sees another boy with pale skin and a red mouth, coughing blood into a napkin. She sees the red-mouthed boy floating away on harmonics and dissonance and brutal love. She sees another—her *other*—dissembling, dissolving, despairing daily.

She is formless substance. She is light. She is song. She is the art behind art—which is to say, *infinite*. As formless substance, she sees her other kneeling in the doorway. As light she pours through the door. As song she slides what used to be her fingertips into the secret grooves of his throat. She plucks out melody and harmony—line, phrase, dissonance, and counterpoint. As art she lands upon his open mouth. She lays her mouth upon his mouth, space and negative space. He tastes of lilac and lavender, oil and smoke. He sings of bent metal and burning wood and beautiful soldiers and poisoned waters and multitudes of airships hurling themselves against the geodesic sky. He sings of a war that seems as though it will never end. He sings of lost love, lost art, lost music, lost nations, lost women, and lost men.

He sings her name. He never, ever stops.

THE
DEAD BOY'S
LAST POEM

A YOUNG GIRL LOVED A POET. *LOVED* HIM. SHE LOVED THE graphite stains on his fingers, the thick cowlick that covered his left eye, the hand-rolled cigarette dangling from his open mouth. She loved the way he pressed himself against her in the dark and scratched poems into the soft skin of her long, bare back.

"Don't date poets," her mother said. "More trouble than they're worth. Open them up and there's nothing more than a wad of torn-up paper at the heart."

To the poet she said, "Why settle down yet? You're young; she's young. A broken heart will burn you alive. You hear me?"

But the girl didn't listen and the boy didn't care. The girl came home with sonnets scribbled on her arms, first draft villanelles veining their way up her lilied thighs. At night her mother heard the off-pitch wail of love songs through an open window, a bed creaking to lines that did not scan.

But he was a poet, so his fate was sealed: seventeen; cigarette spewing ash into his eyes; a launch of metal; gasoline blooming like roses at the side of the road. A screaming boy, flung into the darkening sky.

He left her his poems. He had already promised that he would, and so the girl was waiting by the window. Expecting. Boxes arrived filled with smudged notebooks, stacks of torn paper, inked sections of box tops, envelopes marred by off-kilter metaphors and mostly apt allusions.

"We don't want them," her mother said when the truck arrived. But the girl insisted, and men delivered the poems into her room, leaving her mother grumbling downstairs. The poems lined the walls and blocked the window light; they assembled into chairs and chaises, into curtains hanging from the walls, lamps hanging from the ceiling.

"Well," her mother said. "I hope you're happy."

And the girl was. At first. She slept on a bed of poetry, felt the click and beat of internal rhythms moving up her legs as she slept, the slick of rhyme in her mouth each time she inhaled. She let the color of his words rest against her eyes as she dreamed and dreamed. Each night she saw a boy made of paper—scribbled eyes, a lettered mouth. She saw a body that formed and unformed as the wind blew, and a mind that insisted on revising itself—words written and unwritten, arranged and scattered, a poem that would never be finished. And somewhere inside that paper boy, a flesh heart quivered, and swelled, and pumped, and beat, beat, beat, beat.

She woke each morning stained with graphite and cut by paper. She stopped eating. Love satisfied her. She stopped wearing shoes. Handwritten letters cushioned the space between her soft toes and the hard ground. She wore a dress made from notebook paper. Stanzas bound her hair. Her mother shook her head. Worried.

"It isn't right," her mother said as the girl drifted to the breakfast table, followed by a flurry of unbound papers. "Girl your age shouldn't be tied down." The poems shivered in horror, but the girl gathered them in her arms, curled her pink lips, and crooned as though hushing a child. "She didn't mean it," the girl said.

Her mother handed her coffee, juice, plates heaped with food, but the girl refused. She stood, the poems standing with her, and walked away. "You're just jealous," she said.

"As *if*," her mother grunted.

In the doorway, the poems crinkled their edges in disgust.

Time passed, and at last the girl ate. Her mother wept in relief.

The next day, she bought a red dress. The notebook pages fluttered sadly to the ground. The girl skipped to the door as a horn blasted outside. The girl's mother, watching from the window, heard a car shudder and spurt before rumbling into view on the street. The pages tumbled toward her, assembled themselves into a stack, and peered over the sill.

"Don't say I didn't warn you," the mother said, giving the pages a sympathetic pat. "Nothing lasts forever."

The next day, the girl bought new shoes. The poems were heartbroken. They swirled into the basement to sulk.

Days passed.

A whole week.

"You should do something about that boy," the mother finally said one morning at breakfast.

"What are you talking about?" the girl said, shoveling eggs and sausage into her mouth. Sinking her teeth into bread and butter and sugared fruit. "He's wonderful."

"Not *that* boy," the mother said, impatiently. She jerked her head toward the doorway. "*That* one." A thousand bits of torn paper—each one bearing a tiny love poem, so smudged as to be illegible—gathered themselves into the silhouette of the dead boy, wavering hopefully in the shadows. A paper cowlick draped over a handwritten, hopeful eye.

"Oh. Him." The girl shrugged. "He'll take the hint eventually." She gulped her juice. "Right?"

But he didn't. He made himself into cardboard shoes with haiku on the toes. He unraveled the spiral spines of his notebooks into fingers, and at night he etched his name on the insides of her arms, the soles of her feet, and even the pulsing curve of her throat.

"Knock it off," the girl said firmly one night, hurling her pillow into his papery middle. He scattered and sobbed. Tear-soaked couplets landed on her bed. Sonnets drenched in misery and snot hurled themselves in wads onto the ground.

That morning when she showered, he fingered words through the steam. "Ode to Things Unfair," read the bathroom mirror as she slipped her nakedness from stall to mat. "The Beautiful and the Cruel" proclaimed the sink with toothpaste letters. She wiped the wetness from her face, threw her towel on the ground, and ran her fingers through her long hair.

Paper hands curled around the edge of the door. Paper eyes peeked in. They ogled.

"That's *it*," she said. And she meant it.

She invited her girlfriends to a bonfire. They drank sticky-sweet wine coolers in clear bottles and vodka-spiked cranberry juice, filled high and sloshing over the rims of their plastic cups, spilling onto their hands. They drank to sisterhood. They traded stories of past lovers, painstakingly detailing each excruciating inadequacy. The girls were brutal, and specific. In the box next to the fire, the poems winced.

The girls promised to never date poets again. They pinkie swore. They sat close together, bare shoulders touching bare shoulders; they cocked their glossy heads and sighed as, one by one, they tossed the poems into the fire. Their young skin glowed in the firelight; their pearl teeth glinted through the smoke.

Inside the flames, the poet composed in their honor. His words were now a burning thing, as his life burned and his soul burned and the whole world burned and burned. He sang of the shiver on the neck at the touch of a lover's mouth, the taste of breath in the ear, the agony of a finger's brush against a lonely hand. He sang of breasts and skin and throats and thighs and mouths in mouths on mouths.

He sang of a girl, mostly true.

He sang of a boy, his smudged, smoky scream, his life cut short: a poem flung out, pinned onto the cruel, dawning sky.

DREADFUL
YOUNG LADIES

1. Fran

It was easy enough to lose a child by accident. To do so on purpose turned out to be nearly impossible.

The child slid his grubby, slick fingers into her hand. Hung on for dear life. He rubbed his face on the seat of her skirt, and hooked his arm into her purse's glossy leather strap. Meanwhile, people passed by without a glance, their hands full of drooping cotton candy or oversized stuffed dogs with weak seams or shrill whistles in the shape of a bird. Aggressively unattractive parents wooed their children with sweets and grease and cheap toys. Fran pressed the fingers of her free hand to her mouth and choked down bile.

The child stumbling next to her hip was not her own. This child, with thick lips and the watery squint of dull eyes, was her lover's. Or, more specifically, her lover's wife's child.

If a child was an anchor on a good man's soul, Fran reasoned, *if it kept him from daily loving his love, would it not be better if such a child disappeared?*

Children disappear every day. Just watch the news.

When Fran was fourteen, she took her little sister to the park. The little girl flew higher and higher on the swing—lace bobby socks, black mary janes, a dress lined with crinoline flapping about her spindly legs like white and pink wings—while Fran leaned against the elm tree and let Jonah Marks slide his hand into her shorts. Let him hang on tight.

Watch me, the little girl cried. *Watch me.* Her voice bounced against the basketball court, rustled the leaves, floated on the breath of Jonah Marks, on his wet lips and insistent tongue. *Watch me.*

When she turned, the little girl was gone. The swing still arced back and forth, a memory of her body. *She flew away*, Fran told her mother, her father, the social worker, and the police. *I heard the rustle of lace and the flapping of wings. I heard a voice echo within, around, and above. She flew away.*

And she may have done. Really, who's to say?

But Fran's little sister was a pretty child. No one ever snatches the ugly ones.

Fran's lover's son was not a pretty child. He whimpered and wheezed. He chortled and pleaded. An endless litany of wants.

Grant me a snow cone.

Grant me a foot-long.

Grant me a deep-fried candy bar on a stick.

Fran tried to dash away at the restroom, but the child appeared like magic at the doorway and grasped the hem of her skirt. Fran tried to dodge him in the haunted house, but he kept close to her heels in the dark. He hid in her pocket. He slid into her shoes. The weight of him swung from side to side. She heard him flapping and flying. *Watch me!*

Fran sent the child to the top of the giant slide hoping for an opening, but a convention of police officers gathered without warning to look appraisingly at the hordes of ugly children hurtling down yellow humps, their faces lit by the misplaced love of their fawning parents on the ground. Fran was, she saw, surrounded by idiots. And she couldn't slip away.

The child at the top of the slide—her lover's wife's child—shivered and shook. He gripped the burlap sliding sack the way a skydiver hangs on to his defective parachute before his final bounce upon a pitiless ground. Fran looked up. Felt her shoulders hemmed in by police.

She flew away, she wanted to say to the cop on her right. *Children disappear every day*, she nearly said to the cop on her left, *especially the pretty ones. It isn't my fault that the boy is hideous.*

The ugly child peered down at Fran, held her gaze. She imagined him in black mary janes. In bobby socks with lace at the ankle. She imagined him on the arc of a swing, unhooked from gravity, bumping against the sky. The wind lifted his pale hair like the crinoline lining of a fluttering skirt. Fran felt her breath catch. *Watch me!* the ugly child mouthed. *Watch me!* He swayed and swayed, and Fran found herself swaying too.

Grant you feathers, murmured her lips.

Grant you wings.

Grant you light and wind and helium.

Grant you cloud and moon and star. The vacuum of space. The infinite distances between lover and love.

The child sat on his burlap and pushed off.

And somewhere inside, Fran grew wings.
She flew away.

2. *Margaret*

Red lips invite trouble, when trouble requires an invitation. Which it usually doesn't. Margaret knew that trouble hid under dirty rugs and scratched coffee tables. It lurked behind heavy drapes like in old vampire movies. It gathered in great clouds like pollen in the spring and fall and settled like dust in between.

Margaret stood in front of the mirror painting black around the eyes, muting acne scars and fresh pustules with muddy makeup, and crafting a false beauty mark at the hollow where her chin met her neck.

She wore pink lips to school, black lips to visit her grandparents, and red lips for everything else. She wiped Vaseline across her small, white teeth to prevent stains—like a barrier against blood on crisp new sheets. The color of the lip is significant, Margaret knew. The color matters.

Margaret's teacher, for example, was terrified by a red lip. He pulled at his earth-tone tie until his face went red, then purple, then green. He stammered and hesitated before shooing the girl away.

Pink, though. Pink was a different story.

Two weeks with pink lips. Only two. By then he was weak and trembly, his fingers fluttering gently as they grazed her neck.

They found him the next day. Heart attack. Hard-on. Pink lips. Really, who's to say? Margaret offered no opinion.

Her mother snored in the next room, her new boyfriend at her side—also snoring. The room stank of liquor and sex, and Margaret wrinkled her nose as she slipped inside.

Margaret intended the black lips for her grandfather, but it was her grandmother who, somewhere between the tuna casserole and the Cool Whip surprise, began to nervously run her fist through the porcupine spikes of her black-and-white hair. And shiver.

"I was a Girl Scout once, did you know," her grandmother said. Margaret curved her black lips into a grin. She slipped her supple fingers into her grandmother's rice paper hand, felt the old woman's soul leak out in a long, slow sigh as she leaned inexorably in.

Grandmother still wore her oven mitts when they found her. Black lipstick on her mouth.

Borrowed time, people said.

Margaret crawled in between her mother and her mother's boyfriend. Her mother slept openmouthed, wet breath catching in her throat.

It's only a matter of time, her mother had said earlier that day, as she checked the fit of Margaret's new bra. Her thumbs lingered on the dense, round breasts as though checking for freshness. *Every Tom and Dick'll want a taste. A kiss, I mean.*

The boyfriend had leaned in the recliner, his hands occupied by a cigarette and an icy highball glass. But his fingers itched. Margaret could tell.

A kiss is a dangerous thing, the boyfriend said. *I feel sorry for the poor son of a bitch. Won't know what's hit him until it's too late.*

Still, he said, dragging deep on his cigarette, *not a bad way to go.* He had given Margaret a full-handed smack on her rear as she passed.

Margaret leaned over, placed a hand next to each of his shoulders, peered into his sleeping face. *Too late for you*, she whispered in the dark. His face was calm, his jowls slack. The stubble on his chin stood at attention. His lips were full and slightly parted, the corners twitching with each breath. She licked her lips.

Too late.

She licked her lips again. Tasted musk and cinnamon, and *oh god*, salt, sweat, and lemon juice, and *oh god*, grass and wheat and meat and milk. Tasted youth and birth and decay.

She licked her lips again. Felt her body shudder and buck. *What is it*, she wondered, *about death that makes us feel so alive?*

3. Estelle

Reginald curled his body up the length of the radiator pipe. Winked one yellow eye. Winked the other. He tested the air with a quick flick of the tongue.

"Mind your own business," Estelle said, returning the gesture, though she knew he wouldn't notice.

Estelle sat at a desk with one hundred and two different file folders on the surface—all color coded, labeled, and stacked neatly according to year. This is what she had been told to do. To prepare. *They don't look out for your best interests, so don't expect it*, her friends said. *They care about numbers and procedures and forms. They care about quotas. If it were up to them, they'd swallow you whole.*

"They can try," Estelle chuckled, as she pulled Andrew and Arnold from their hiding place in the bottom drawer and draped them heavily on the ground. They lifted their flat heads and gave her twin looks of indignation before sliding across the floor and under the upholstered chair.

The young man appeared in the doorway. He had long, white hands, tapered fingers, narrow hips. A blue suit and a blue tie and a haircut both severe and modern.

"I see you've been busy, Ms. Russo. I appreciate your work, but I assure you it was not necessary. I'm top in my field."

He remained in the doorway. From his position on the radiator pipe, Reginald tasted the air. He leaned closer and unhooked his jaw.

"No, no," Estelle said firmly. Reginald pulled back, chastened.

"Oh, yes, I assure you I am," the young man said. "May I come in?"

"Please do," she said, winking one yellow eye.

He sat on the upholstered chair, resting his briefcase on his knees. Estelle stood. Her body was long and supple. She slid like oil across the room to the chair opposite the young man. Offered a slow, mesmerizing grin. Flicked her tongue.

Arnold unfurled from underneath, elevating hungrily behind the chair. Robin, Mae, and Chavez peeked their heads from the grooves of the couch cushions.

"No, no," Estelle said again.

"I'm sorry?" said the young man.

"Nothing," Estelle said, winking her other eye. Arnold sniffed and slumped to the floor, while the other three retracted without commentary. The young man glanced at the floor, but saw nothing.

"Look," he said, "it doesn't really matter what you have organized in what file. I've already seen it. How you've slid under the radar for as many years as you have is a mystery to me, but it doesn't matter now. There are consequences."

"Nibble, nibble, little mouse," Estelle said. "Always nibbling on the things that aren't yours."

"The government," he said primly, "is not a mouse."

The new brood woke and came tumbling out of the hole in the wall. At a hand signal from Estelle, they fell upon one another and played dead, as they had been trained. Diana, Elizabeth, and Eleanor glided in through the open door and moved regally toward the guest. Their golden eyes glittered like crowns. Estelle breathed deeply through her nose, flicked her tongue again. The young man smelled green and young. Like tight fiddleheads before they unfurl. The budding of spring. The tang of green apple on the tongue.

"Who said anything about the government?" Estelle said. "I'm talking about you." She leaned in. "Little mouse." She unhooked her jaw.

Gagged.

Gulped.

Swallowed him whole.

4. Annabelle

"My father says I can't play with you anymore," the boy said.

Annabelle shrugged. "He's not the boss of me."

"He says your mother isn't raising you right."

"Could be," she said, squatting on the ground. She spat on the bare dirt. Drew with her finger.

"He says you'll grow up just like her. He says the neighborhood doesn't need another one."

Annabelle drew a picture of a house with a sun and a heavy cloud. She drew a man inside with a woman. The man was on his knees. The woman had her head tossed back.

"He says you're all the same. He says I'm not supposed to chase a dirty skirt."

Annabelle drew heavy drops coming out of the cloud. She drew a flood that bent beams and rotted floors. She drew swollen banks and ruptured dikes and water that would not be bound. She drew a broken house tumbling down the river and floating off to sea.

She washed the land clean with the back of her hand.

"Um." He kicked at a clump of weeds with his sandal. "Do you know where my dad is?"

"With my mom. At my house." She looked up and smiled. "They floated away."

He bent down, rested his rear on his heels. Annabelle drew a boy and a girl in limitless space. She gave them wings. The boy arched his back as though it itched.

"Can I go with you then?"

"Suit yourself," she said. She took his hand. Hung on tight. *They flew away.*

THE TAXIDERMIST'S OTHER WIFE

1.

Not one of us has ever stepped inside the Taxidermist's house. We have no need to do so. We already know what we'll find.

2.

On the center of his desk in the mayoral suite of the town hall (though it is not much of a suite anymore, and not much of a hall; the old town hall burned down years ago, and was replaced by a temporary double-wide) stands a mounted howler monkey, one of the finest specimens from the Taxidermist's vast collection. Its mouth is open, lips curled outward like the rim of a trumpet. Its head is cocked sweetly to one side, as though reconsidering what it was just about to say. Its knees are bent, toes pigeoned inward in the classical stance, and—though this is a violation of protocol and is generally frowned upon by most who practice the art of taxidermy—its left hand is curled, poised just above the monkey's bum, as though about to scratch.

Or, perhaps it *does* scratch. Really, who's to say?

In any case, it is a frivolous gesture, but so furiously ruddy with life (or the side effects of life), that it takes the viewer aback. People have petted the howler monkey. Spoken to it. *Loved* it. They've checked its body for nits. They've unaccountably wanted to scratch their own backsides—and they *have*, when they've thought no one was watching.

The Taxidermist is always watching.

And later, at night, when they've left the office, when they've left the howler behind and returned home, they've tossed and shivered in bed, dreaming of that lonely howl across the empty fields, the yawning trees, and the wide, cold sky. And sometimes, they've howled in return.

The howler makes them forget why they came to the Taxidermist's office in the first place. They wander away, complaints unfiled, petitions undelivered, pieces of mind ungiven.

The Taxidermist loves his howler monkey. His secretary, on the other hand, does not.

"Sir," his secretary says, bringing in a file. "For the meeting." She says the word *meeting* with a certain accusation. She lets the file hover over the desk before fanning her fingers, letting the thing hit the desk with a slap.

"Did you know," the Taxidermist says, "that when Pliny attacked Carthage, he entered the Temple of Astarte and found it filled with no fewer than thirty mountain gorillas? Each one was exquisitely mounted, painstakingly preserved, and, apparently, terrifying. The poor man turned on his heel and ran from the temple, claiming it had been seized by Gorgons."

He sits at his desk, ancient books opened to different pages and stacked for ease of access. The secretary presses her lips into a long, tight line. She is the former librarian of the former library. She disapproves of the wanton opening of books. She shudders at the splay of tight spines, the heedless rustle of unloved pages like the whisper of lifting skirts.

The Taxidermist presses his fingers to his mouth to suppress a burp, though he pretends to clear his throat. He continues. "It is, they believe, the first indication that the art of specimen preservation is not a modern pastime as previously thought. I wonder if the Carthaginian priests thought to re-create the minutiae of the mundane as we do now. I wonder what they thought they were preserving."

The secretary flares her nostrils, forcing her gaze away from her employer. The Taxidermist closed the library. Everyone knows this. Everyone blames him. The secretary answers his phones and files his documents and maintains his correspondence and organizes his meetings. But she hates the Taxidermist. *Hates* him.

"I'm not certain your research is correct," the secretary says. "But gorillas have nothing to do with your meeting tonight."

"My dear Miss Sorensen," the Taxidermist says, peering into a heavily diagrammed book, its ancient dust rising from its pages like smoke, "it has everything to do with the meeting tonight. You'll see."

3.

The Taxidermist is the mayor, and has been for the last fifteen years. We did not vote for him. We've never met anyone who *has*. And yet he has won, term after term. Always a landslide. We never offer our congratulations, nor do we bring casseroles or home-made bars to his house, nor do we come to his Christmas parties or summer barbeques. (We already know what's in that house. We *know*.)

This, we are sure, hurts the Taxidermist's other wife. What wife wouldn't be wounded by such a snub? She is a sweet, pretty thing. Young. Large eyes. Tight, smooth skin. She grew up four towns over, though no one can say in which one, exactly. Each day she pushes open the large, heavily carved front door of the house and stands on the porch. She brushes a few tendrils of shellacked hair from her face with the backs of her fingers. She adjusts her crisp, white gloves.

She is *perfect*. Her symmetry jostles the eye. Her body moves without hesitancy, without the irregular rhythm of muscle and bone.

Each day she walks from their house at the center of town, past what used to be the butcher shop and what used to be the hardware store and what used to be the Shoe Emporium and what used to be the offices of our former newspaper, until she reaches her husband's office at the Town Hall. She wears high heels that click coldly against the cracked sidewalk. She wears a skirt that skims her young thighs and flares slightly at her bending knees. She used to smile at us when she passed, but she doesn't anymore. We never smiled back. Instead, she keeps her lovely face porcelain-still, her mouth like a rosebud in a bowl of milk. A doll's mouth.

We want to love her. We wish we could love her. But we can't. We remember the Taxidermist's first wife. We remember and remember and remember.

4.

Taxidermy is more than Art. It is more than Love. The Taxidermist has explained this to us, but we have closed our ears. We change the subject. We scan the sky for signs of rain.

Still, words have a way of leaking in.

"If the artisan does not love the expired subject on his table, it is true, the final product will be a cold, dead thing. A monstrosity. A hideous copy of what once was unique and alive and *beautiful.*"

We told ourselves we weren't listening. Still, we found ourselves nodding. We found ourselves *agreeing.* It *is* hideous when a thing isn't loved.

"But the love is not enough," the Taxidermist insisted. "*Desire,* friends. *Desire.* When God leaned against the riverbank, when he pressed his fingers into the warm mud and pulled out a man, what was the motivation? *Desire.* God saw mud and made it Man. He *made* Man because he *wanted* Man. We see death and desire life. Love isn't enough. You have to *want* to make it live."

5.

There was no funeral for Margaret, the first wife.

We learned she was dead in the "Fond Memories" section of the newspaper. That was when we had a newspaper. He never mentioned it out loud. He never told anyone. He never even held a funeral. We tried to grieve. We wanted to drape our arms around the Taxidermist, to feel his tears wetting the shoulders of our shirts, to wrap his hand with our hands and squeeze. Then we took frozen hotdishes and bar cookies and flowers and sliced ham and left them on the porch when the Taxidermist refused to open the door.

"Here," we shouted. "We've brought food. Wine. Whiskey. We brought our presence and our ears and our love. Let us in and we'll feed you. We'll share a drink and share a song and make you live again. And *she* will live in the spaces between word and word, between breath and breath, between your tears and our tears. She will *live*."

But the Taxidermist would not open the door. The next morning, we saw our gifts heaped in the trash bin outside the house. We never mentioned it again.

6.

We listened to the old men in Ole's Tavern suck down shots and chasers and fuss over the meeting in the school. Or the building that will soon *not* be a school.

"Not much use pretending we're still a town if the school's gone."

"We stopped pretending we were a town after the grain elevator closed."

"And when the butcher shop shut its doors. Can't call yourself a town if you can't get a fresh hock for supper. If you don't have a locker to put your winter's buck."

"Taxidermist's got a lot of damn gall closing the school midyear. If he was any sort of a man, he'd set aside his own salary rather than pull the rug out from underneath a bunch of little kids."

"Not much of a bunch. Just fifty. On a good day. When was the last good day?"

"We stopped pretending we were a town when the hardware store closed. And the seed store. And the gas station. And the green grocer. And the shoe shop. At least we still can pickle ourselves at Ole's. Soon, he'll just shove us into a bunch of damn mason jars and line us up on a shelf. He'll keep us topped up with nice, clear vodka so we can see. Folk'll come in looking for the town and find it looking right back at 'em, shelves and shelves of blinking eyes." Arne says this. He's always been a morbid fellow.

"The Taxidermist'll like it, though," Zeke Hanson says. "He'll like it very much."

We agree.

7.

Night falls early in November. In those waning moments of light, the sky paints its face like a harlot (overripe rouge, stained lips, unbuttoned taffeta spreading outward like wings), before opening itself wide to the void of space. Each jagged shard of light in the darkness is a tiny message sent from the recesses of time. "You are alone," the stars say. "You are alone. You are still alone."

We pull our coats tightly against the howl of the wind and start our cars.

The school is slightly outside the town, and it sits on a small rectangle cut out of Martin Hovde's sod farm. The schoolyard is packed earth with a single metal swing set for the children to play on. The yard is dusty from their feet, every speck of green crushed by the insistence of play. Just outside the schoolyard is the endless grass of the Hovde farm. Martin steamrolls it twice a year to keep it as flat as any floor and then he burns it, to give the grass a good, rich start. It is green as snakes, and softer than a lie.

We park our cars next to the school but do not lock them. No one locks their doors. This is a small town. A good town. Or it was, anyway. We hold our coats closed tightly at our throats and bend our backs against the wind. The stars are cold and sharp above our heads and the wind howls across the wide, empty fields.

8.

Taxidermy must embrace imperfection. It is a weak practitioner who feels the need to extend the leg of a lamed cougar cub or repair the jagged scar above the eye of an ancient wolf. Taxidermy, in its soul, is the celebration of life, the re-creation of a single moment in a sea of moments. The taxidermist must build motivation, history, consequence, action, reaction into one, perfect gesture.

The taxidermist's diorama is a poem.

A song.

A short story.

"We are all just a collection of faults," the Taxidermist told us once. "A myriad of imperfections through which shines divine Perfection. You see? It is our flaws that make us beloved by heaven. It is our scars and handicaps and *lack* of symmetry that prove that we are—or once were—alive. The more we attempt to force our corrupted idea of the Perfect and the Good upon what is *actually* and *deeply* perfect and good, the farther we are from the divine.

Reveal the subject as the subject *was*, and you reveal the finger-prints of God."

We have shut our ears to the Taxidermist. We have stopped listening to his hypocrisy. We know what he has done. We have *seen* it.

This is the very reason why we can never love his other wife.

9.

The Taxidermist's other wife greets us as we come in. Her eyes light upon each coming person and dim when they pass. Her lips spread open into a smile. We shudder at those straight, white teeth. We turn our gaze from that flawless skin. She tilts her head to one side and blinks her large eyes.

(*There!* We gasp. We grab one another's shirts and pull. We whisper in one another's ears. *Did you hear that? The whir of metal. The click of motor. She doesn't clear her throat. She doesn't sigh. She doesn't lick her lips, or adjust her skirt. She doesn't pass gas, or snort when she laughs, or cough.*) We have examined her skin. We have watched her pass. We've looked for clues but have come away with nothing.

"The efficient preservationist leaves no trace of his hand," the Taxidermist told us once. "It is a dim fellow who has the tools of the trade, who has centuries of experience to guide his practice, and still leaves evidence of stitching. Who still leaves a seam to mar the life that he sets out to create. Do not repeat the blunder of that poor fool in Austria. Do not let the Doctor's mistakes be your mistakes."

We would not expect to see scars.

We would not expect to see seams.

The Taxidermist's other wife lays her hand upon our arms as we pass. We shiver. Even through our coats, we can feel the stony cold of those fingers. Even through our scarves, we can smell the formaldehyde on her breath.

10.

The Taxidermist takes the podium. His other wife sits in a folding chair just behind. She crosses, then uncrosses, then crosses her legs. She rests her hands, one on top of the other, on her knees. She cocks her head to one side, a studied look of wifely admiration on her face.

(We know! We know what she is. Look in her eyes. Look under her skin. We know what we'll find.)

The Taxidermist taps his microphone three times. He smiles at the audience. The audience does not smile back.

"My friends," the Taxidermist says.

(You are no one's friend. You closed the library. You're closing the school. We are pickled in memory, preserved on porches and in church basements and bars. We blink through worlds of liquor and mason jars. You have frozen us in time.)

"This isn't easy for me to say," the Taxidermist says easily. "We are down to fifty students. That's all. What we get from the state isn't enough to cover the heat for the building. It doesn't cover the health insurance for the employees. Our school, once the pride of the county, is falling apart. It is dying."

(We are dying. We are dying and we don't know why.)

"Now, I recognize that, with the school closed, we will be forced to bus our children all the way to Harris, and I recognize that it is a long ride for little ones, but I'm afraid it cannot be helped. Those who do not want their children going so far away can consider homeschooling. We can all come together to help make that happen. This is a *community*."

(It was a community. Now it is a cold, dead thing. We are alone, we are alone, we are so alone.)

"It is true that we loved the school."

(We loved Margaret.)

"And it is true that we will mourn its passing."

(We wanted to mourn her. We wanted our grief, to prove that we aren't alone. We wanted our grief to show that we are—were—alive.)

"But we now have an opportunity. Preservation, my friends. The dead are not gone when we preserve what is left."

The Taxidermist's other wife lifts her hands, preparing to clap. Her lips unfurl in a mechanical smile. Our eyes dazzle and spin in the glare of those perfect teeth. She splays her fingers out and brings her hands together.

But once her palms are half an inch apart, they stutter and halt. The lights behind her eyes flicker and dim. Her lips freeze in that lovely smile—pink lips insinuating themselves into the white mounds of her cheeks. She is porcelain. She is glass. She is stone and milk. She doesn't move. The Taxidermist doesn't notice.

"We, right now, are sitting on holy ground. How many of us first fell in love on this very schoolyard? And here in these halls, how many of us first discovered the tools that would make us the men and women that we are today? Our lives are written on memory. We preserve the memory—in its perfection, in its state of bliss, and we preserve our*selves*."

The Taxidermist's other wife does not move. She does not blink. She is lifeless, breathless, perfect. She is memory and history and longing.

There are stitches hidden under her collarbone.

(We know! We know what's in there! We know what we'll find!)

There are seams sliding along the curve of her spine.

(A gesture. A moment. Proof of life, or the memory of life.)

"My wife," the Taxidermist says.

(Margaret. We wanted to mourn you. We wanted to grieve. We wanted his tears on our shoulders, his hands in our hands. We wanted to sing songs and tell stories and let you live in the spaces between word and word, between breath and breath.)

"Thinks I'm crazy."

(She doesn't think. She simply is. A memory. A state of bliss.)

"But it can work. We can preserve what we have. We can turn our loss into a single perfect moment. We can turn this school into a memory of a school. A moment in time. The fingerprints of a thousand hands, and the mingling of a thousand breaths. And it will be proof forever that we are not alone."

(We are alone.)

"We are not alone."

(We are alone. We are still alone.)

The Taxidermist's other wife does not move.

(Margaret.)

She does not clap.

(Margaret.)

And we feel ourselves lifting. We feel our souls unfurling like wings. We feel the howl of the wind and the vastness of space and the tiny voices of the distant stars. We feel our stitching and our seams, the clean line of empty bones, the weight of plaster and spun glass. We taste arsenic and salt, the grease of leather, the dust of hair. We feel the beat and the longing of our broken, paper hearts. And we love the Taxidermist's other wife.

Love her.

— ELEGY to GABRIELLE —

PATRON SAINT of HEALERS, WHORES + RIGHTEOUS THIEVES

++++|+| |+++|||+

*C*URATOR'S NOTE: *THE FOLLOWING PAGES WERE FOUND IN A cave on an islet eleven miles southwest of Barbados. The narrative is, of course, incomplete, disjointed, and unreliable, as is the information contained within its pages. There is no record of Brother Marcel Renau living in the Monastery of the Holy Veil during the years in question. There is a record of the order for the execution of a Gabrielle Belain in St. Pierre in 1698; however, no documentation of the actual execution exists. Some of this narrative is indecipherable. Some is lost forever. Most, if not all, is blatantly untrue, the ravings of a lost sailor gone mad without water. As to the conditions in which these writings were found: this too remains a puzzle. The cave was dry and protected and utterly empty except for three things: a human skeleton, curled in the corner as though sleeping; a two-foot length of human hair, braided tightly with a length of ribbon and a length of rope, laid across the hands of the dead man; and an oiled and locked box made of teak, in which these documents were found. Across the lid of the box the following words had been roughly scratched into the wood, as though with a crude knife or a sharp rock: "Bonsoir, Papa."*

Two days before Gabrielle Belain (the pirate, the witch, the revolutionary) was to be executed, a red bird flew low over the fish market, startling four mules, ten chickens, countless matrons, and the Lord High Constable. It flew in a wide spiral higher and higher until it reached the window of the tower where my beloved Gabrielle awaited her fate. People say that she came to the window, that the shadows from the bars cut across her lovely face. People say that she reached out a delicate, slightly freckled hand to the bird's mouth. People say that she began to sing.

I stood in the hallway with the two guards, negotiating the transfer of food, water, and absolution across the threshold of the wood and iron door that blocked Gabrielle from the world. I did not see the bird. I did not hear song. But I believe them both to be real. This is the nature of existence: We believe, and it *is*. Perhaps God will turn His back on me for writing such heresy, but I swear it's the truth. Gabrielle, like her mother before her, was a Saint Among Men, a living manifestation of the power of God. People believed it, therefore it was true, and no demonstration of the cynical power of bureaucrats and governments and states could unbelieve their believing.

Gabrielle Belain, at the age of ten, walked from the cottage where she lived with her mother past the Pleasure House to the shore. The moon, a thin slash on a glittering sky, cast a pale light on the foamy sand. She peered out onto the water. The ship, hidden in darkness, was still there, its black sails furled and lashed to the tethered boom, its tarred hull creaking in the waves. She could *feel* it. Actually, there was never a time when she could not feel it. Even when it was as far away as Portugal or Easter Island or the far tip of the continent, she knew where the ship was. And she knew she belonged to it.

Four porpoises bobbed in the waves, waiting for the child to wade in. They made no sound, but watched, their black eyes flashing over the bubbling surf. A mongrel dog, nearly as tall as the girl, whined piteously and rubbed its nose to her shoulder.

"You can't come," she said.

The dog growled in response.

Gabrielle shrugged. "Fine," she said. "Please yourself. I won't wait for you." She waded in, caught hold of a porpoise fin, and swam out into the darkness, the dog paddling and sputtering behind her.

The sailors on the quiet ship watched the sky, listened to the wind. They waited. They had been waiting for ten years.

By the time Gabrielle was thirteen, she was the ship's navigator. By the time she was fifteen, she was captain, and a scourge to princes and merchants and slave traders. By the time she was eighteen, she was in prison—chained, starved, and measured and weighed for hanging.

At night, I see their hands. I do not see their faces. I pray, with my rattling breath, with the slow ooze of my blistered skin, with my vanishing, worthless life, that I may see their faces again before I die. For now, I must content myself with hands. The hands of Gabrielle, who thwarted governors, generals, and even the king himself, and the hands of her mother, who healed, who prayed, and God help me, who loved me. Once. But *oh! Once!*

Gabrielle's mother, Marguerite Belain, came from France to Martinique in the cover and care of my order as we sailed across the ocean to establish a new fortress of prayer and learning in the lush, fragrant islands of the New World. It was not our intention to harbor a fugitive, let alone a female fugitive. We learned of Marguerite's detention through our contacts with the Sisters of the Seventh Sorrow, several of whom waited upon the new and most beloved lover of the young and guileless king. Although the mistress had managed to bear children in her previous marriage, with the king she was weak-wombed, and her babes flowed, purple and shrunken, into her monthly rags with much weeping and sorrow in the royal chambers. Marguerite was summoned to the bed of the mistress, her womb now quickening once again.

"Please," the mistress begged, tears flowing down those alabaster cheeks. "Please," she said, her marble mouth, carved always in an expression of supercilious disdain, now trembling, cracking, breaking to bits.

Marguerite laid her hands on the belly of the king's beloved. She saw the child, its limbs curled tightly in its liquid world. The womb, she knew, would not hold. She saw, however, that it *could*, that the path to wholeness was clear, and that the child could be born, saved, if certain steps were taken immediately.

But that was not all she saw.

She also saw the child, its grasping hands, its cold, cold eye. She saw the child as it grew in the seat of authority and money and military might. She saw the youth who would set his teeth upon the quivering world and tear upon its beating heart. She saw a man who would bring men to their knees, who would stand upon the throats of women, whose hunger for power would never cease.

"I cannot save this child," Marguerite said, her leaf green eyes averted to the ground.

"You can," the mistress said, her granite lips remaking themselves. "And you will."

But Marguerite would not, and she was duly imprisoned for the duration of the pregnancy, until upon the birth she would be guillotined as a murderess if the child did not live and as a charlatan if it did.

It did not. But it did not matter: Marguerite had been spirited away, disguised in our habit and smuggled onto our ship of seafaring brethren before the palace ever did turn black with mourning.

I helped her escape, my Brothers and I. I placed our rough robes over those blessed shoulders, and helped her to wind her hair into the darkness of the cowl. I pulled it low over her face, hiding her from the world, and took her hand as we hurried through the city's underground corridors, never stopping until we made it to the harbor, and hid her in an empty wine barrel on our ship. I told myself that the thudding of my heart was due to the urgency of our action. I told myself that the hand that I held in my hand was beloved because we are all beloved by God. To be human is to lie, after all. Our minds tell lies to our hearts and our hearts tell lies to our souls.

It was on the eighteenth day of our voyage that Marguerite gave me leave into her chamber. It was unasked for and yet longed for all the same, and came to me the way any miracle occurs—in a moment of astonishment and deep joy. On that same day—indeed, that same moment—a storm swirled from nowhere, sending the wind and sea to hurl themselves against the groaning hull, and striking the starboard deck with lightning.

Was it the feeble lover, I wondered, or the lightning that produced such a child when she bore a babe with glittering eyes?

Gabrielle. My child. I am supposed to say the issue of my sin, but I cannot. How can sin produce a child such as this?

On the morning of the forty-first day, a ship with black sails appeared in the distance. By noon we could see the glint of curved swords, the ragged snarl of ravenous teeth. By midafternoon, the ship had lashed itself to ours and the men climbed aboard. In anticipation of their arrival, we set food and drink on the deck and opened several—although not all—of our moneyboxes, allowing our gold to shine in the sun. We huddled together before the mainmast, our fingers following prayer after prayer on our well-worn rosaries. I reached for Marguerite, but she was gone.

A man limped from their ship to ours. A man whose face curled in upon itself, whose lashless eyes peered coldly from a sagging brow, whose mouth set itself in a grim, ragged gash in a pitiless jaw. A mouth like an unhealed wound.

Marguerite approached and stood before him. "You are he," she said.

He stared at her, his cold eyes widening softly with curiosity. "I am," he said. He was proud, of course. Who else would he be? Or, more importantly, who else would he desire to be? He reached for the cowl that hid the top of her head and shadowed her face and pulled it off. Her hair, the color of wheat, spilled out, poured over the rough cloth that hid her body from the world, pooled over her hands, and around her feet. "And you, apparently, are she."

She did not answer, but laid her hands upon his cheeks instead. She looked intently into his face, and he returned her gaze, his hard eyes light with tears. "You're sick," she said. "You have been for . . . ever so long. And sad as well. I cannot heal the sadness, but I can heal the sickness. He too suffers." She pointed to the pock-marked man holding a knife to the throat of our beloved Abbot. "And he, and he." She pointed to other men on the ship. Walking over to the youngest man, who leaned greenly against the starboard gunnels, she laid her hand on his shoulder. "You, my love, I cannot save. I am so sorry." Tears slipped down her cream and nutmeg skin. The man—barely a man, a boy, in truth—bowed his head sadly. "But I can make it so it will not hurt." She took his hand, and squeezed it in her own. She brought her pale lips to his smooth brown cheek and kissed him. He nodded and smiled.

Marguerite ordered a bucket to be lowered and filled with seawater. She laid the bucket at the feet of the captain. Dipping her hands in the water, she anointed his head, then his hands and his feet. She laid her ear upon his neck, then his heart, then his belly. Then, scooping seawater into her left hand, she asked the pirate captain to spit into its center. He did, and immediately the water became light, and the light became feathers, and the feathers became a red bird with a green beak who howled its name to the sky. It flew straight up, circled the mainmast, and spiraled down, settling on the captain's right shoulder.

"Don't lose him," she said to the captain.

In this way she healed those who were sick, and soothed the one who was dying, giving each his own familiar: a one-eared cat, an air-breathing fish, a blue albatross, and a silver snake.

When she finished, she turned to the captain. "Now you will return to your ship and we will continue our journey."

The captain nodded and smiled. "Of course, madam. But the child in your womb will return to us. She was conceived on the sea and will return to the sea. When she is old enough we will not come for her. We will not need to. She will find us."

Marguerite blinked, bit her lip so hard she drew blood, and returned to the hold without a word. She did not emerge until we made land.

Our brethren that had preceded us met us on the quay and led us to the temporary shelters that crouched, like lichen, on the rock. That the new church with its accompanying cloister and school were unfinished, we knew. But the extent of the disorder was an unconcealed shock to all of us, especially our poor Brother Abbot, whose face was stricken at the sight of the mossy stones upon the ground.

Brother Builder hung his head for the shame of it. "This is a place of entropy and decay," he muttered to me when the Abbot had gone. "Split wood will not dry, but erupts with mushrooms, though it has heated and cured for days. Cleared land, burned to the ground, will sprout within the hour with plants that we cannot identify or name—but all our seeds have rotted. Keystones crack from the weight of ivy and sweet, heavy blossoms that were not there the night before. The land, it seems, does not wish us to build."

The Abbot contacted the Governor, who conscripted paid laborers at our insistence—freemen and indentured, Taino and grim-faced Huguenots—to assist with the building, and soon we had not only church and cloister, but library, bindery, stables, root cellars, barrel houses, and distilleries.

Desperately, I hoped that Marguerite would be allowed to stay. I hoped that the Abbot would build her a cottage by the sea where she could keep a garden and sew for the abbey. Of course, she could not. The Abbot gave her a temporary shelter to herself, forcing many of the brethren to squeeze together on narrow cots, but no one grumbled. At the end of our first month on the island, she left without saying good-bye. I saw her on the road as the sun was rising, her satchel slung across her back. Her hair was uncovered and fell in a loose plait down her back, curling at the tops of her boots. I saw her and called her name. She turned and waved but said nothing. She did not need to. The sunlight bearing down on her small frame illuminated at last that to which I had been blind. Her belly had begun to swell.

Gabrielle was born in the vegetable garden that separated the Pleasure House from the small cottage where Marguerite lived and worked. Though the prostitutes gave her shelter in exchange for her skills as a cook, a gardener, and a healer, it soon became clear that her gifts were greater and more numerous than originally thought. As Marguerite's pregnancy progressed, the gardens surrounding the Pleasure House thrived beyond all imaginings.

Guavas grew to the size of infants, berries spilled across the lawns, staining the stone walkways and steps a rich, dark red, like blood coursing into a beating heart. Vines, thick and strong as saplings, snaked upward along the whitewashed plaster, erupting in multi-colored petals that fluttered from the roof like flags.

Marguerite, when the time came, knelt among the casaba melons and lifted her small hands to the bright sky. Immediately, a cloud of butterflies alighted on her fingers, her heaving shoulders, her rivers of gold hair, as the babe kicked, pressed, and slipped into the bundle of leaves that cradled her to the welcoming earth.

The girls of the Pleasure House saw this. They told the story to everyone. Everyone believed it.

After Gabrielle was born, Marguerite scooped up the after-birth and buried it at the foot of the guava tree. The girls of the Pleasure House gathered about her to wash the baby, to wheedle the new mother to bed, but Marguerite would not have it. She brought the baby to the spot where the placenta was buried.

"You see this?" she said to the baby. "You are rooted. Here. And here you will stay. The captain can believe what he will, but you are not a thing of water. You are a child of earth. And of me. And I am here." And with that she went inside and nursed her baby.

Though I assume it was well known that the babe with glittering eyes was the product of the one time (but *oh! Once!*) that Marguerite Belain consented to love me, we had chosen to believe that the child was a miracle, conceived of lightning, of sea, of the healing goodness of her mother. And in that believing, it became true. Gabrielle was not mine.

For months, the Abbot sent a convoy of monks to the little cottage behind the Pleasure House to argue in favor of a baptism for the child. Marguerite would not consent. No water, save from the spring that bubbled a mile inland, would touch Gabrielle. She would not bathe in the sea. She would not taste or touch water that came from any but her mother's hand.

"She will be rooted," she said. "And she will never float away."

After a time, the girls of the Pleasure House emerged to shoo us off. They had all of them grown in health and beauty since Marguerite's arrival. Their faces freshened, their hair grew bright and strong, and any whiff of the pox or madness or both had dissipated and disappeared. Moreover, their guests, arriving in the throes of hunger and lust, went away sated, soothed, and alive. They became better men. They were gentler with their wives, loving with their children. They fixed the roof of the church, rebuilt the washed-out roads, took in their neighbors after disasters. They lived long, healthy, happy lives and died rich.

Gabrielle Belain was never baptized, though in my dreams, I held that glittering child in my arms and waded into the sea to my waist. In my dream, I scooped up the sea in my right hand and let it run over the red curls of the child that was mine and not mine. Mostly not mine. In my dream, a red bird circled down from the sky, hovered for a moment before us, and kissed her rosebud mouth.

When Gabrielle was six years old, she wandered out of the garden and down the road to the town square. Her red curls shone with ribbon and oil, and her frock was blue and pretty and new. The girls of the Pleasure House, none of whom bore children of their own, doted on the child, spoiling her with dresses and hats and dolls and sweets. To be fair, though, the girl did not spoil, but only grew in sweetness and spark.

On the road, Gabrielle saw a mongrel dog that had been lamed in a fight. It was enormous, almost the size of a pony, with grizzled fur hanging about its wide, snarling mouth. It panted under the star apple tree, whining and showing its teeth. Gabrielle approached the animal, looked up at the branches heavy with fruit, and held out her hand. A star apple, dark and smooth, fell neatly into her little hand, its skin already bursting with sweet juice. She knelt before the dog.

"Eat," she said. The dog ate. Immediately, it stood, healed, nuzzled its new mistress, shaking its tail earnestly, and allowed her to climb upon its back. In the market square, people stopped and stared at the pretty little girl riding the mongrel dog. They offered her sweets and fruits and bits of fabric that might please a little child. She came to the fishmonger's stall. The fishmonger, an old, sour man, was in the middle of negotiating a price with an older, sourer man, and did not notice Gabrielle. A large marlin, quite dead, leaned over the side of the cart, its angled mouth slightly open as though attempting to breathe. Gabrielle, a tender child, put her hand to her mouth and blew the fish a kiss. The fishmonger, satisfied that he had successfully bilked his customer out of more gold than he had made all the week before, looked down and was amazed to see his fish flapping and twisting in the rough-hewn cart. The marlin leapt into the air and gave the customer a sure smack against his wrinkled cheek, before hurling itself onto the cobbled path and wriggling its way to the dock. Similarly, the other fish began to wiggle and jump, tumbling and churning against each other in a jumbled mass toward freedom. People gawked and pointed and gathered as the fishmonger vainly tried to gather the fish in his arms, but he had no idea what to do without the aid of his nets, and his nets were being mended by his foulmouthed wife in their little hovel by the sea.

Gabrielle and her dog, realizing that there was nothing more to see, moved closer to the fine house and tower that served as the Governor's residence and court and prison. To the side of the deeply polished doors, carved with curving branches and flowers and images of France, was the raised dais where men and women and children in chains stood silently, waiting to be priced, purchased, and hauled away. The man in the powdered wig who called out the fine qualities of the man in chains on his left did not notice the little girl riding the dog. But the man in chains did. She looked up at him, her freckled nose wrinkled in concentration, her green eyes squinting in the sun. She smiled at the man in chains and waved at him. He did not smile back—how could he?—but his eye caught the child's gaze and held it. Gabrielle watched his hands open and close, open and close, as though grasping and regrasping something invisible, endurable, and *true*. Something that could not be taken away.

The child began to sing—softly at first. And at first no one noticed. I stood in the receiving room of the Governor's mansion, waiting to receive dictation for letters going to the governors of other Caribbean territories, to the Mayor and High Inquisitor of New Orleans, and to the advisors to the king himself. This was our tribute to the Governor: rum, wine, transcribed books, and my hands. And for these gifts he left us mostly alone to live and work as pleased God.

Through the window I saw the child who came to me nightly in dreams. I heard the song. I sang too.

The people in the square, distracted by the escaping fish, did not notice the growing cloud of birds that blew in from the sea on one side and the forest on the other. They did not notice how the birds circled over the place where the people stood, waiting to be sold. They did not notice the bright cacophony of feathers, beaks, and talons descending on the dais.

Two big albatrosses upset the traders' moneyboxes, sending gold spilling onto the dirt. A thousand finches flew in the faces of the guards and officers keeping watch over the square. A dozen parrots landed on the ground next to Gabrielle and sang along with her, though badly and off-key. And hundreds of other birds—and not just birds of the island, birds from everywhere, birds of every type, species, description, and name—spiraled around every man, woman, and child, obscuring vision and confounding hand, foot, and reckoning, before alighting suddenly skyward and vanishing in the low clouds. Gabrielle, her song ended, rode slowly away, as though nothing out of the ordinary had happened. It was several moments before anyone realized that the dais was now empty, and each soul waiting for sale had vanished, utterly. All that was left was an assortment of empty chains lying on the ground.

For weeks after, the Governor, who had invested heavily in the slave-bearing ship and had lost a considerable sum in the disappearing cargo, sent interrogators, spies, and thieves into every home in the town, and while no one knew what had happened or why, everyone commented on the strange, beautiful little girl riding a mongrel dog.

From his balcony atop the mansion, the Governor could see the road that led away from the town, through the groves of fruit trees, through forest, to the Pleasure House and the little cottage surrounded by outrageously fertile gardens. He could see the golden-haired woman with her redheaded child. His breath was a cold wind, his face a merciless wave. A storm gathered in the town, preparing to crush my little Gabrielle.

I went with the Abbot to the cottage behind the Pleasure House, prepared to plead our case. It was not the first time. As the grumblings from the mansion grew louder and more insistent, we wrote letters in secret, sending them to the other islands and to France. Marguerite, dressed in a plain white linen shift, her golden hair braided and looped around her waist like a belt, laid out plates laden with fruit and bread and fish. Gabrielle sat in the corner on a little sleeping pallet. She was nine now and able to read. She came to the abbey often to look at Bibles and maps and poetry. What she read, she memorized. Once she was heard reciting the entire book of Psalms while perched high in a tree gathering nuts.

"Eat," Marguerite said to us, sitting opposite on the wooden bench and taking out her sewing.

"Later," the Abbot said, waving the plate away impatiently with his left hand. "Your child is not safe here anymore. You know this, my daughter. The Governor has his spies and assassins everywhere. We could hide her in the abbey, but for how long? It is only at my intercession that he has not come this far down the road, but neither of you is safe within a mile of the town."

"We need nothing from town," Marguerite said, filling our glasses with wine. "Drink," she commanded.

I brought my fist to the table. Gabrielle sat up with a start. "No," I said. "She cannot stay. I will accompany her back to France, and the Sisters of the Seventh Sorrow will protect her and educate her. No one will know whose child she is. No one will know of the Governor's hatred. She will be safe."

Marguerite took my fist and eased it open, laying her palm upon my palm. She looked at the Abbot and then at me.

"She is rooted here. I rooted her myself. She will not go to the sea. There is nothing more to say. Now. Eat."

We ate. And drank. The wine tasted of flowers, of love, of mother's milk, of sweat and flesh and dreaming. The food tasted like thought, like memory, like the pale whisperings of God. I dreamed of Gabrielle, growing, walking upon the water, standing with a sword against the sun. I dreamed of the taste of Marguerite's mouth.

The Abbot and I woke under a tree next to the abbey's stable. There was no need to say anything, so we went in for matins.

The next day, a ship with black sails appeared a mile out to sea. The girls of the Pleasure House reported that Marguerite went to the shore, screaming at the ship to depart. It did not. She called to the wind, to the ocean, to the birds, but no one assisted. The ship stayed where it was.

Soldiers came for Gabrielle. Marguerite saw them come. She stood on the roof of her house and raised her hands to the growing clouds. The soldiers looked up and saw that the sky rained flower petals. The petals came down in thick torrents, blinding all who were outdoors. With the petals came seeds and saplings, rooting themselves firmly in the overripe earth. The soldiers scattered, wandering blindly into the forest. Most never returned.

The next day, a thicket of trees grew up around the Pleasure House and the little cottage behind, along with a labyrinthine network of footpaths and trails. Few knew the way in or out. Whether the girls of the Pleasure House grumbled about this, no one knew. They appeared to have no trouble negotiating their way through the thicket, and trained a young boy, the son of the oyster diver, to stand at the entrance and guide men. If an agent of the Governor approached, the boy darted into the trees and disappeared. He was never followed.

The morning of Gabrielle's tenth birthday, a storm raged from the west, then from the north, then from the east. Everyone on the island prepared for the worst. Anything that could be lashed was lashed. We boarded ourselves in, or ran for high ground. Outside, the wind howled and thrashed against our houses and buildings. The sea churned and swelled before rearing up and crashing down upon the island. Most of the buildings remained more or less intact. At the abbey, the chapel flooded, as did the library, though most of the collection was saved. Several animals died when the smaller stable collapsed.

Once the rains subsided, I journeyed through the thick and cloying mud to check on Marguerite. I found her kneeling in the vegetable patch, weeping as though her heart would break. I knelt down next to her, though I don't think she noticed me at first. Her pale hands covered her face, and tears ran down her long fingers like pearls. She turned, looked at me full in the face with an expression of such sadness that I found myself weeping though I did not know why.

"The guava tree," she said. "The sea took it away."

It was true. Instead of the broad smooth trunk and the reaching branches, a hole gaped before us like a wound. Even the roots were gone.

"There is nothing to hold her here," she said. And for the first time since the night in the ship's hold during the storm all those years ago, I reached my arm across her back and coaxed her head to my shoulder. Her hair smelled of cloves and loam and salt. Gabrielle stood on the rocks at the shore, gathering seaweed into a basket to be used for soup. Her dog stayed close to her heels, as though Gabrielle might, at any moment, go skipping away. From time to time, the child peered out at the water, her eyes fixed on the rim of the ocean, or perhaps on something hovering just past the horizon—something that Marguerite and I could not see.

Two weeks later, Gabrielle Belain was gone. She slipped out to sea on the back of a porpoise, and she did not return to the island, except at last in chains in the belly of a prison ship.

From the window in the library, I saw the ship with black sails unfurl itself, draw its anchors, and sail away. From the forest surrounding the Pleasure House, a sound erupted, echoing across the shore, down the road, and deep into the wild lands of the island's interior. A deep, mournful, sorrowing cry. A dark cloud emerged over the forest and grew quickly across the island, heavy with rain and lightning. It rained for eighteen days. The road washed away, as did the foundations of houses, as well as gardens and huts that had not been securely fastened to the ground.

The Abbot went alone to the place where Marguerite wept. He brought no one with him, but when he returned, the sun reappeared, and Marguerite returned to her work healing sickness and coaxing abundance from the ground.

Every day, she made boats out of leaf and flower and moss, and every day she set them in the waves and watched them disappear across the sea.

Some years later, shortly after Gabrielle reached her fifteenth year, the captain called Gabrielle to his quarters when the pain in his chest grew intolerable.

"The weight of the world, my girl, rests upon my chest, and even your mother wouldn't be able to fix it this time. That's saying something, isn't it?" He laughed, which became a cough, which became a cry of pain.

Gabrielle said nothing, but took his hand between her own and held it as though praying. There was no use arguing. She could see the life paths in other people, and was able to find detours and shortcuts when available to avoid illness or pain or even death. There was no alternate route for her beloved captain. His path would end here.

The red bird whined in its cage, flapping its wings piteously.

"I thought that bird would die with me, but he looks like he's in the prime of his life. Don't lose him, girl." He did not explain, and she did not ask.

The captain died, naming Gabrielle his successor, which the crew accepted as both wise and inevitable. As captain, Gabrielle Belain emptied many of the ships heading toward the holdings of the Governor, as well as redirected ships with human cargo, placing maps, compasses, swords, and ship wheels in the palms of hands that once bore chains, and setting the would-be slavers adrift with only a day's worth of food and water and a book of prayers to help them to repent. The freed ships followed flocks of birds toward home, and Gabrielle prayed that they made it safely. The Governor lost thousands, and thousands more, until he was at the brink of ruination, though he attempted to hide it. This caused the pirates no end of delight.

The red bird remained in his cage for two years next to the portal in the captain's quarters, though it hurt Gabrielle to see it so imprisoned and alone. Finally, after tiring of his constant complaining, she brought the cage on deck to give the poor thing a chance to see the sun. The mongrel dog growled, then whined for days, but Gabrielle did not notice. There the bird remained on days when it was fine, for another year, until finally, Gabrielle whispered to the bird that if he promised to return, she would let him out for an hour at sundown. The bird promised, and obeyed every day for ten days. But on the eleventh day, the red bird did not return to its cage.

The next morning, a mercenary's ship approached from the north, and fired a shot into the starboard hull. It was their first hit since the crew's meeting with Marguerite Belain eighteen years and nine months earlier. The ship listed, fought back, and barely escaped intact. Gabrielle stood on the mast step and peered through her spyglass to Martinique. A storm cloud churned and spread, widening over the thrashing sea.

Down in the ship's hold, Gabrielle rummaged and searched until she found the empty rum barrel where she had placed the boats made of leaf and flower and moss, which she had fished out of the water when no one was looking. She took one, then thought better of it and took ten and threw them into the water. In the waning light she watched them move swiftly on the calm sea, sailing as one toward Martinique.

Gabrielle Belain (the witch, the revolutionary, the pirate) became the obsession of the Governor, who enlisted the assistance of every military officer loyal to him, every mercenary he could afford, and every captain in possession of a supply of cannons and a crew unconcerned about raising a sword to the child of a Saint Among Men. The third, of course, was most difficult to come by. A soldier will do as he is told, but a seaman is beholden to his conscience and his soul.

For many years, it did not matter. Ships sent out to overtake the ship with black sails, navigated and subsequently commanded by the girl with red hair, flanked as always by a mongrel dog, found themselves floundering and lost. Their compasses suddenly became inoperable, their maps wiped themselves clean, birds landed in massive clouds and ripped their sails to shreds.

In the beauty and comfort of the Governor's mansion, I took the dictation of a man sick with rage and frustration. His hair thinned and grew gray and yellow by degrees. His flesh sagged about the neck and jowls, while swelling at the middle. As he recited his dictation, he moved about the room like a dying tiger in a very small cage, his movements quick, erratic, and painful.

When Gabrielle was a child and still living on the island, she was to the poor Governor an unfortunately located tick, a maddening bite impossible to scratch. When she boarded the pirate ship and gained the ear of a captain who was both a matchless sailor and ravenous for French gold, she became for the Governor an object of madness. He outlawed the propagation of redheaded children. He made the act of bringing fish back to life a crime punishable by death. He forbade the use of Gabrielle as a given name, and ordered any resident with the name of Gabrielle to change it instantly. He sent spies to infiltrate the wood surrounding the Pleasure House, but the spies were useless. They could have told him, of course, that Marguerite Belain went to the surf every morning to set upon the waves a small boat that sailed straight and true to the far horizon, though it had no sail. They could have told the Governor that every night a blue albatross came to Marguerite's garden and whispered in her ear.

They told him no such thing. Marguerite instead led the spies into her home, where she fed them and gave them drink. Then, she led them to the Pleasure House. They would appear a few days later, sleeping on the road, or wandering through the market, examining fish.

The Governor, gesticulating wildly, dictated a letter to the king, asking for more ships with which to capture or kill the pirate Gabrielle Belain. He detailed the crimes of the pirate—twenty-five ships relieved of their tax gold, eighteen slave ships either freed or vanished altogether, rum houses raided, sugar fields burned— all these things I wrote to his satisfaction, confident that the king would, as usual, do nothing. In the midst of our audience, however, a young man threw open the doors without announcing himself and without apologizing. The Governor, sputtering with rage, threw his fist upon the desk. The young man did not stop.

"The black ship," he said, "has been lamed."

The Governor stood without breathing. "Lamed," he said, "when?"

"Last night. They hailed the *Medallion*, who brought the message presently. They have taken refuge on the lee of St. Vincent. The injury to the black ship is grave and will take several days, I am told, to remedy."

"And the ship who lamed it. Is it sound?"

"They lost a mast to cannon fire, but the ship, crew, and instruments are sound. Nothing lost, nothing." The young man paused. "*Strange.*"

The Governor walked across the room, threw the doors open with such force that he cracked one down the middle. Whether he noticed or not, he did not acknowledge, nor did he take leave of me. The young man also left without a word. I laid my pages on the table and went to the window, the prayers for the intercession of the Blessed Mother tumbling from my lips. I stood at the window and watched as rumors of lightning whispered at the sky.

On the first of May, 1698, the ship with black sails was surrounded and beaten, its deck boarded and its crew put in irons. Messages were sent to the islands of France, England, and Spain that Gabrielle Belain (the pirate, the witch, the revolutionary) had been captured at last, and her execution had been duly scheduled. The citizens of Saint-Pierre brought flowers and breads and wine to the edge of the wood surrounding the Pleasure House. They lifted their children onto their shoulders that they might catch a glimpse of the woman who was once the girl who brought the fish to life, and who rode on the back of a porpoise, and who inherited the saintly, healing hands of her mother.

The day before Gabrielle Belain was to be executed, a large red bird visited the window, hovered on the sill, and kissed her mouth through the bars. This the people saw. This the people believed. In that moment, Gabrielle began to sing. She did not stop.

The Governor, as he welcomed representatives from neighboring protectorates and principalities, attempted the pomp and protocol befitting such a meeting. He heard the song of the girl pirate in the tower. His foreign guests did not, even as it grew louder and louder. The Governor rattled his sword, ran a shaking hand through his thinning, yellowed hair. He attempted to smile, as the song grew even louder.

The people in the market square heard the song as well. They heard a song of flowers that grew into boats that brought bread to hungry children. They heard a song of a tree that bore fruit for anyone who was hungry, of a cup that brought water to any who thirsted. She sang of a kiss that set the flesh to burning, and the burning to seed, and the seed to sprout and flower and heavily fruit. The people heard the song and sorrowed for the redheaded child, barely a woman now, who would die in the morning.

The song kept the Governor awake all night. He paced and cursed. He made singing illegal. He made music a crime worthy of death. Were it not for the celebrations planned around the scheduled execution of the pirate, he would have slit her throat then and there, but dignitaries had arrived for a death march, and a death march they would see.

In the moments before the dawn crept over the edge of the sky, the Governor consented that I would be allowed into Gabrielle's cell to administer baptism, absolution, and last rites. Gabrielle stood at the window where she had stood all night and the previous day, the song still spilling from her lovely mouth, though quietly now, barely a breath upon her tongue. I offered her three sacraments, and three sacraments she refused, though she consented to hold my hand. I thought she did this to comfort herself, a moment of tenderness for a girl about to die. When the soldiers came to take her to the gallows, she turned to embrace me for the first time. She placed her mouth to my ear and whispered, "Don't follow."

So I did not. I let the soldiers take her away. I did not fight and I did not follow. I sat on the floor of the tower and wept.

Gabrielle, still singing, walked without struggle in the

company of soldiers, all of whom begged her for forgiveness. All of whom told her stories of how her mother had saved a member of their family or blessed their gardens with abundance. Whether she listened, I do not know. I remained in the tower. All I know are the stories people later told.

They say that she walked with her eyes on the ground, her mouth still moving in song. They say she stepped up onto the platform as the constable read the charges against her. He had several pages of them, and the people began to shift and fuss in their viewing area. As the constable read, Gabrielle's song grew louder. No one noticed a boat approaching in the harbor. A boat made of flowers and moss and leaves. A boat with no sail, though it moved swift and sure with a woman standing tall at its center.

Gabrielle's song grew louder, until with a sudden cry, she threw her chained hands into the air and tossed her red hair back. A mass of birds—gulls, martins, doves, owls, bullfinches—appeared as a great cloud overhead and descended over and around the girl, blocking her from view. The Governor ordered his men to shoot. They did, but the flock numbered in the thousands of thousands, so while the square was littered in dead birds, the cloud rose nonetheless, the girl suspended in its center, and moved to the small craft floating in the harbor.

The Governor, his rage clamping hard around his throat and heart, ordered his ships boarded, ordered his cannons loaded, ordered his archers to shoot at will, but the craft bearing the two women skimmed across the water and vanished from sight.

This I learned from the people in the square, and this I believe, though the Governor issued a proclamation that the execution was a success, that the pirate Gabrielle Belain was dead, and that anyone who claimed otherwise risked imprisonment. Everyone, of course, claimed otherwise. No one was imprisoned.

That night, I stole gold from the coffers of the Abbey and walked down the road to the harbor. My beloved Abbot knew, I'm certain. The stores where such treasures are kept are always locked, but the Abbot left them unlocked and did not send for me after my crime. I purchased a small skiff and set sail by midday.

I am, alas, no sailor. My map, one that I copied myself, paled, faded, and vanished to a pure white page on the third day of my voyage. I dropped my compass into the sea, where it was promptly devoured by a passing fish. I have searched for a boat made of leaf, but I have found only salt. I have searched for two faces that I have loved. Gabrielle. Marguerite. The things I have loved. The scratch of quill to paper. The Abbot. France. Martinique. Perhaps it is all one. One curve of a wanton hip of a guileless god. Or perhaps my believing it is one has made it one. Perhaps this is the nature of things.

I do not know—nor, indeed, does it matter that I know—whether these words shall ever be read. It is not, as our beloved Abbot told me again and again, the reading that saves, but the writing: it is in the writing that the Word is Flesh. In our Order, we have copied, transcribed, and preserved words—both God's and Man's—for the last thousand years. Now, as I expire here in this waste of water and wind and endless sky, I write of my own disappearing, and this, my last lettering, will likely fade, drift, and vanish into the open mouth of the ravenous sea.

I have dreamed of their hands. I dream of their hands. I

dream of a garden overripe and wild. Of a woman gathering the sea into her hands and letting it fall in many colored petals to a green, green earth. I dream of words on a page transforming to birds, and birds transforming to children, and children transforming to stars.

Notes on the Untimely Death of Ronia Drake

*

1.

The last sound she heard was water. It bubbled and flowed from the masses of decaying snow piles, slicked the path, and fanned into the spongy turf and sleeping grass. Bits of puddle splashed up on her white socks and white-and-red legs—a spangle of gray salt drips curving up to the knee. She did not mind, but continued to run across the park, gaining speed as she went. She ran with ease, with a surety of motion and grace. She did not worry about growing tired or hurting herself. She ran without fear.

Both the path and the park were empty, which surprised her because the day was warm at last after an endless winter of endless cold. She wore shorts and a T-shirt that said "Big Mama's Bar," which she thought she had been to once. The westerly breeze nipped at her upper arms and thighs, and while it was warm enough to melt the snow, she probably should have worn leggings or a windbreaker.

Should have.

In truth, it didn't really matter either way. In about ten minutes, Ronia Drake's life will end. She will not see death coming, nor will she see it scuttling away—its large mouth damp, drooping, and satiated. She will only know a sharp knock, a flurry of feathers and fur, a whisper of her name, and a sharp, curved finger at her throat.

Or perhaps it will be a burst of light.

Or perhaps it will be nothing at all.

2.

Once upon a time, there was a little girl who wanted to be a princess. She wanted a pretty ring that glimmered on a pink-tipped finger, a tiny foot slipped neat and tight into a smart, beaded shoe. She wanted a crown of curls framing a delicate face.

But, alas, she was large-footed and ungainly. Her face was broad and fleshy and unbalanced. Nothing about her twinkled. Nothing.

Once upon a time, there was a little girl who came into a little bit of magic. Well, perhaps *came into* is the wrong phrase. Perhaps *stole* would be more apt. Either way, the girl felt, it was nothing more than semantics. When people inherit money they say *came into*, and since the magic's previous owner was as dead as could be, *came into* was as good a description as any.

There once was a little girl who wanted to be a princess, and learned magic to make it happen. Magic—stolen, inherited, or otherwise—is an unwieldy tool, but like any other useful thing, can be mastered by anyone who bothers to learn it.

After several attempts on unsuspecting proxies, the girl turned her magic on herself. She marveled at her tiny feet, snug in lovely beaded shoes with heels that clicked over a blue tile floor. She marveled at her face, milky soft and delicately boned. A princess's face. She looked longingly at her hands, her long-fingered hands, as pale as pearls. There should be, she felt, a ring on her finger. With a diamond that glittered. And a prince to go with it.

Once upon a time, there was a princess who stole a prince. *No*, she thought, *not stole. Came into.* And so what if she used her little bit of magic? Her little inheritance. So what if he needed some encouragement to turn his head? No one cared, anyway. If she could have her way, and she often did, she would tell a new story—the right story—and she would write it like this:

Once upon a time there was a princess. A very pretty princess. Prettier than you. Once upon a time, a very handsome prince stole the very pretty princess.

No, not stole. Came into. And he would not get out.

3.

The moment Ronia Drake died, her daughters turned to their stepmother and pointed.

"Girls," the stepmother said, "don't point."

"You," the girls said, their small fingers pointing to the stepmother's pale gold curls, cropped prettily under her ears.

"You," the girls said, pointing at the stepmother's swollen belly, which had enlarged upon itself, doubling, then tripling its size until people joked that it must be a medicine ball shoved under her skin. Or a go-kart. Or a truck.

"Girls," she said again, but she stopped. She never called them by their names. She only called them "girls" when she was feeling petulant and "ladies" when she was feeling fine. Now, with the pointing and the accusations, she was feeling petulant. But when she reached for the first one, the one with the scar over her eye (and if only she could remember which one had the scar over her eye), she caught sight of her own hand and drew it back with a sharp cry. The stepmother had always had lovely hands the color of pearls. Or, at least it seemed like always. She told people that when women let themselves go, the first place it shows is in their hands. No man wants to make love to a woman with red knuckles and cuticles jutting out like spikes. No man wants a woman with quick-bitten fingernails, or fingernails rimmed with dirt, or spots or wrinkles or cracks.

Ronia Drake had dreadful hands. It was no wonder her husband had left her. The stepmother said this as though it were true. No one noticed the way a smile slicked across her milk-pale skin. No one noticed the strange glitter of her terrible beauty. Or, at least, they pretended not to notice. Instead they nodded to her comment about hands. So true, they said. So very, very true.

But now. Now as the stepmother reached for one of the girls she saw a hand, her own, covered in blood. A hand missing a pinkie and a thumb. And what was worse, it wasn't her own hand at all. It was Ronia Drake's hand.

4.

As Ronia Drake ran along the path, the wind seemed to curve around her, twisting like yarn. Her hair wouldn't stay tied back and instead wisped free, tickling her eyes and ears and nose. The left side of the path was a strip of grass that soon would be green but was currently brown, and though it looked prickly, she knew that if she removed her running shoes, the ground would be spongy and cold and soaking wet. Beyond the grass the ground fell away in a tangle of leafless branches and trunks and thorns that wove through each other in their tumble toward the river below. Ronia Drake always warned her daughters to stay out of those woods.

You never know who might be living in those woods.

As Ronia Drake ran, she did not notice the eyes in the woods. She did not notice the way the ravens gathered and re-gathered only just behind her as she ran. She did not notice the pale reflection that glimmered on the edges of the oil-slicked sheen of the dark puddles. Pale curls dancing on the rippling water. And a delicate mouth slashed open in a grin.

Every once in a while a bench made of river rocks held together by gravelly mortar with a few splintery planks set across for sitting on appeared along the path. So did occasional ancient barbeques and fire pits with chimneys that pointed effortlessly toward the sky. These too were made of river rocks. Once, when she had taken her daughters here for a picnic, Anna, or perhaps it was Alice, shinnied to the top of the chimney, her long, bare arms and legs moving with the chaotic grace of an insect. Now that she thought about it, it was both Alice and Anna, but it was Anna who fell, slicing the tender skin between her eye and brow on a particularly sharp piece of granite. Alice remained on top, crying, and Ronia never knew if she cried because her sister fell, or if she was frightened, or if she simply did not like to be separated from the girl who shared her face. A man called nine-one-one on his cell, and a fire truck came to bandage Anna and pluck

Alice from the sky. The girls, reunited, wrapped their long, pale arms around each other, whispering soundlessly in each other's ears.

That night, Ronia dreamed that the girls lived in a nest at the top of the chimney. Their hands gripped the edges of the rocks like talons and they peered down at the people on the path. When Ronia walked along the path looking for her children, the girls threw bits of twig and feathers and dry grass at their mother, but it did not reach her. It blew up in a twisting wind and vanished over the edge of the empty trees. She called to the girls to come down, but they were no longer girls. They stared down at her with large, complicated eyes, their gentle antennae clasping and unclasping, their long, thin, green legs folded under their bodies, ready to spring. Ready to fly away. And they did fly. Over her head, her girls, or her grasshoppers, or her grasshoppers who once were her girls, vaulted across the sky in a buzz of leg and song.

When she woke, she did not remember the dream.

"I had the strangest dream," she told people.

"What was it?" the people asked.

"No idea," she said.

5.

The police were called, more than once, although no one could tell them why they called. People dialed the emergency number and found themselves staring at the place where Ronia Drake once lived and breathed, but now did not. One man vomited on his phone, ruining it forever. A girl tried to explain what she saw, but she fell to her knees and began speaking in tongues instead.

An older woman began to have heart palpitations, and asked the dispatcher—a kind woman named Eunice—to send out an extra ambulance while she was at it. When the ambulance arrived, the EMTs found the old woman seated under a tree, her legs stretched out in front of her, her body pressed to the trunk of the tree as though pinned. She had faced herself away from the remains of Ronia Drake, which seemed sensible enough, but had died anyway, pressing one hand against her eyes and one on her heart. The girl remained in the center of the path, kneeling, her hands and face pointing to the sky. Her voice had gone hoarse by the time the ambulance came, and the second ambulance, and the fire truck and police car. But her lips continued to move.

One paramedic knelt by some of the remains of Ronia Drake. A severed ponytail, a bit of T-shirt that said "Mama." The paramedic picked up the ponytail and brought it to his nose. He smelled bread and long-limbed children and cut grass and a curved pink lip exposing white teeth that had been sharpened to points. He smelled bright green grasshoppers tenderly washing their faces. He smelled a slim, long-legged deer, bending sweetly to feed upon the damp grass. A deer with two grasshoppers balanced on her delicately boned head. A deer with a blue eye.

"Ronia Drake," he said to the others. "Her name was Ronia Drake." He did not explain how he knew this, and no one asked. The others began looking for any kind of identification, though they would find none. They did find a shoe, ten toes (in ten places), a shoulder, a blue eye. Each part was sliced cleanly, as though with a scalpel. There was little blood. "And this," the paramedic said, picking up the two hands clasped together as though praying. One hand was red-knuckled and quick-bitten. The other was pink-tipped and pale as pearls, with a diamond that would have gleamed were it not for the drop of blood that had landed on the stone. "This," he said, "is not her hand."

Above their heads an unkindness of ravens gathered and dispersed and gathered again. They landed on empty branches, on signs declaring which path was for biking and which for walking, and on the wet ground. They opened their black beaks and called to one another, and back, and back again. The paramedic looked into the glinting eye of the biggest, shiniest of them all. Although he knew it was crazy, he could have sworn the ravens were calling "Ronia, Ronia, Ronia."

6.

The stepmother locked herself into the bathroom.

"You," the girls said on the other side of the door. They did not knock or bang.

"Shut up," the stepmother whispered, her voice like glass in her ears.

"You," the girls sang. No, screeched. No, sang. Sang like birds—*no*, like bugs. They sang with the voice of something small. Something scuttling. Something with a damp, satiated mouth.

"Tzzz, tzzz, tzzz," they sang, their voices reverberating on the tile and porcelain, shaking the walls, vibrating the stepmother's perfect house.

The stepmother covered her ears, felt the coagulating blood gum up on the side of her cheek. Her left hand was bloody still, and still not her own. Ronia Drake's hand. Ronia Drake's hand missing a pinkie and a thumb. With the hand that was her own, she gripped at her belly, swollen so taut and tight that it threatened to split down the middle. The child inside did not move. It had not moved all day.

When Ronia Drake was pregnant, the girls' father said, her belly twisted and rumbled from morning to night. He said that the girls were a constant tumble of arms and legs and wings. He said that if you placed your ear on Ronia Drake's belly, you could hear the girls singing.

"What did they sing?" the stepmother asked, not because she was interested, but because she felt it would be polite.

"Tzzz, tzzz, tzzz," her husband sang on the tips of his white teeth. The teeth that she insisted he bleach.

"That's not a song," she said.

"Oh, but it is," he said, and he sang it again. "Tzzz, tzzz, tzzz." He sang it gorgeously, lovingly, magnanimously. He sang it with a smile curving across those white, white teeth. He never sang that way for her.

As her belly grew, swelled, puffed, she bought a stethoscope, and listened for the sounds of her own child singing. She heard silence.

And the stepmother hated the girls.

And the stepmother hated Ronia Drake.

7.

As Ronia Drake ran, she did not miss her daughters. She knew she should feel guilty for this but she did not. When she was young, she was afraid of being alone and filled the empty spaces of her life with boyfriends and best friends and intimate acquaintances. But now. Now, it was different.

Ever since her husband learned how to bleach his teeth, how to artfully tousle his hair with pomade, and how to love the woman who would be her daughters' stepmother, Ronia had her children on Wednesdays through Saturdays, and her husband had them on Sundays through Tuesdays. This arrangement worked for a long time while the stepmother did not conceive. But the stepmother wanted a baby. Of course she did. Pretty girl like that would want to pass it on. Ronia Drake, when she was young and slick with love, wanted a baby as well. She got two, and her body showed it. Then her husband left.

So it goes, she told people.

Finally, the waist of the stepmother swelled prettily. She bloomed, blossomed, was ripe and happy. At first. But after a while the growth was more rapid and uncontained. She doubled and tripled. She grew out of her maternity clothes and hired a woman to sew new shirts to cover her enormous middle.

You're fine, the doctors said, you have a healthy boy—and just one, so don't worry. But the stepmother worried and Ronia Drake could tell.

For two weeks, the stepmother had avoided allowing the girls into her home.

I'm so tired, she said.

My back hurts, my ass hurts, my belly hurts, my legs hurt, she said.

You understand, of course you do, she said.

Ronia Drake held her tongue. *Lazy,* she thought but smiled kindly instead. Of course she understood.

Ronia Drake loved her daughters. *Loved them.* She loved the mown grass scent of their matching scalps. She loved their reedy arms and matching pale lips, and how, no matter what color they wore, the mind's eye dressed them in green. She loved the way they pressed their fingertips on her cheekbone when she pretended to sleep. They were her girls, and she loved them.

But when her husband—no, ex-husband—and sometimes her husband's new wife, came to pick up the girls in the brand new Audi, Ronia Drake kissed their mown grass heads, and straightened their pink shirts and brown pants (though in her memory, they would only be wearing green), and told them to be good girls as she caressed their delicate faces, pressing her fingertips gently along their cheekbones. She stood on the curb and waved to them. They watched her through the window, their faces drawn and solemn. They waved back, the car rumbled then glided away, and her children disappeared.

Then, Ronia Drake did not miss her children. She painted. She worked. She ran—long runs along the river, or the creek, or from one end of the city to the other. Sometimes she ran for hours without tiring. She felt unfettered, faceless and unnamed. Lost, yes, but there was a freedom in being lost. There was a freedom in abandonment too, if you thought about it right.

She painted the walls in large, complicated murals that changed when she felt it was time for them to change. In the girls' room, she painted a collage of important women, to inspire them. But when the girls found them boring, she covered up the severe suffragettes and resistance organizers, and painted bugs instead—delicate diplopods, luscious butterflies as they pleasured trembling flowers, and sure-footed arachnids pulling filament upon filament from their bellies. She painted figures that looked like girls if you looked at them in one way and bugs if you looked at them in another.

In the living room, she painted a girl sitting on a park bench with an old woman. The girl was unattractive, and would have been in an agreeable way, if it weren't for the unpleasantness in her eyes and the slice of her mouth. The old woman was so old, the folds of her skin so complicated and fragile, as to render her shockingly beautiful.

People asked Ronia: "Does she glow in the dark? How did you get the old woman to shine like that?"

"I don't know," she said truthfully.

People asked, "Is it just me, or is that the ugliest looking ugly girl you've ever seen?" They saw the way the girl had just moistened her lips with her cracked tongue, the way the tip lingered under her sharp teeth. They noticed the way her knuckles were bent, ready, itching to strike.

"And look," the people said. "The branches look like eyes."

"And look," the people said. "The grass looks like a mouth. A grassy mouth with hungry teeth and a large damp tongue."

"Oh," Ronia said. "I hadn't noticed."

8.

Once upon a time, a little girl sat next to a witch on a park bench as the sun set over the park. The witch was old and kind, with fragile skin that folded and creased upon itself like a complicated map. When people walked by, the witch would smile, and though they did not notice, they began to relax, soften, become unaccountably happy.

"You see," the witch said to the girl. "It is neither good nor bad. It is itself, but can extend our goodness or badness, our foolishness or our intelligence. It's difficult to use. It has consequences. It is not a toy for children." She said this kindly, gently, attempting to put the girl off without being off-putting. She inquired after the girl's studies, after her friends, but there was little to say in that department.

Besides, the girl was busy rewriting the story:

Once upon a time, there was a princess under a spell. A wicked spell. Cast by a wicked witch. The witch had magic that should not have been hers, while the princess was denied the honor of beauty. In order to break the spell, the witch's magic needed to be stolen away. The princess broke the spell. She reached into the complicated folds of the witch's throat and squeezed.

The girl felt the old woman's magic (neither good nor bad but unwieldy, with consequences) surge into her open, astonished mouth.

9.

The police arrived and scratched their heads, wondering where to begin. The paramedic told them what he knew, though he did not say how he came into that knowledge. *Better to be vague*, he thought. They began to mark the places where the body lay scattered in the damp, brown grass. The paramedic was worried about the ravens that gathered in greater numbers on every branch, on every park bench, on every sign. But they did not make for the meat. In fact, they had stopped calling altogether. They watched silently: a gathering, black-coated crowd.

The girl speaking in tongues was coaxed onto a gurney and examined. Her eyes, dilated and wild, circled the sky while her mouth continued to make words that were not words.

"All right, sweetheart," the paramedic said. "In we go." But the girl sat up, her long brown hair falling into her face. She grabbed the paramedic's uniform and looked directly into his face.

"Tzzz, tzzz, tzzz," she said.

"Don't worry, honey," he began, but she shook her head.

"Tzzz, tzzz, tzzz," she insisted.

The paramedic ignored this, and with a one, two, three and a heave, he and his coworkers inserted the gurney into the open maw of the ambulance. He patted the back, and the driver took the girl away. The ravens watched her go.

The paramedic walked to his bag and was reaching for it when he noticed a large, shocking green grasshopper on his hand.

"Hello," he said to the grasshopper, bringing his hand to his face. The grasshopper did not move, but stared at him with its iridescent eyes, its long legs gently wiping its mouth.

"Tzzz, tzzz, tzzz," said the grasshopper.

"That seems to be a popular song these days," the paramedic said, and then stopped. Because the song wasn't just coming from his hand. It came from the grass, then the tree, then the tangled forest tumbling down to the river. Then it was everywhere.

10.

The stepmother leaned her expanding bulk against the door. She knocked the back of her head against the teak veneer, which she had ordered herself and had polished to a high gloss. Outside, inside, or perhaps in her head, the girls' voices went from accusation to song to accusation again.

"You," they said, their voices sharp as scalpels.

"Tzzz, tzzz," they sang, their voices an insistent whir.

"You're doing it wrong," she shouted. "This isn't how the story goes." Her hand itched. Except it wasn't her hand. Ronia Drake's hand itched. But that couldn't be right. Ronia Drake was dead. The stepmother watched it happen in a slick of water, and water can't lie. The old woman told her so. And a dead woman can't itch.

And yet the hand did itch, and it was driving her mad. That and the constant drone of the girls outside the door. She rubbed Ronia Drake's hand on the lump of her belly. The child inside did not move. It never did. And it did not sing. She rubbed harder, trying to block out the itch, trying to block out the sound that whirred in the tile, in the air, in her bones. As she rubbed her belly grew. Her buttons popped off and cracked the far window with a sharp ping. Her knees buckled under the weight, and she crashed to the ground.

She looked at the hand. Ronia Drake's hand. A thing she did not expect. *(Unwieldy. With consequences.)* It had to go.

With great effort, she grasped the edge of the sink and lifted herself up. She threw open the door to the medicine cabinet, cracking the mirrored surface against the wall. Grabbing her husband's razor, she hacked at the skin that bordered Ronia Drake's ugly hand with her own pale and creamy skin. It wasn't enough, of course. How could it be?

"More," she said to the razor. "Be more, goddamnit."

And the razor was more. First it was a butcher knife. Then a machete. Then a scimitar. The blade was so sharp it glinted and sang in the air.

"Tzzz," sang the blade.

"Shut up," commanded the stepmother. "Just cut." And it cut. The skin cut quietly. The bone sliced with a short, quick snap, and Ronia Drake's hand fell softly to the ground with a thud.

As the stepmother reached for a towel to stop the bleeding, the glossy surface of the door split apart and the air sang. Grasshoppers, electric green and delicate and utterly wild, swarmed into the bathroom. They covered the shower curtain, inundated the sink, blanketed the toilet. They blocked out the light, crawled into her mouth, stopped up her nose, crowded onto her eyes. And they were beautiful. The stepmother thought, *You look just like Alice.* Then she thought, *No, perhaps it's Anna.* But before she could decide, darkness thundered all around her and she was lost.

11.

The paramedic shaded his eyes, even though it was overcast. One cloud, dark, thick, and undulating, approached quickly over the tops of the empty trees. The cops stopped scratching their heads and looked up at the sky.

"What the hell is that sound?" one of them asked.

The cloud moved faster and faster. When it arrived, the

paramedic saw that it wasn't dark at all. It was green. Deep green, like a still pool. And not a cloud, either.

Grasshoppers landed lightly on the brown grass. They balanced on the beaks of the motionless ravens and buzzed wildly in the air around the cops and paramedics and everyone else who stopped at the edge of the police line to watch.

The paramedic cupped his hands around his eyes. He crouched down to get a better view. The grasshoppers seemed familiar, though he did not know why. He seemed to recall a girl perched on the top of a stone chimney, and another girl who shared her face crying on the ground beneath. He remembered a woman, tall, with long, dark hair and shockingly blue eyes, kneeling next to the girl on the ground, her eye fixed on her child clinging to the edges of the stone.

"Ronia Drake," he started to say, but a grasshopper flew into his mouth.

"Hush," he thought he heard it say. Or maybe it was "Tzzz."

A moment later, the cloud lifted as quickly as it came, tumbling over the twisted bramble and down to the river. By the time the cops and paramedics registered their astonishment and looked down at the ground, at the places where they had marked the locations of the remains of Ronia Drake, the markers still lay on the grass, untouched, but the severed, bloodless pieces of the body were gone.

12.

The night after her husband left her, Ronia Drake lay alone in her bed and cried herself to sleep. During the night she had a dream. She dreamed she had fallen off the path in the park and then tumbled in the bramble as it fell to the river. She rolled until she reached a narrow ledge, where she found a table and two chairs. She sat down. An old woman sat on the other side. She had hair so white it seemed to glow and delicate skin that folded again and again upon itself.

"Tea," the old woman said, handing her a cup.

They drank.

"Watch out for puddles," the old woman told her.

"All right," Ronia Drake said, her mouth inside the teacup.

"And take this." She reached across and fastened a pendant around the neck of Ronia Drake.

"What is it?"

"Change," the old woman said. "Change is good."

When Ronia Drake woke up, her legs were covered in red scratches and cuts, and a pendant was fastened around her neck. She never took it off.

13.

Once upon a time, there was a man who had a wife that he lost and another wife who was locked up and was therefore as good as lost. He could not remember his first wife, though he knew he should. He had an inkling of daughters, as well, but that came and went.

Still, he felt lonely.

Still, he felt lost. Once, someone told him that there was a freedom in being lost. And in abandonment too, if he thought about it right. But he could only think about the blank spaces where a family ought to have been.

The man's other wife lived in a tower far away. He rode to see her when he could. Once upon a time, this wife was pretty. Pretty as a princess. But not anymore. Not since they plucked the baby, purple and twisted and waterlogged, from her distended womb. Not since she was found in the bathroom with the hand of a dead woman and razor slices up and down her arm. Now she lived in a white tower with white walls and a long white gown that tied in the back. Now, her feet were large and ungainly, her face lopsided and haphazard, like a potato left too long in the ground. Now, she whispered stories of witches and insects and a wicked, wicked woman named Ronia Drake.

Each time he heard that name, he felt a jolt in his heart. *Ronia Drake*, the man thought, and though he could not place it, he liked the sound of that name. It had a comforting heft and weight. It was familiar, somehow.

Once, the man went walking in the park and fell off the path. He had been warned never to stray from the path, you never did know who lived in those woods. Although for the life of him, he could not remember who had warned him, if anyone had. He fell off the path and tumbled into the greening wood. Halfway down, he reached a ledge of sorts and stood. The ledge became a path that switched back and forth. He followed it. He couldn't go up, but he assumed the path would lead him to a boat landing, or maybe a road.

As he walked, he became aware of something following him, something with soft, sure steps. He turned.

A deer stood in front of him, brown and sleek and lovely, her coat shining like a queen's. Her narrow head tilted slightly to the right, and breath clouded prettily from a damp, black nose. Her eyes were wide and intelligent and blue.

Do deer normally have blue eyes? He couldn't remember.

Above each eye rested a grasshopper, glimmering like a green jewel. The grasshoppers tilted their iridescent faces toward the man, and he could have sworn that one of them winked.

"You," he said.

"Tzzz," said the grasshoppers. Or perhaps it was the deer. Or perhaps it was the wood.

Once upon a time there was a prince who searched for his lost love in the deep, dark forest. He never returned.

THE INSECT

and the

ASTRÖNOMER

A LOVE STORY

++++++/////+++++

1.

The Insect has never been in love.

The Astronomer has never been alive.

It is important that you understand this.

2.

The Insect paces his office, allowing the tips of his forelegs, the ooze and suck of the pulvilli between his tiny, delicate claws, to graze against the stacks of books, the stacks of papers, the stuff and rustle of a life dedicated to learning and study and endless pontification. He has been, until now, and in his own estimation, a grand professor and a great scholar. Until now. *Shed scales,* he thinks. *It is only shed scales. And abandoned husks. The remnants of word and lecture and useless thinking.* He listens to his lower feet as they scuttle against the old stone floor—a thin, cold, lonely sound.

The Hon. Professor Pycanis Educatus—called the Insect, or the Pyca, or the Bug-in-Spats, or the Insectus Insufferabilis, or the Hon. Doctor Please-Swat-Me Creepy-Crawlie, by his students and former students and current colleagues—was one of only nine of his kind when he was born. Now, he is the only one. At one time *Pycanum bellus gigantis* were numerous in this part of the world—and widely known for their devotion to the arts and sciences, as well as the noble pursuits of athleticism, skepticism, gnosticism, and algorithmic recalculations. Not anymore. They are gone now. All, all gone. And he is alone.

If it is wrong for Man to be alone, the Insect muses in the solitude of his room, *must it not also be wrong for Insect? If I share the intellect and soul of Man, should I not also share in his joy?*

There must be a logical answer, he tells himself. A proof for the theorem. And so the professor puts his brain to work.

The Insect, in his way, has always sought solutions in the study of opposites. Does not light, he asks, counter darkness? Does not plenty vanquish want? *Contraria contrariis curantur,*[1] he reasons silently. Hippocrates, as dependable as the rising sun, provides the answer, as always. Surely his loneliness must have an antidote. Surely if the fact of him*self* has been the source of his terrible singularity, the cure would be found in companionship with his own antithesis—one as wholly unlike himself as to become him. Light, after all, cannot know itself to be light until it first knows darkness; and music cannot know itself without coupling with silence. It is, he feels, astonishingly obvious, and he sits down with his notes and his ledgers and scratches out the beginning of his next treatise—one of many that he will never complete.

---

[1] Opposite is cured by opposite.

Later that night, the Insect dreams of the Astronomer. He wakes in a sweat.

That same night, in a faraway country, the Astronomer dreams of the Insect. He wakes with a shiver and a cry, and, as usual, consults the stars. He does not breathe (he never does); he does not blink (how can he? He has no tears). The stars, as usual, are silent. The Astronomer watches without moving.

The Insect and the Astronomer have never met.

But they *will*. The Insect is sure of it.

3.

It has been many years since the Bug-in-Spats last set foot in Vingus Country—land of his birth, land whereby he received his extensive and thorough education (by the hand of one Professor Ignatius Pedantare, at whose name the Pyca clasps his delicate tarsus to his brightly clothed thorax and sighs prodigiously), and land that, despite its tendencies toward backward thinking and provincial blindness, he still refers to in his more nostalgic moments as his home. He had thought at one time that he would never return. Indeed, he swore that he would not.

Still, as he traverses the land where the green of the hills begins to lighten and sparkle, where it finally, thinly protesting, gives way to endless hills of yellow and yellow and yellow—the glow of his country, the shimmer of home—the Insect feels his soul begin to shudder and shake. He feels his bound wings begin to tremble and moan. He raises his curled fingers to his enormous black eyes and discovers a hidden reservoir of tears.

How odd, he thinks. He brings a single tear to his mouth and tastes the salt on his long, prehensile tongue. It tastes, he knows, ever so much like an ocean, though he has never seen an ocean, nor tasted it for comparison. He knows there are oceans some-where, just as there is an ocean inside him, inextricably linked to his heart.

The heart breaks and an ocean flows; this is the way of things.

"*Abyssus abyssum invocat*,"[2] he whispers out loud. And he believes it too. The abyss of his soul has pulled him here, on this path, toward the one who ponders the abyss of the sky.

The Astronomer, his dreams have told him. *The Astronomer will know what to do.*

The Insect has brought little for the journey. Only a flutter of hope in his heart. And something else, in the regions beyond his heart. A quiet something that he could not identify or name. But it is heavy, and dark, and *alive*.

The journey has been long and his feet are tired. He sees no one on his first day home. Still. It is *home*. And that flutter in his heart feels like an ocean's gale. And the salt lingers on his tongue.

4.

The moment that the Insect crosses into Vingus Country, the Astronomer freezes in his tracks. The people in the village see him halfway up the yellow hillside where his terrible tower stands. His left foot hovers over the ground in an aborted step. His right hand is nearly to his mouth. His lips remain parted, as though he is about to smile. Or speak. Or cry out.

---

[2] Deep calleth unto deep; or—Sea calls to sea.

The village folk see this, but they do not offer to help. Those who have business dealings with the Astronomer (and they are many) simply turn on their heels and hurry back down the hill. They do their best not to look at the Astronomer. Of course, this is nothing new.

His chest don't rise and it don't fall, the people have whispered.

There's not a thing on that hill what's alive, they've grumbled since he first arrived.

It's not natural. All that star looking and planet tracking. It's not natural with his infernal machines. It's not natural at all. They seethe and seethe and seethe. Every day they watch the Astronomer turn the keys in his tower and mind the gears in his automatons and polish his instruments until they gleam. They know that he used neither an iota of magic nor a whiff of witchcraft in its construction and maintenances. What he uses is something *else*. And they don't trust it.

As the sun begins to set, one of his automatons walks out of the tower, its gears in need of tuning and grease, and hoists the Astronomer onto its back, hauling him inside. The next day, the Astronomer is back to normal.

Or mostly normal.

The village notices that a smile has begun to play on the Astronomer's lips. One that has not been there before. It is fixed into his face as though with paste or paint or solder. And what's worse, he has started muttering.

"Wings," the Astronomer whispers over and over again. "Wings, wings, wings. Thorax and segment and luminous eye. But, oh! *Wings!*"

Sunup to sundown, he mutters without ceasing.

And the villagers begin to worry.

5.

By the beginning of the Bug's second day in Vingus Country, the loneliness of the journey has begun to take its toll. Now when he sees the figure of a man moving in the same direction that he, himself, is traveling, the Insect increases his speed, his long legs bounding down the road in great, leaping strides. He adjusts his five pinces-nez on his long snout and smooths his finely tailored waistcoat. He ignores the itching of his tightly bound wings. He clears his throat. He knows the value of a good first impression.

"*Tempora mutantur et nos mutantur in illis*,"[3] the Insect says to the man—a farmer, by the look of him. He dearly hopes that the man is impressed by this greeting. Indeed, it is terribly impressive, as well as being profoundly *true*. Has not the Pyca been changed by his time away? Has not his home country been changed as well?

It is nearly noon, and the Hon. Professor is feeling peckish and overly warm. He would not mind an invitation to lunch on a blanket in the shade, or, even more desirable, to lunch in a farmhouse with cold milk and cold ale and a highly solicitous farmwife. He waves to the farmer and uncurls the final segment of his right arm to shake the man's hand. With his left, he adjusts the two final pinces-nez at the end of his impressively long proboscis and gives what he is sure must be a winning smile.

(The winning smile is important. After all, did Professor

---

[3] The times are changed, and we are changed in them.

Pedantare not implore his students over and over with the same sage proclamation: *Ut ameris, amabilis esto*[4]? Surely, after all this time, the lesson still stands.)

"Come again?" the farmer says. He is an aged fellow. His face is deeply creased and his back is bent. The Insect, in possession of a sensitive heart and a loving soul, is moved to pity. He reaches into his pack and pulls out a brightly colored parasol and proffers it to the farmer with a flourish. The farmer jumps backward and screams. "Attack an old man, will you?"

"Pardon?"

"I have no money if that's what yer asking."

The Pyca peers at the parasol, its bright point gleaming dangerously in the midday sun, and understands. "My apologies," the Bug says. In the Capital City—a cosmopolitan, *forward-thinking* place—his appearance is, while unusual, rarely commented on. No one finds him particularly *dangerous*. Why would they? The Hon. Professor spent his career cultivating his erudition and his appearance. To see an insect standing eye to eye with a man must surely be a surprise for the uninitiated, but seeing him decked in a perfectly tailored waistcoat of the finest brocade and a top hat imported from the Lands Beyond the Sea—*well*. Clearly the man is in shock. The Pyca decides to try a different tack.

"My good man," he says, "it occurs to me that my appearance alarms you. Fear not. I seek education and nothing more. As the scholars tell us, *scientia potentia est*.[5] Have we not found such

---

[4] Be amiable, then you'll be loved.

[5] Knowledge is power.

pearls of wisdom to be more than true? And if not, who are we to argue with scholars?"

"Yer lookin' for the Astronomer?"

"My good man," says the Pyca. "That is exactly who I seek. *Quaere verum*,[6] my good professor once said to me. If I am to seek the truth, I believe the truth must rest in the hands of the man who watches the stars."

"Hmph," the farmer grunts. *"Astra inclinant, sed non obligant."*[7]

So startled is the Professor that all five of his pinces-nez fly from his proboscis and tumble to the ground. One shatters irrevocably. "Why," he sputters, pressing his hands to his heart, "my dear sir! You are a scholar!" In all his years in Vingus Country, he had never heard anyone respond in Latin—except glumly, in school, before the headmaster's downward stare. It was the custom to, instead, bear the weight of learning with the patience of a snapping turtle, and leave it behind as soon as possible. This, after all, is why the Insect left.

"No," the farmer says darkly. "That man in the tower's the scholar. If you can call him a man." He pauses, rubs his hand over the gnarl of his face, expels breath through pursed lips. "It is rude, I know, but I hope you'll forgive me if I won't share the road with you, Mister . . . whatever you are. I'll not invite you to my home, nor to my table, neither, but you're welcome to the lunch my good wife packed for me in this sack." He lets his sack fall to the ground, and he backs away. "This road'll take you right to where you want

---

[6] Seek the truth.

[7] The stars incline us, but do not bind us.

to go. Walk 'til you find that infernal tower. It's unnatural, is what it is. Stars. The Astronomer. All of it. Unnatural. And I'll bid you good day."

And the farmer turns on his heel and walks down the road in the opposite direction. The Bug does not call out to him, nor does he beg him to return. "A strange sort of fellow," he says, and pulls a hunk of meat from the satchel. He eats it slowly and presses onward through the shimmering hills.

6.

The Astronomer lives alone. He has always lived alone.

The Astronomer, it is generally thought, first came to Vingus Country four decades ago. Or, perhaps it was four years. Or maybe a month. No one knows for sure. When the Vingare try to puzzle it out, when they try to count the years on their fingers and toes and hash out the months on bits of paper, or perhaps a wall, they find themselves drawing a blank. Their eyes lose their focus and their minds turn to thoughts of faraway dust clouds, the bright accretion of swirling nebulae, of planets made of water or ice or storm, and quietly pulsing stars. Their eyes gaze skyward and they forget why they questioned in the first place.

The Astronomer has always been here.

The Astronomer has just arrived.

Both are true.

No one knows where he traveled from, nor his country of origin, and he has never told. His accent is obscure, his clothes unusual, and his many trunks of fragile equipment unsettlingly strange.

The Vingare asked him when he arrived—as they watched him carefully remove item after item from his line of trunks, inspecting each one for damage and wear—what his many tools were for, but he simply smiled vaguely and gave a delicate wave of his small, pale hand. "Oh, you know," he said, over and over again, "work, work, work." And then he would say nothing.

The Vingare were unused to obscure answers. They are a concrete people. It became clear to the Vingare that the new resident was not like them, did not belong, and should probably leave their country, so they did their best to give him the cold shoulder. Or, as best they could. The Vingare are a welcoming people by nature, and usually not prone to open confrontation. They opted for subtle hints. Therefore, they did *not* line his walkway with rose petals, as was their custom, opting instead for a measly bundle of wildflowers (surely they would wilt soon) tied up in a ribbon that was not new, and presented in a vase. They thought certainly the Astronomer would feel the depths of their non-welcome, but he did not. He thanked them profusely for their kindness and declared the flowers the most beautiful thing he had ever seen in his life.

The Vingare decided more drastic measures were needed. They brought him neither meat pies nor sugared fruits nor brightly colored jellies, opting instead for common foods like bread and cheese and wine. He did not take the hint. He declared that Vingus bread was better than the finest pastries in the Capital City, and that Vingus cheese and wine would rival the sundries produced in the most gastronomically famous cities in the Lands Beyond the Sea. The Vingare were flummoxed. They had never met so dense a fellow. They then threw no banquet in his honor, gave him not a single key to any city—high, low, or middling—and neglected to organize a welcoming parade. He refused to notice these slights as well.

It was infuriating.

Meanwhile, the Astronomer told anyone who would listen how much he admired the Vingare people, and how much he desired to become one of them. To that end, he altered his appearance to fit in with his adopted countrymen (his hair, his dress, even the color of his eyes and skin). He mimicked their mannerisms, their habits, their way of walking, and tried desperately to integrate the linguistic oddities peculiar to that region into his patterns of speech, but the results were disastrous. The more he tried to assimilate, the more strange he became to his neighbors.

He never gave up his desire to become as near-to-like his chosen kinsmen as he could, however. And while he would never be *Vingare*, he would have to settle for *Vingare-non-Vingare*, and that would be that. And he would be alone.

And in time, the Astronomer was—if not accepted—at least tolerated. He was to the Vingare like a rare bird, flown into their region by mistake, and too lost to find another way home. Not *of* them, or even *with* them, but *near* them. And the Astronomer had to content himself with that.

To build his tower, the Astronomer contracted fifteen Vingus laborers, five Vingus draftsmen, nineteen ironworkers, twenty-two tinsmiths, three surveyors, two engineers, and one overseer. He set up a small tent—(There were stars inside, people said. Real stars that rose and set in tandem with the actual stars they represented.)—on the top of a hill and marked out a shape on the ground. It was said that before work began, he sat for hours in the center of that shape, staring at the sky.

It took nearly five years to build the tower. (Or was it ten? Or twenty? No one can remember.) The Astronomer set up a second tent where matters of business and construction could be discussed. It was filled with drafting tables and chalkboards and narrow-drawered cabinets to accommodate and organize his meticulously drafted—and entirely inscrutable—plans.

The Vingare soon realized that it didn't matter how much they failed to understand the instructions laid out for them. The tower had a mind of its own.

The hill upon which the tower slowly grew was tall and bald—a knob of rock in the center of a broad, flat yellow prairie. As a result, most Vingare were able to watch the tower as it progressed, floor by shining floor. They watched the silvery skeleton of each story uncurl from the struts below and hook together like a web. They watched as the substrate of machinery grew like lichen from the base.

They held their hands to their open mouths. It was beautiful— but not in a way that they could name. It was a beauty that stopped their voices in their throats and held them silent.

The tower had hollow walls with a complicated network of steam pipes, humming engines, tiny levers, and delicate gears. There were dumb waiters and smart waiters and waiters of unknowable intelligence. There were automatic ottomans that rolled toward any visitor who needed to put their feet up for a moment or two. On each floor were copper-plated mechanized arms, each with four elbows and nine fingers. These were placed at the four corners of each room, each one with a different function. One arm set up the desks and work tables each morning with razor sharp precision, one saw to the dust, one fetched things (books, pencils, napkins, drafting tools, toothpicks) moments before a person actually felt the need for them, and one took hats and coats and shook the hands of weary travelers.

In addition to the mechanical arms on the inside, there were three on the outside, and these would lift materials and supplies to the laborers on the upper floors, as well as fetch lunch boxes, jugs of water, afternoon tea, notes from home, and—if a particular laborer looked as though they needed encouragement or were simply having a bad day—offer a sympathetic pat on the back.

The Vingus laborers went home each evening, their mouths heavy with stories they could not tell. Not that they were forbidden—the Astronomer had told them he had no secrets that he minded sharing and no aspect of his tower that he'd rather keep hidden. No, they simply had no words. And so their husbands and wives and children and neighbors pestered them with questions that they lacked the language to answer.

"What is in that tower?" their loved ones said. "What is he building?" they needled.

"Nothing," said the laborers. "Everything," they countered.

Both were true.

7.

The Insect lies on his curved, shining back and rests his head on the torso of a fallen tree. He tilts his head toward the domed sky and watches the clockwork movements of the glinting stars. He had grown accustomed to the luxury afforded to him at the university, but he does not miss it now. No featherbeds or scented sheets here, yet the Vingus soil gives way to the ease of his back, and the Vingus winds blow gentle and warm on his skin. He has never been more comfortable.

The hills have flattened into prairie. He is so close. Perhaps midday tomorrow he will see the singular bluff standing alone in a sea of yellow and yellow and yellow, and the tower that has, for months now, infected his dreams.

Go to Vingus Country, his dreams told him. *Find the Astronomer. You'll understand when you arrive.*

Now that he is this close, the Bug-in-Spats is not so sure. Certainly, the philosophers said, *in somnis veritas*.[8] Surely his dreams would speak truly to him if the philosophers claimed it so.

Still, after his decision to leave his post at the Royal College of Athletic and Alchemical Arts, he has never wavered on the *veritas* of his dreams and the truthfulness of his inexplicable inclinations.

The Astronomer will know, he told himself. *The Astronomer will understand.* And he lay there the rest of the night, awake and staring, his great black eyes reflecting the endless glitter of endless stars.

8.

The Astronomer has built nineteen automatons—all named Angel—who roam the tower and the grounds, and even explore

---

[8] In dreams there is truth.

the depths of Vingus Country, and do the Astronomer's bidding. Angel #11 is the one who has haggled at the flea markets and book dealers for rare volumes. Angel #9 goes to the forests to find specific herbs and fungi.

Angel #4 was sent into the schoolrooms to give lectures on the wonders of the stars. The automaton has no mouth. Its eyes are painted on like a doll's. The children covered their ears. They closed their eyes. It was so terribly *wrong* that the children wept silently and hid their faces until it finished its programmed speech and stuttered out of the room.

Not all of the Astronomer's automatic creatures walk on two legs, however. The tower itself is an automaton of sorts. The windows and the doors possess a delicate and precise gear work, both internal and external, that anticipates their use and opens and closes them with the gentlest whirring to let in the day or to keep out the wind. Light boxes show images of the stars and screens and display maps of places no one has ever heard of and books in languages that do not exist. All the floors turn on a central axis, at differing speeds and seemingly random directionalities. One floor makes a full turn every hour and another floor turns so slowly that a person standing by the window would have no knowledge of its movement, until realizing that the window now faced north, when it had surely faced south earlier in the day. Some floors' windows follow the sun, while other floors' windows fear it.

The Astronomer does not call his automatons by their names, even though each one has a name welded to its metal lapel. He calls each one "brother." He calls the tower "brother" as well.

The Mayor of the Township of Lin, during his yearly Visit of Friendship to the Astronomer—a ghastly, tedious affair, in which both parties consume foodstuffs that they do not care for (the Mayor, because he is of Vingus Country, a land not known for its cuisine, but famous for its cultural habit of complaining about the food; and the Astronomer, because he does not eat, though he understands that other people do, and has done his best to understand it, without yet learning the knack of replicating it) and engage in topics of conversation that do not interest them, all in the name of cooperation—once asked, in a rare moment of candor (one that has not been repeated), "Can you tell me the reason for the intricacies of the tower?"

Immediately upon asking, the Mayor found himself choking on a particularly insipid piece of pastry. *What was he thinking?*

The Astronomer, for his part, was so stunned that he forgot to drink the foul-smelling liquor that was so typically served at that wretched function with any kind of relish or gratitude, and instead allowed himself to grimace. The Mayor noticed the grimace, took it as an indication of a shared moment of honesty, and carried on.

"I mean to say," he said, "that I mean no harm. I simply notice that your work—from my point of view—requires no special equipment. Indeed, it seems to me that your work only needs your two flesh eyes and your one living brain and your own beating heart."

The Astronomer looked at his companion in surprise.

"My dear sir!" he said. "But surely you know I possess none of these. I never have! My machines serve only to lure the one who might lend me his flesh eyes, his living brain, his own beating heart. My machines are my beacon of hope."

"What?"

"D-did I . . ." the Astronomer faltered. "I m-mean to s-say . . ." But he said nothing after that. His eyes flickered and dimmed. His fingers pressed to his lips and stuck tight. He did not move for the rest of the luncheon.

The Mayor said nothing. He took his liquor. He ate his food. He left without another word.

He never returned to the table at the Astronomer's tower. His eyes and brain and beating heart hurt just at the thought of it.

9.

The Insect agrees to stay the night at the home of an aged couple in the village that sits in the shadow of the Astronomer's tower. They are extraordinarily kind. They have tender smiles and searching hands and glittering eyes. The Insect loves them. Their house is cozy and warm. Their food makes him sleepy.

He has never been so sleepy.

He takes another drink of wine. The room swims.

"Look at you," the old woman says, her hand resting on the fourth segment of the Insect's arm. "As light as a feather. And after such a long journey and all! Do you see him, my love? Do you see the state that he is in?"

There is a rumble in the ground. A squeak of gears. A scuttle of metallic legs. The Insect does not notice. The old man and old woman do not notice either. The man sharpens his knife. The woman checks the heat in the oven.

"Is someone coming?" the Insect asks.

"Only you, my dear," the old woman says. "And you have already arrived. Lucky us."

The old woman fills the Insect's goblet. The old man cuts his meat. The Insect curls his fingers around berries and breads, he pours tea and milk and ale and wine into his open throat.

"Thank you. My heart thanks you. *Cor ad cor loquitur.*"[9]

The old man puts another slab of cheese on the Insect's plate. "I don't know what from *cors*, but you're in a sorry state, my friend. A sorry state is what," the old man says. "They work you too hard in that there city. All those buildings! All those people! That's no way to live. And you just a young bug."

"Not so young," the *Pycanum bellus gigantis* says sleepily.

"Young and supple," the old woman says. She smells his skin and smells his head and smells each of his hands. The Insect assumes this must be some sort of custom. "Did you see the shine on him, darling?" she asks her husband. "Did you see?" And to the Insect: "Eat. You must recover your strength. And your vigor. Your journey has sapped you dry."

The Insect, it's true, is still starving. *Starving.* He feels he will never be full. His tongue lolls and his head rolls back. "*Propino tibi salutem,*"[10] he garbles. He can hardly get the words out. "*Abyssus somethingus proboscis,*" he yawns. "*Slurpus, durpus, interpus.*"

"Of course, dear," the old woman says.

[9] Speaking heart to heart.

[10] Cheers.

She turns to her husband. "You did sharpen my needle, didn't you, darling?"

"As you said, precious," the old man replies.

"*Vescere bracis meis,*"[11] the Insect yawns. He is not making any sense. His words are dry leaves. They are a cold wind in an empty field.

In his mind's eye the Astronomer's tower stands against the night sky like a beacon. At its pinnacle, the Astronomer himself balances on the needle spire and calls his name.

Come to me, the Astronomer calls into the gale. *Come to me.*

There are salt tears in the Insect's eyes. An ocean surges in his heart.

"*Provehito in altum,*"[12] he whispers to the tower in his dreaming.

"Wake up now and eat," the old woman soothes. She pulls a tape from her apron pocket and measures the breadth of his abdomen. She peers into his mouth to scan for disease.

Butterflies line the walls, each one pierced at the thorax and preserved under glass. Bright purple billie-bugs too. And occulaflies and snankets and whirlibeetles, and three-headed crickets and trupalapods. Swamp moths and apple moths and moths-of-paradise and moths defying description or name. And they are beautiful. And they are everywhere.

"Your collection . . ." the Insect begins.

[11] Eat my shorts.

[12] Launch forward into the deep.

There are no *Pycanum bellus gigantis* that he can see. The old woman moves in closely.

"I've caught other genera of the *Acanthosomatidae* for years. A fine suborder. One to be proud of, dear. Bright, beautiful things. But I've never seen such a fine fellow as you." The Insect notices the delicate beading on the woman's blouse. He hears the whispers of the fragile husks that ring her wrists.

"Are they wings?" he asks. "Do you have wings?"

"You are . . . *so lovely*," she whispers.

"Around your wrists." The marching is closer. Metal on stone. Metal on dirt. Metal on damp gravel. Doors slam and shutters rattle and people shriek in alleyways. "Are they wings?"

"We all have wings, my darling. Mine are invisible. Yours are under your waistcoat. How I long to see them!"

A scramble of gears. A moan of rust. He hears a rocky hillside giving up its scree, the scree tearing up its soil, the soil submerging its trees and tumbling into an avalanche.

"More wine?" she asks.

The Insect woozes and burps. He can hardly keep his eyes open. He blinks and blinks and blinks again. The old man and the old woman see their reflections in his inky, shining eyes. They see their shoulders hunch, their arms rise, their features loom.

The hill is there. It waits in the darkness. It calls him home.

The old man holds the shine of the knife next to the Pyca's throat. He pauses, gazes into the bug's large eyes, and smiles.

"It won't take but a second. If we thought we could trust you to stay put under the glass, we'd do that. We don't want you wandering off."

"I'll get the needle," the old woman says. "Mind you don't muss up his waistcoat. We can make use of it later. Such a fine fellow. A fine, fine fellow."

His eyes roll back.

The ceiling, he realizes, has a curious sheen. It flutters and shines like wings.

There is salt in his mouth.

There is salt in his eyes.

The old woman screams and the old man shouts, "I'm armed!" and the Insect says *armed, armas, armat, armamus. Armaments. Arm-and-a-leg. Men-at-arms. Armies. Amis. Amigo. Amante.*

The *Pycanum bellus gigantis* says *amo. Amat. Amamus.*

There are arms and legs and arms and legs. There is metal and flesh—muscle and exoskeleton and snapping bones. There is the shine of a needle in the hand of the woman on the top of a tower on a lonely, windswept hill with the Astronomer balanced atop it like a flag.

Amo. Amas. Amamus. Amant.

I love. You love. We love. They love.

I am coming for you, the Astronomer says. *I am coming for you. I am already here.*

In his dream, the Insect lifts into the air on a cloud of metal and dust. In his dream he arcs around a burning star again and again and again. What is time to a planet? What is time to a star? Does the light from the star love the darkness? Does the darkness love the light?

Darkness and light thunder and thunder and thunder inside the head of *Pycanum bellus gigantis*. And he is gone.

10.

When the Insect awakens, he is on the roof of the tower. His eyes are open. He feels the glint of each star like a needle. He is pinned in place.

He is terribly cognizant of his wings. This has been a growing problem. He has kept his wings bound by his vest and morning coat for so long that he can hardly remember the sensation of the sun warming the membranous shimmer of his forewings and mesothorax. There was a time, before his education, that he went without clothing—a round-hulled marvel of color and light. How strange it seems to him now! How foreign! His wings itch. They ache. They long to be free.

The Astronomer lies next to him, his hand as close as possible to the Insect's arm to almost-touch without touching. There is no heat from the Astronomer's hand. His chest does not rise and fall.

"Are you alive?" the Insect says.

"Are you?" the Astronomer counters.

"I eat and I breathe and I rest. I yearn and I ache and I wonder. I rage and lust and feast. I imagine and fear and mourn and journey. I am very much alive, thank you." His voice is a trifle sniffier than he had intended. Embarrassed, he clears his throat.

The Astronomer turns his face to the sky. "*Pulvis et umbra sumus*,"[13] he says.

"*Quaecumque sunt vera*,"[14] the Insect counters.

The Astronomer laughs. "May I take your hand?" he asks.

---

[13] We are dust and shadow.

[14] Teach me whatever is true.

"You may," the *Pycanum bellus gigantis* says primly. As he had assumed, the Astronomer's hand gives off no heat. But it is not cold. It feels like a stone that has been warmed by the sun all day and is only just starting to cool—pleasant to touch, pleasant to hold. Cooler than the body, but guilty of no chill. The Astronomer's skin has an elasticity similar to the Insect's own wings. He rarely displays his wings—he is, after all, terribly modest. And shy. And when he undresses at night in the privacy of his room and lets his delicate fingers run down the length of his glittering wings, he shivers with pleasure.

As he shivers now.

You called to me, the Insect thinks. *And I came.*

I loved you, the Astronomer thinks in reply. *And you loved me in return. Rare bird yearns for rare bird. Things that have no opposite. Each to each.*

"The question still stands: are you alive?" the Insect asks.

"Whoever made the stars," the Astronomer says, "imbued them with the life of a machine. They follow their courses. They implement their programs. They operate as they were designed to do. They are made of dust and return to dust and remake themselves from dust again. They recuperate, reincarnate, regenerate. Their gears do not rust. Their steps do not stumble. Their workings intersect and dialogue with the workings of their billions of brothers and sisters burning their way through courses of their own. To watch the sky is to watch the most intricate of clockworks, the most perfect of machines. They are unalive. And yet. They are terribly alive."

"So?"

"That's all there is."

"You did not answer my question."

"You want to know too much."

"I want to know everything."

"*Qui totem vult totem perdit.*"[15]

"You don't mean that."

The Astronomer laughs ruefully. "You're right. I don't."

"Did you call me here?"

"I did."

"Why?"

"I needed your eyes so that I may see the reflection of the stars that I love in the eyes that I love. I needed your hands to steady my hands and your mind to temper my mind." The Astronomer closes his eyes. He does not breathe. He does not swallow. The *Pycanum bellus gigantis* can hear the whirl of his gears. He can hear the pulse of the bellows and the tine of the spring and the click of each finely jeweled tooth into each delicate groove. "A heart burns like a star—perfectly, patiently, selflessly. It lights the sky and it invigorates the land and it asks nothing in return. I have no heart. But I love yours. Is that enough?"

The Insect does not blink. He does not move. He is shadow. He is dust. He is bound by stars. He is particle hooking to particle hooking to particle. He is accretion and convection and radiation. He is heat and light and heat and light. He is sky and wind and deep, deep sea. There is salt in his mouth. There is an ocean in his eyes. There is an abyss in his heart and an abyss overhead. An

---

[15] He who wants everything loses everything.

abyss teeming with stars moving like clockwork across the deep, deep sky.

His waistcoat buckles and splits. Its perfectly tailored seams rip wide open.

"Wings," the Astronomer says. "Wings, wings, wings."

"Yes," the Insect says. "Wings." And it is true enough.

The stars say nothing in return.

THE UNLICENSED
MAGICIAN

1. *Now.*

The Vox sputters to life, on schedule, at four a.m.

Even the chickens are asleep.

"CITIZENS!" it shouts. "ROUSE YOURSELVES! THROW OFF YOUR BEDCLOTHES! PREPARE FOR A MESSAGE FROM THE MINISTER HIMSELF. TODAY, BELOVED CITIZENS, IS A GLORIOUS ONE! RUB YOUR EYES! CLEAR YOUR THROATS! THE ANTHEM IS AT HAND!"

Every citizen has a Vox. It's the law. Everyone knows the schedule by heart. Still, the jangly arrival of the announcer's voice is a jolt in the nationwide quiet. In households across the country, traitorous pillows cover otherwise patriotic ears. And in the darkness, thousands of children feel their inconstant eyes well up, mourning the loss of yet another night's rest.

The junk man's daughter stares up at the scattered stars, the harsh glint of planets cutting into the black. The hay under her back has clumped and matted over the course of the night, and everything is damp. Her father—well, her foster-father—is lying on top of the heap of gathered treasures, head below hips, arms splayed over cracked urns and dead radios, skinny legs hanging over the side in unlikely angles. He snores prodigiously, and even from where she lies a few yards off she can smell the decaying drunkenness; her eyes burn from the alcoholic cloud emanating from his mouth and off-gassing from his skin.

He calls it whiskey, but it is not whiskey. It is a homemade alcohol that he brews in a boot and distills in small batches in a miniature coil that he designed himself.

His daughter is amazed that he hasn't gone blind. Or blown his hands off. She knows that it has something to do with the unintentional protection that she affords him simply by existing.

What will happen to him if she is discovered? How will he survive without her? Who will take care of him if she is gone?

(Not *if,* her heart knows. *When.*)

The junk man groans in his cart.

"Did you say something, my Sparrow?" he slurs.

"No, Papa," she says. "Go back to sleep." By the time she finishes the word *papa*, he is already snoring. Still she says it. "Papa." Her voice is like the clasp of fingers curling around a living heart and holding on for dear life. He has been her papa since she opened her eyes for the second time, fifteen years ago. But will he even remember her when she is gone? She doesn't even know.

The anthem blares—a long, plodding, minor-key affair, like a funeral dirge. It is sung this time by two old men, their voices tired and sagging.

Former generals, the girl knows without trying. *And today is their last day.*

Being a general is a risky business, after all. Little failures are more likely to catch the Minister's eye, and no one wants to catch the Minister's eye. Not if he wants to keep his own head. The two men heave a great sigh the moment the song ends. One begins to sob.

"DO YOU SEE, BELOVED CITIZENS, HOW PATRIOTISM STIRS THE HEARTS OF EVEN THE MOST HARDENED OF MEN? LET US ALL TAKE A MOMENT TO WIPE OUR OWN FLOWING TEARS! LET US ALL PAUSE TO BLOW OUR LEAKING NOSES!"

The Vox devolves into a chorus of fake sobbing. Someone makes a honking sound like a dying goose, or a broken horn.

The junk man's daughter sighs. She pulls herself to her feet, wraps what used to be a boiled-wool blanket, but now is little more than a scrap, around her shoulders and tiptoes, barefoot, across the frost-kissed lawn to the window of the farmhouse. She shivers, but not from the cold. The inhabitants do not know that she spent the night on their lawn with her beyond-drunk father. Even if they looked out the window, they would see *him* and they would see the cart, but they likely wouldn't see *her*.

Hardly anyone can see the junk man's daughter. Those who can do so, she can count on one hand. Others can see her from time to time, but without any regularity. (And most don't like her much, when they do. She is the junk man's daughter after all. Tainted, clearly, by his drinking and shiftlessness.) It is lonely, this invisibility. Of course it is lonely. But safe. *Safe.*

(*But for how long*, she finds herself wondering more and more lately. *And for what purpose?* Even now, having lived this way for fifteen years, she still has no idea.)

She leans her chin on the sill and rests her forehead against the glass. She can feel the vibrations of the Vox's voice buzzing in her skull.

"BELOVED CITIZENS! HAS THERE EVER BEEN SO GREAT A NATION?" The Vox chuckles at the very thought of it. "NOW, GATHER CLOSE. WE HAVE ITEMS OF BUSINESS TO DISCUSS BEFORE OUR DEAR MINISTER COMES TO BRING YOU HIS MESSAGE OF HOPE AND PEACE!"

The farmhouse inhabitants have ignored the Vox and have kept their lights off and bedroom doors closed. Likely, they have fashioned earplugs for this very purpose. (These cannot be bought, of course. Earplugs are illegal. Ignoring the Vox is also illegal. This family, like many this far away from the capital, sometimes lives by its own rules. For now, anyway. The junk man's daughter finds this charming.) The Vox drones on for a bit—new regulations for the sale of homemade baked goods. New regulations for the admission of young children into Obedience School. (There is, the Vox assures the people, no place in this great nation for disobedient toddlers. All children over twelve months of age must now report to Obedience School. No exceptions. Starting today.) New regulations for the sale of liquor. (The punishment for unlicensed sales is no longer life in prison, but is now, as it should be, death. A righteous and glorious decision. All hail the Minister.)

The farmhouse is warm and cozy. Hand-stitched crazy quilts draping over the sagging sofa and rough-hewn chairs. A wide, hand-planked wooden table with a bowl of field flowers in the center.

There are five people who live in this house—two parents and

176

three boys. The youngest, not quite eleven, still attends Obedience School. The older boys are thirteen and seventeen, and they both work the farm.

The junk man's daughter knows this family well. She has sat with them at their dinner table as they ate. She has listened at the foot of the boys' shared bed as their mother or father took turns snuggling in and reading the stories from ancient copies of illegal books. (Books with numbers and diagrams. Books with stories and histories. Books with plants and microbes and far-off galaxies and sliced-open stars. Old volumes. Carefully rebound. Remnants from another world. The family regards them as precious.) She has peered over the mother's shoulder as she worked through the arithmetic of farming, weeping as the numbers didn't add up. She has lain on the floor while they made music in the living room with homemade instruments. They never see her. They have no idea.

The oldest boy, Jonah, seventeen years old and taller than his father, has taken to building contraband telescopes in the backyard. The junk man's daughter has stood near him as he peered into the sky in the darkest hours of the night, her breath clouding before her face like ghosts. She has listened as he muttered to himself—rattling names that she has never heard—Antares, Canis Majoris, Andromeda.

She has peered over his shoulder. She has watched him fuss over his own charts. She has listened to his whispery voice. He has no conscious memory of her.

And yet.

He wears a locket around his neck. He doesn't know where

it came from. He wears it anyway. She has watched him wrap his fingers around the locket and hang on tight. She has felt how their breathing in and their breathing out becomes synchronized. Noticed moments when he speaks into the darkness. A question, always.

There are moments when she almost answers back.

But there is no Jonah this morning. And no Isaac and no Benjamin. There is only the voice of the Vox, and its announcer's excitement reaching a fever pitch.

"Can you turn that thing down, my Sparrow?" the junk man slurs, though she can tell that he is still dreaming. No one can turn down a Vox. And dismantling them sets off an alarm.

Whole families have disappeared following Vox infractions.

"I've already done it, Papa," she says. "*Sleep.*" And her voice, heavily laden with intention, does what she hopes it would do. The junk man sinks into unconsciousness. He will not rouse before noon.

"HE IS HERE, CITIZENS!" the announcer nearly screeches. His voice is hoarse. He trembles and panics. "THE MINISTER IS HERE! ALL HAIL THE MINISTER!"

The junk man's daughter, the Sparrow, the child that never lived, the guttersnipe, the tramp, the trash-spawn, the dirty thief, the tart-in-training, and every other name that has been assigned to her in her young life, presses her hands against the glass. The family may notice her fingerprints. She hopes they do.

The Vox scrambles a bit, static scratching the quiet world. The Minister has no magic, of course, but he has spent enough of his overly extended life in the presence of magic. And it interferes with radio signals. His voice stutters and halts. It is far away. It is in a cloud.

The girl holds her breath.

"Are you listening?" the Minister says through the Vox. His voice is tender. Loving. Stern. And underneath it all, terribly, terribly afraid.

The junk man's daughter nods.

The Minister clears his throat. "It has come to my attention, my beloved children, that . . ." His voice trails off. He clucks his tongue. Even his bodiless voice seems to shake its head. "Well. It seems so crazy to say it out loud."

A bugle, very far away, plays the anthem. Its long, sad notes slide under the Minister's voice.

"Have I not loved you, my children? Have I not cared for you? Have I not kept your bellies full and your wounds healed and your homes safe from harm?"

His voice, she can hear, is amplified, not by the radio, but by magic. Whose magic, she has no idea. The last remnants from the depleted magic children—dying now, if they aren't dead already. The Sparrow shivers, thinking of them.

"Nonetheless, I have heard reports of . . . *oddness*. Here and there. Things that *have no right to be happening*. It is astonishing to me that there could be, somewhere in this nation, an unlicensed magician. Laughable, even. It is beyond ludicrous to believe that such a level of *flagrant rule-breaking* could exist here, in this *most blessed nation*."

The junk man's daughter's heart gives a little thrill. She presses her lips lightly against the glass. Gives it a kiss. The house shivers.

"And yet, the facts prove otherwise. An unlicensed magician now walks among us. But not for long. Not if we can help it. You and me together."

His voice trembles. He worries. He yearns. He fears. He is beside himself. The girl is moved with compassion.

"To you, my beloved citizens, I say this: *Watch. Observe. Report.* Even small things. I am relying on you."

She loves the house. She loves the family. She loves the Minister too. She is suffocating from so much love. Her very skin is stretched tight with it, like a balloon about to burst.

"And to you—*little magician.*" His breath rattles. There is a hiss in his voice. He is afraid. She can feel his fear in her very skin.

Poor baby, she thinks.

"You have no name."

I have a name, she thinks. *My mother whispered it before I was born. And then she forgot it. I am the only one who knows my name.*

"You have no place. You are lost. You are a lost lamb in a dark, cruel wood."

No, she thinks. *It is you who is lost.*

"But I am coming."

I am waiting for you.

"I will find you, my darling," the Minister says.

I will lead you to me. As a spider leads a fly.

"I will catch you. I will claim you. I will love you to bits."

As I love you, the junk man's daughter thinks. *As I love you and love you and love you.* And she does. She loves him *so much.* As she loves everyone. It is dangerous, this love, and she can't control it. It is ever so much bigger than she, and growing by the day. It is a river. An ocean. The sky. Her love crushes planets, shatters suns, burns whole galaxies to cinders and dust.

"And then, child, I will drain you."

Yes, she thinks. *You can try.*

"Do you hear me? I WILL DRAIN YOU DRY."

Try, she thinks. *Try and you will drown in it. You will drown, and drown, and drown.*

And for the first time, she knows it is true.

2. Then.

The first appearance of the Boro comet and the subsequent appearance of magic children occurred shortly after the Minister first began his long and fruitful rule.

No one can say how long ago—how very, very long—this was. Only the Minister knows. And he won't tell.

The comet simply appeared one day in the eastern skies, fat and shining like a pendant on the neck of the horizon. Astonished astronomers clamored over one another, elbowing their colleagues out of the way in an effort to be the first one to name it. In the end, it was named in honor of the Minister's father—a dear man who had met an unfortunate and untimely end a decade earlier in a tragic firing-squad accident (all condolences to the Minister). No one knew at the time—aside from the comet's mysterious and surprising appearance—the impact the object would have on them all.

No one knew that the whole world was about to change.

First, it was the dreams, crowding thick and fast, night after night, into the slumbering skulls of the populace. No one mentioned it, but everyone knew—every man, woman, and child was marked by pale faces and darkened eyes and mouths slack from dreaming. *And oh!* What dreams!

And then, shortly after the comet disappeared, the babies arrived—one hundred and two of them in counties all around the nation. Magic babies.

They all had, to a one, a curious birthmark curling out of their navels—a strange spiral that glowed in the dark. They were volatile, some of them, liable to make doors explode or syringes vanish or to catapult their mothers from one side of the room to the other. There were broken bones. Cracked teeth. Annoyed nurses.

Other babies were more benign, liable to make their teddy bears sentient, so as to see to the important work of infant cuddling when their busy families could not. Or they made lullabies come gurgling out of bedsheets and cradles. Some endowed their panicked fathers with new, round breasts, laden with milk. And others, remarkably, grew wings.

The Minister, thinking fast, sent his massive landships (each one large enough to house and transport several battalions), gouging the earth as they went. In each town, swarms of soldiers poured out, invading nurseries and bassinets, checking for the magic mark. The children were to be rounded up and sequestered for study.

"They could be dangerous," the Minister explained.

"They could be sick," he went on. "Or contagious."

He paid the families, of course. Handsomely. They were in no position to argue. He had all the guns.

"So many things," the Minister mused, "can be accomplished with guns. How many more things might be accomplished with magic?"

And thus his experiments began.

He used earplugs to keep out the screams.

3. *Now.*

There are signs all over the marketplace.

UNLICENSED PRACTICES OF **MAGIC**
ARE PROHIBITED BY LAW.

BE A MODEL CITIZEN.
WATCH.
LISTEN.
REPORT.

FAILURE TO REPORT
IS A FAILURE TO YOUR COUNTRY.
FAILURE IS NOT TOLERATED.

The signs appeared the night before, sometime after midnight. No one knows who hung them. The people in the marketplace are doing their best not to notice the signs. Their eyes slide from side to side. They talk about the weather. They talk about their children's need for new shoes. They talk about their recent teeth extractions. Why would they mention the signs? They have done nothing wrong. They are not breaking the law.

(They say this over and over, in the silences of their hearts, until it feels true.)

The junk man does not have a stall, and pays no tax to the mayor—never has. The mayor has never forced the issue. If he did, the junk man would simply sell elsewhere, and then the populace would revolt, and then—after both tarring and feathering him, because that's what happens to mayors who fail their constituents—they would find themselves a replacement. Or maybe they'd just report him to the Minister, and have him disappeared quietly. These things happen.

It's tricky work. Being the mayor. Times being what they are.

It snowed the day before, but now the winds have slowed and the sky has cleared and the day is fine and warm, with the easing dampness of a world still soft, but readying itself for a freeze.

The junk man's daughter eats an apple. She sits on the edge of the cart while the junk man stands off to the side, conferring with a matron in low, hushed tones.

"As you can see," the junk man says, pulling an apple out of the empty bowl, and holding it with a flourish on his open palm. He tosses it without looking at his daughter, who plucks it from its high, clean arc, and places it with the rest of the apples on her apron. Each apple came from the empty bowl. "It's just a bowl. Lovely, yes. A couple chips, sure, but the ceramic is of good quality and you don't find that kind of glaze-work nowadays." He reaches in. The bowl is empty. He grabs another apple. This one he bites. The skin is red and firm and the flesh is a creamy white. A burst of sweet apple smell hangs between the two of them. He grins.

"Delicious. Would you like one?"

The matron nods slowly, her eyes wide.

"Well. Help yourself." He winks. She reaches in. The bowl is empty. Her fingers find an apple—this one golden in color. She bites. It tastes like honey—the junk man's daughter can tell just by looking at her face. The matron closes her eyes and her lips spread across the crushed apple in a smile.

"How much?" the matron says with her mouth full.

It takes fifteen minutes to negotiate a price. The junk man's daughter tires of the conversation and returns her gaze to the marketplace. There is a toad on her lap, and two identical chickens pecking the ground at her feet. The toad settles itself in the folds of her skirt. She caresses its head absently.

The matron leaves with the bowl balanced on her hip, pulling apple after apple from its empty depths and shoving them into her pockets. The girl shakes her head. It was a mistake, that bowl. Like so many others. Her eyes slide back over to the signs.

She doesn't want anyone to get into trouble. She never has.

The junk man waves as the matron disappears and counts his earnings, dropping each coin into his purse with a pleasant jingle. "Oh, my Sparrow, my Sparrow, my Sparrow!" he croons at his daughter. "And oh, the cleverness of me!" he enthuses, throwing his arms wide open. He wobbles and giggles and gives a little hiccup.

"You stole that line," the girl says, though it isn't exactly true. The junk man cannot read very well, and even if he could, he would never have encountered such a turn of phrase in a book. In theory, only the books that the Minister has approved exist anywhere in the country. And the Minister doesn't approve of much. Still, there is much that is suddenly available to the junk man when his daughter is nearby. Images pop into his head. Proverbs. Quotes. Even a song or two. And worlds and worlds of stories. He collects them the way he collects his junk, which is to say, *joyfully*. His daughter gives him a snort. "And, anyway, you are not that clever, Papa."

He gives her a bow and blows her a kiss and it nearly breaks her in two. It is a good life they have, the two of them. It will kill her to leave it behind. She knows a change is coming. She can feel it hover, just out of reach, as surely as a coming storm.

The church pastor wanders over, his steps weighted and slow. Sweaty skin, hooded eyes, and a red, red nose.

"Ah!" the junk man says. "Reverend! Do I have the perfect thing for you!" He ambles into the square, all bony knees and elbows. He is barbed wire and braided grass holding up a patched suit, and greets the half-drunk pastor with a foxy grin and a conspiratorial wink. With a wave of his hand he reaches into one of his many pockets and produces a bottle that, as far as he can tell, will never run dry. The pastor licks his lips and stares with interest.

The Sparrow shakes her head and turns away. She cups her hands and ladles the toad onto the ground between the identical chickens, first giving the top of its head a quick kiss. The toad bellows indignantly—not for the kiss, but for the separation from the girl. He loves that girl. Desperately. So do the chickens. And she loves them back.

She slides into the crowd. There are people who can see her today—unusual, though it's been happening more and more lately. And it's not always pleasant. An old man tips his hat and then puckers his lips at her.

"Oh, come now, guttersnipe," he says. "One kiss."

She shakes her head and darts away.

She bumps into an old woman with a basketful of muffins for sale.

"Hmph," the woman says. "Watch where you're bumping, little tramp." She picks up the muffins and brushes the grit off with her fingers, checking this way and that to make sure no potential customers noticed. "Off with you now. Shoo!"

The woman doesn't notice that the number of muffins in the basket has inexplicably doubled. She will only realize something is wrong much later when she counts her earnings at the end of the day and finds her purse nearly twice as full as it should be. She will have no explanation for it. She will not remember the girl.

The Sparrow tries to buy meat from the butcher with the coins she lifted from the junk man's purse. The butcher gives her a poisonous glare.

"Oh!" he says, throwing his hands up. "You're paying me this time, are you? Well. Maybe we should have a party."

She presses her lips together and says nothing. She *has* stolen from him. Before. She's surprised he knows. Sucking her lips between her teeth and biting down hard, she points at a good-looking bit of salt pork, which he wraps for her begrudgingly.

I'm sorry, she wants to say. But she doesn't.

He has a wound on his shoulder. It is wrapped, but the wrappings are soaked with a yellow fluid, and red streaks seep across his skin. He is sweaty and shivering. The Sparrow tilts her head to the left.

Yellow, she thinks. *Yellow, yellow, yellow.*

The red streaks start to shrink.

"Thank you," she says when he hands her the meat and she hands him the money. "Thank you for everything."

And she slips back into the crowd and disappears.

Well, the butcher thinks. *She didn't disappear. I just suddenly wasn't able to see her. With all the people. She was sucked into the crowd.*

Except that's not exactly what happened. She wasn't moving. And the crowd didn't suck her anywhere. She simply vanished.

Wait, the butcher thinks. *What am I saying? Who vanished? I haven't seen anyone all day.* He shakes his head. He has no memory of the junk man's daughter. He stares at the coins in his hand, confusion clouding his face.

And even more confusing, the wound on his shoulder has begun to itch. He is crazed with itching. He throws off the bandages, and realizes that his wound is gone, and his skin is whole. Nothing shows where the injury was. His skin is firm and smooth as a baby's.

And even stranger: On the spot where the wound once was: a coin. A big, gold coin.

Yellow, the butcher thinks. *Yellow, yellow, yellow.*

The junk man's daughter watches his face. She hasn't moved. The butcher simply doesn't see her. She shrugs and continues on her way.

She stops at the cheese maker's and the breadsmith's and the beekeeper's, buying enough to keep her father fed and whole. The marketplace is crowded today—it's harvest time, and everyone's yields are impressively high this year. The beekeeper's stall is crowded with jars and she sells honeycombs by the barrel. The pigs are fatter, the milk has twice the cream, and the potatoes are as big as boulders.

It will all go away, unfortunately. The rest of the nation is in a food shortage. This province has been the only one oddly blessed with abundance, which means that soon it will all be gathered, crated, and shipped off.

There is a frenzy of buying, people getting what they can afford before—

"Sparrow!"

The girl looks up and sees Marla, the egg woman—all broad shoulders and wide hips and hardened biceps—tossing her neighbors out of the way as she hurries across the square.

Marla has loved the Sparrow for as long as she can remember. And the Sparrow loves her back.

"Marla," the girl says with the beginnings of a smile—one that fades the moment she sees the look on Marla's face.

"Run, child!" the egg woman says. "Soldiers. The soldiers are back."

She throws out her arms, blocking the girl from view. As though all that was needed to keep the girl from harm was the formidable presence of her own body.

"But my father—"

"I'll see to him. The Constable is distracting the soldiers. He won't let anything happen to you. None of us will. Run. Now."

And the egg woman turns and walks toward the soldiers, strong as a tank. She has a basket of homemade cheeses hooked in the crook of her arm. She has a basket of astonishingly fine eggs from her battalions of Most Remarkable Hens. Indeed, there are no hens quite like them, thanks to her little Sparrow.

She'll use them if she has to.

And the Sparrow hesitates. She looks to the greengrocer and the cobbler. She looks to the berry man and the candle maker. No one sees her. The soldiers stand on the far side of the square, their electronic eyes focused on the eggs in the basket.

"Whips up like none other," the egg woman says loudly. "Thick as cream." They also cure acne, heal burns, mend shoes, seal cracks, and make meringues that will melt in the mouth. (They can also, in a pinch, secure a lover for the night. Very powerful, these eggs. Not magic, though. Surely not.)

The Sparrow calls for her father. She calls for the Constable. She calls for the egg woman. No one comes. She wobbles. She flickers. And she flies away.

Later, people will say that they saw a flash of a patched apron catch a breeze and fly above the heads of the crowd.

"No," someone will counter. "It wasn't an apron. It was feathers."

"Not feathers," someone else will say. "Wings. Patchwork wings."

"Hogwash," a third will swear. "It was a flock of sparrows. Sparrows and sparrows and sparrows. And then they were gone."

4. Then.

The Sparrow couldn't remember being born.

She *could* remember, however, parts of her life within the watery womb of her mother. She could remember the sound of her mother's worry. She could remember the soothe of her father's voice, and then the bite of her father's rage. And the silence he left behind. She remembered the Boro comet, though she could not see it. She remembered it like a flash in the dark, and the surge of . . . *something* . . . coming up from under her like a wave.

And then she was something *else*. Even then, she knew. She knew her hands, she knew her mouth, she knew her toes, and she knew her magic. She knew these things without the power of names.

She heard the fear in her mother's voice at the mention of *Boro comet*. But it wasn't the comet that made her like this.

It wasn't the flash that changed her, it was the wave. The wave from underneath. The Boro comet doesn't *make*. It *draws*. She knows it in her bones.

5. *Now.*

Every Vox in the nation sputters to life at once.

"CITIZENS!" it screeches. "YOUR COOPERATION HAS BEEN NOTED. YOUR MINISTER ASKED AND YOUR MINISTER HAS RECEIVED. LONG LIVE THE MINISTER. THOUSANDS OF PATRIOTS FLOODED OUR MESSAGE LINES AND OUR VIDEO CENTERS AND OUR OFFICES. SO MANY BEAUTIFUL ACCUSATIONS. SO MANY JUSTIFIABLE CONCERNS. YOU WILL BE REWARDED—MEN, WOMEN, AND CHILDREN ALL. YOU WILL BE REWARDED."

A crackle.

A breath.

A beat.

"AND FOR THOSE OF YOU WHO KNOW AND DO NOT TELL."

Another breath. And another. The Vox is silent. Until—

"Oh citizens," the Vox whispers. "Oh, my precious citizens. *I cannot, cannot say.*"

6. Then.

The Minister had never counted on the wind. He built his tower higher and higher—a wobbly, twisty, unlikely looking structure, uncurling like seaweed toward the shimmering limit of the sky. Dark stones, blackened windows. Impossible without magic, without his little magicians.

He loved them.

He couldn't bear to think of them.

He shoved them out of his mind.

And look. His tower. A marvel! It was higher than any structure in the history of the world. The Minister knew the history of the world. He had all the history books, after all. The ones he hadn't burned, anyway. And while the books told of impressive structures, they never mentioned the winds.

The wind at the top of the tower nearly sent him careening to his death, which would have been unfortunate seeing how long—how very long—he had spared himself the unpleasantness of dying. Fall off his own tower? Certainly not! He started binding himself with straps to keep him in place as he gazed at the sky through his stargazer, and watched for the first glimpse of the returning Boro comet.

Four times a century it came. The Minister had seen it more times than he could count. And now he would see it pass by once again—*and so close*—but he still would not be able to catch it. Not yet, anyway. How many more magic children would he need until his tower was tall enough? Ten? Hundreds? Thousands? How many enhancements would he need before he could pluck the comet from the sky and carry it in his pocket forever? It sickened him, of course, this business with the children. But the sickness in his heart didn't interfere with the surety of his will. Besides, the first act of cruelty made the thousands that followed infinitely easier.

He needed that comet. He needed it desperately. It was all he could think about.

There were large red flowers growing along the edges of the walls defining the rooftop patio—a gift from one of his magic children, right before she died. "To help you breathe," she said kindly, before she breathed her last. Her lips were pale, her eyes were the color of milk, her hair had fallen out months before. He usually did not learn the names of his magic children—or anyone, really. People die so quickly when they are not enhanced, and only the Minister is enhanced. He has seen to that. But the magic children. They die quicker. Best not to know them.

This one, though. This one he knew. Not her name, of course, just the *fact* of her—that inscrutable bit of the Self that cannot be drawn or recorded or named. And after all these years, he still mourned her. A raw, painful, immediate feeling of loss.

Red flowers, his heart whispered. *Red, red, red, red.*

He picked a flower, breathed deeply, and felt a tightening in his throat. He inserted the flower stem into his lapel and returned his gaze to the stars.

"Soon," he said, waiting for the first glimmer of the comet to come into view, "soon." And he shivered, thinking of the coming magic, blessing the land. Thinking of the women with bellies about to swell with children imbued with the power to assist their Minister. Living only for him until they died.

"Soon," he said, and he imagined himself plucking the comet from the sky as though it were a candied fruit atop a large, luminous pastry. A delight meant for him and him alone.

He fell asleep at the top of his tower, wrapped in wind, as the taste of sweetness and magic and promise lingered on his tongue.

7. Now.

The boy named Jonah makes his way to the egg woman's house. Very few people know the way. Indeed, Marla the egg woman can count those who do on one hand. And Jonah is not one of them. She removes the small pistol she keeps in her ample brassiere and points it at the boy.

"Give me three reasons why I shouldn't shoot you, son." She says this casually, as though asking his opinion on whether bulbs should be planted in September or October. The gun in her hand is small and bright. She holds it perfectly still.

The boy puts up one hand. The other grips a locket around his neck. "I—"

"I can give you one why I *should.*" A mild smile. A narrowed eye. "Trespassing."

"I—"

She rolls her eyes. "Really? That's the best you can do?"

"I'm sorry, miss," the boy says. "I truly don't know what brought me here. I—" He shakes his head as though to dislodge sleep from his brain. "I've certainly never been here before."

Marla gives a sidelong glance to her right. She shakes her head with a harrumph.

"You're Laney Tice's oldest boy, yes?"

He nods.

"Your mother's a good woman. A clear mind in a sea of puddingheads. She'd miss you if you didn't come home." She sets the gun back in her lap. "Greet her for me, will you?"

He nods again. His face is muddled. Darting eyes in a tangled brow.

"Well," she says firmly. "Off you go."

"Yes," Jonah says. "Off I go." He is about to say something more. His voice catches and he says nothing. He turns, takes two steps away, and then freezes.

Marla groans.

He spins around. "Scorpio!" he nearly shouts.

"What's that child?"

"Orion's belt!"

Marla sighs and shakes her head. "Jonah Tice, what are you on about?"

"Delphinius and Draco and Cassiopeia! Polaris. The arm of the Milky Way." He closes his eyes and presses his hands to his face. "I came here with a girl. I've seen her before."

Marla feels her stomach drop and her mouth go dry. "Now," she rasps, "that's enough of this silliness."

The boy's face is glowing. He holds his hands open before him, as though wanting to catch something that might fall from the heavens. "She wore no shoes."

"It's cold." The acidic bite of panic in her throat. "No one goes barefoot in this weather. You imagined it."

"She wore a dress made of scraps and a coat that was too big and a face made out of sky." His breath comes in quick gasps.

He loves her, Marla thinks, her skin going cold.

"Now that's just foolishness." She tries to scoff. It is a thin, brittle sound.

"Sparrow," the boy whispers.

"No."

Shut your mouth, she thinks. Her heart screams it. *Shut your stupid mouth.*

"Sparrow." The boy's face falls into itself, like a sleeper waking up.

"A trick of the light," she says. "I mean an active imagination. I think you should go."

"Sparrow," he says with more insistence. As though it is the most important word in the world.

Marla points her pistol at the ground to the left of the boy's feet and pulls the trigger. He yelps.

"Get out." Her voice is dead calm. Her face is a stone. She shoots again, this time on his right side. And slightly closer.

He turns and runs as though pursued by wolves.

"Don't come back, or I'll sic my dogs on you!" This, of course, is an empty threat. Years ago, maybe, her dogs could have torn the poor child limb from limb. But not anymore. They are impossibly old. Plus they are drunk. Drunk in love with the Sparrow.

The Sparrow sits on Marla's right, leaning her head on the older woman's muscular shoulders. She has not just arrived. She has been there the whole time.

"I told you," the girl says.

"This proves nothing. The boy is nothing but a bundle of junk and sighs and juicy thoughts and sweaty socks. It's not magic that drew him. It's pheromones. I knew boys would be sniffing around in your vicinity someday, so it's no surprise. Pay him no mind. He's one of many."

"Don't be mean," the Sparrow says. "He's nice."

"God," Marla snorts. "Please."

"I must go find Papa." The girl stands and stares down the path. Marla gives her a narrowed eye.

"*Really*," she says, glaring at the spot where the boy had just stood. "You're off to find Simon, and not . . . *anyone else?*" Marla is the only person in town who refers to the junk man by his proper name. Always has. Even before the Sparrow came into their lives.

The girl smiles and gives the egg woman a kiss. "Hug my hens, will you?" She waves at the chickens in the barn, the Most Remarkable Hens. Each one regards the girl with their loving, identical eyes. The egg woman waves her off with a grunt.

"I wish you didn't have to go," Marla says. "And don't follow that boy home."

"I won't," the girl lies.

She disappears down the trail.

"Don't go," Marla whispers to no one in particular. "Please."

8. *Then.*

The Boro comet appeared in the sky four times a century, which meant that four times a century pregnant women in his country would fuss and worry over the possibility of bearing a child with magic. And, four times a century the government sent operatives into the hospitals and clinics. They listened to rumors and hired spies and tattletales and read furtive glances. They measured the middles of women of child-bearing age. They banned prophylactics. They made lists of the names of pregnant women and their due dates. No one knew how many children would be born marked by magic—it was different every time. But the papers were ready and the payouts accounted for.

The nation's women did their best to protect themselves. They made their husbands sleep in yards and outhouses and sheds. They researched herbs to promote impotence and snuck them into sandwiches. They developed headaches. Those who found themselves pregnant anyway drew runes on their doorways and draped white sashes over their bellies. They prayed and prayed for unmarked babies.

Not a magic child, they whispered. *Please not a magic child.*

Magic children were, after all, *expensive* children, the price of them measured in heartbreak and loss. They were taken, worked, and depleted, and then they died young. They were children who belonged not to their families, but to the government. And no one wanted to bear a government child.

The Sparrow was conceived under the spell of the Boro, of course. Two months before she was born, her mother had been rounded up with the other pregnant women and held in a high-security maternity ward, with nurses trained in martial arts and doctors who were excellent marksmen.

Even the orderlies had military training.

"No security measure is too great when it comes to protecting these precious mothers and their blessed progeny," the Minister intoned on the Vox.

Staff stylists coiffed the hair of the expectant mothers, aestheticians de-clogged their pores, manicurists pampered to their quick-bitten nails. They were given the best food, the sweetest drinks, and the highest-quality drug cocktails to imbue them with a giddy sense of well-being. The mothers felt as though they were floating through clouds of feathers and bubbles. They forgot about their families, about their bellies, about everything. They were happier than they had ever been in their lives.

The Minister congratulated himself heartily.

"A regular humanitarian!" he said to no one in particular.

The Sparrow's mother couldn't get enough of it. She stole drug patches from the haunches of passed-out mothers in the recreation hall, or in the bathroom, or the morgue. She raided the trash cans, licked them clean.

The Sparrow, in her unborn, watery world, was as addled as her mother. She dreamed of a tower as high as the sky. She dreamed of a jewel hovering over the world, pulling energy toward itself like a magnet, or a black hole. She dreamed of a wave pulling out of the center of the world, of a man riding its crest, a look of ecstasy on his face. She dreamed of a wobbly tower and a wobbly cart and red flowers and yellow coins and of a girl disappearing into the sky.

She dreamed of her mother.

And then there was only darkness.

9. *Now.*

No one sees the junk man's daughter. Not today. At least not so far.

She wears a dress that she made herself from cast-off bits of fabric and a man's belt wound twice around her waist and a large, wool jacket that used to belong to the junk man, but now belongs to her. In theory. She has nothing on her tiny feet. Her soles are black and thick with road dust and farm dust and factory dust. They do her fine and take her where she wishes to go, which is all a body can ask of a pair of feet. And anyway, she hates shoes.

She sits in the back row of the church, listening to the pastor intoning on the virtues of Virtue, and of the beloved Minister—the Parent of Virtue—in his strange, dark tower in the center of the country. Everyone loves the Minister. It's the law.

The entire town packs itself into the pews. Church services are required. Of course they are. How else would the population be reminded to pay homage to the Minister, if it weren't for required services, or the daily adulations, or his face on the money, or his face everywhere else, or the National Radio Broadcasts—blasting into each home at four-hour intervals without invitation, hesitation, or volume control? What better way to be roused in the middle of the night, to have nightmares interrupted, than to be yanked into consciousness with the sweaty, panicked, screaming name of the Minister in the mouth?

The people of the town sit in the church, straight backed, shoulder to shoulder on a rough-hewn bench. To all appearances, they are attentive. It is a practiced attention. Pastor Jenkins clears his throat. His jowls are gray, his eyes hooded, and his hands shake. He hurts. He longs for a drink. This is obvious to everyone. The junk man's daughter gazes at his face and feels her heart breaking with compassion. She feels his need as if it were her own, and experiences the deepness of the pastor's ache in her bones. She traces his face with her eyes, studiously imagining a tumbler full of whiskey—all amber and gold—sliding down his throat, hot and cold all at once. She imagines the heaviness on his tongue. The squeeze of his throat as he swallows. She watches as his tongue darts across his lips. She watches as he swallows. To her satisfaction, she notes the creeping flush of his cheeks and the sudden steadying of his voice. The smell of whiskey wafts through the pews.

She smiles.

No one else notices.

The pastor continues with his sermon.

The junk man's daughter has to pull her knees tight to her chest so that Mr. Brilange and his wife may pass by her in the pew, late as usual. She grabs her bare feet and makes herself as small as she can, in case she is bumped. The Brilanges don't see her now, but they have before, a couple times, and they do not like her. Mr. Brilange called her a guttersnipe, and Mrs. Brilange called her a tramp. Doesn't matter. The junk man's daughter loves them. She loves everyone. She can't help it.

According to the rules, the pastor is required to make note of the tardiness, though that particular statute, like many rules from the capital, has a tendency to be ignored. They are remote here. A backwater. Often forgotten. They do their best not to make waves. Especially recently.

Especially since the onset of the . . . *well*. No one knows what to call it. And certainly, no one mentions it. Little quirks started appearing around town, ten years earlier. The roof that doesn't leak, despite the gaping holes. The jug that makes any water run clean. The old woman who can tell if someone's lying just by touching their right earlobe. The little boy who can talk to horses and sheep and birds. Useful, that little skill.

No one calls these things magic.

How could they be magic?

Magic is against the law.

Martina Strange, two rows up, starts to cough. The cough tears through her chest and sends rhythmic waves coursing over her back. No one responds. She's been coughing for years. And she is old. It's only a matter of time.

The junk man's daughter stands up. She snakes through the pews. No one notices. She lays her hands on the old woman's back. The girl is standing so close to the man sitting behind Mrs. Strange, she is practically in his lap. He doesn't notice. The junk man's daughter feels a pleasant heat between the skin of her hands and the coat of the woman. She feels the coat thin and give way, and the flannel shirt, and the thermal underwear, and the thin jersey that probably belonged to the old woman's husband years ago. She presses until she is skin to skin. There is, the girl notices, a cancer wedged in the lung—black and twisted and oozing. The heat on her hands is so hot, she can feel her fingertips start to blister. She closes her eyes and doesn't move.

The woman shudders.

She lurches.

She gasps, clasps her hand to her mouth, and coughs so hard the sound might have come from the center of the earth. Once, twice, and at that third cough, out of her mouth flies a bird—black and twisted and angry. Oozing pustules for eyes. Talons gripping something bloody. The congregation gasps. The bird hovers in front of Mrs. Strange—all rage and malevolence—spirals four times inside the four walls of the church, and with a tremendous squawk, shatters the third window on the east side and flies out of sight.

Glass spangles the ground.

Bloody, black feathers fall to people's laps. Every mouth hangs open.

The junk man's daughter still doesn't move. Her skin pricks and tingles. She bites her lips and presses her hands to her chest—all hope and anticipation. Still no one notices her. The entire congregation holds its breath. They wait. A beat passes. And a beat. And a beat.

Oh for crying out loud, the girl wants to shout. *Say something. Notice your life!*

A beat. A beat.

A bird just flew out of a dying woman's mouth! You have the proof on your damn laps. The world that you have inherited isn't the world that you have to claim. There is so much, so much more. But she says nothing and they say nothing and eventually Pastor

Jenkins resumes where he left off. The girl sighs and returns to her seat. What else can she do? Shake them?

Marla the egg woman arrives and sits next to the junk man's daughter just as the service concludes. She is a wide, well-built woman—low to the ground and stable as a boulder. As reliable as earth. The pastor gives her a deferential nod and clears his throat. Drunk or not, there is no way he would report Marla. He wouldn't dare.

Marla lays her basket on the ground and casts a sidelong glance at the barefoot girl with the cast-off clothes and the coat that should be burned, by the smell of it. She shakes her head. Reaching over, she lays her hand on the girl's knee and gives it a squeeze. "Hello, my Sparrow," she whispers. Marla can always see her. For as long as she can remember. The girl doesn't know why this is, but she appreciates it all the same.

The junk man's daughter lays her head on the egg woman's shoulder. There is so much love coursing through her body that she can hardly bear it. She loves the town and each person in it, though few of them love her back. And her love rattles and heats inside her. It thrums against her skin and wrinkles her bones. It hurts, this love. And it exhausts her. She will need to take a break in a moment, find a dark corner filled with quiet and loneliness and *thinking*.

She has *so much* to think about.

"Where's your papa?" Marla asks.

"Feeling poorly," the girl says with a shrug.

Marla snorts. "You mean drunk," she says. The junk man's daughter doesn't respond. She gazes at the backs of each head in the pew, lets her eyes graze along their straight spines, their aching shoulders, their swollen joints. She looks inside and sees empty bellies, worried minds, broken hearts. She wants to gather each one in her arms, love them to bits. She wants to help them, heal them, give them strong backs and clear eyes and loud voices. She wants their lives to overflow.

And she can do it too. She knows she can. She just has to figure out how.

The egg woman narrows her eyes.

"Just what are you up to, girl?" she says.

The junk man's daughter closes her eyes. She takes a long, slow breath in through her nose and holds it for a moment. She turns to the egg woman, who instantly clutches her heart. She loves that girl so much it hurts. Her young face is flushed and shining.

"Something wonderful," the girl whispers.

She kisses the egg woman on the cheek and slips out of the church. No one notices her go. No one speaks to Mrs. Strange, nor do they comment on the deepening flush of her cheeks, the growing glow of good health and vigor.

And no one mentions the bird.

10. Then.

There were only twenty magic children born that year. Nineteen, if you subtract the one that died.

The Constable made a show of holding the dead baby's mother down as the Inquisitor weighed the tiny corpse, took photographs of the magic mark curling out of the navel, and filled out the forms in triplicate. But really, it was only a show. The woman in the birthing bed was drugged and exhausted. Her soul was worn thin. She gave no sign of resistance, no indication of struggle. Her shoulders were damp clay in his hands, and her eyes were flat, and dull as porridge.

"Come now," the Constable said. "That's enough," as though just by playacting with the mother he could spark a little life in her. If she fought him, he reasoned, maybe she would heal.

"I have authorization from the Minister," the Inquisitor said, "to gift to your family the full amount, even though his Excellency will be deprived the assistance of this once-blessed child." He adjusted his glasses on his nose. "It is most generous."

"Most," whispered the woman in the birthing bed, "generous." Even her voice was a cold, dead thing. "Can I have my baby back now?"

The Inquisitor squinched his face as though smelling something foul. "Of course not!" he said. "You have been paid. The procedures are done. The child is marked, therefore the child belongs to the Minister."

"But—" the woman on the bed began. The Inquisitor interrupted her.

"Young lady, it doesn't matter whether or not she is alive. Death, in the case of magic children, is irrelevant. A magic child is a government child. And your government thanks you. It says so on this form."

The woman's dead eyes burned to life and her ashen cheeks flushed. It was so sudden, so abrupt, that it seemed to the Constable nothing short of a miracle. *She is alive!* He nearly sobbed in relief.

He was new to the job, and he could tell already there was a reason why no one else wanted it. Still, better that he do it than some Minister's stooge from the capital. This was *his* town, after all.

The woman twisted this way and that. Her feet were still in their straps, and she would not be able to undo them without a nurse. "Take these off!" she shouted.

"As a spokesperson for our precious Minister and his government—"

She spat. "To hell with the government!" She punched the Constable in the eye. "To hell with the goddamned Minister. Give me my dead baby, damnit."

The Inquisitor gaped in horror. "Language, lady!" he sputtered. "This is a hospital! Keep your heresy to yourself."

She thrashed and bit. The Constable got a fingernail in the eye, teeth marks on his bicep, a knee in his groin. He groaned.

"Constable," the Inquisitor said, "please use the cuffs for the wrists of the heretic traitor, and deal with her at a later time. I expect you know what to do with this kind of law-breaking."

The Constable, did, of course, though he suspected that what he had in mind was different from what the Inquisitor meant. They had their own ways of dealing with things, out here in the hinterlands. It was better to keep that information as quiet as possible.

Much later, in the Constable's office, the box containing the dead baby sat on the desk. It had sat there for hours. The Constable opened the lid, and closed it again, wrinkling his eyebrows.

The baby was still dead. That was certain.

The Inquisitor stood next to the wall, a telephone perched

between his ear and his shoulder. For some reason, his communicator had ceased functioning normally, and he was forced to humble himself with the substandard technologies of this outlying town. As if his job wasn't hard enough.

The Constable opened the lid of the box again. Grunted. Closed it.

"Yes," the Inquisitor said. "Yes, yes, yes." A pause. "Of course I'll hold."

The Constable nearly jumped out of his skin. He opened the box. Closed it with a smack. Shook his head.

"Yes," the Inquisitor said, "I understand the Minister is very upset. And for good reason. Imagine that woman! Giving birth to a dead baby. And a magic baby, of all things. It is an insult that cannot be borne. But there is still a question of the corpse itself." Pause. "Yes, I'll hold."

The Constable leaped from his chair and started pacing the room. He shot a glance at the box on the desk. Gave a sidelong glance at the Inquisitor on the phone. Slid his eyes back to the box.

"Is there a problem?" the Inquisitor said.

The Constable shook his head. "Nope," he said. A grimace. "No, I don't believe so."

It took three days for the Inquisitor to get an answer. Three days, the dead baby lay in that box. The Constable didn't sleep a wink. He normally slept on a cot in the back corner of his office. But instead of sleeping, he spent the last three days sitting straight up, his back against the wall, his knees bent under his chin. Staring.

And he heard it.

And he heard it again.

He rubbed his eyes, rubbed his mouth, shook his head. "Stop being an idiot," he told himself. Still, he did not sleep. Still, he kept watch.

Finally, the Inquisitor received an answer. Not a particularly *good* answer, but an answer all the same.

"Come now," the Inquisitor said. "You will accompany me so you may co-sign the form."

The two men, along with the phalanx of soldiers, walked to the rubbish heap.

There it is again!

Don't they hear it?

When they reached the entrance to the heap at the edge of town, the Inquisitor gave the Constable a hard look. "Well," he said, "go on."

"Go on what?" the Constable said.

There! Why doesn't anyone notice?

"Throw the trash on the heap."

"*What?*" the Constable sputtered. He clutched the box to his chest. "That's a horrible thing."

"No," the Inquisitor said. "That is our order. There were nineteen magic children born. They have no names. They do not exist. They live only for the Minister. This one—the twentieth—is a dud. So. The trash heap, then." The Inquisitor was a short man, but he drew himself up, attempted an imperious expression. He pointed to the heap with one, long finger. "Honestly, where do you think the *rest* of them end up? It's not like there's a graveyard for magic children. It would rile people up. Think it through, man."

The Constable thought he might be sick.

"But," the Inquistor added, "not the box. Cardboard is expensive."

"It's been fouled," the Constable said. And it had. The tiny body had already started to leak.

"No matter. It's still usable. Go on now."

The Constable walked slowly out onto the heap, his heart like a boulder in his chest. He knelt down, and scooped the baby out of the box. It would be unrecognizable soon. The flesh would corrupt and loosen and fall; the sinews would be picked away and the bones would bleach until they shone.

The child never was. And that was that.

But as the Constable walked away, holding the reeking box as far away from his body as he could, he heard it again.

A child's voice. He couldn't tell where it came from—the air, the birds, the drizzling sky, or the trash under his feet— but the sound was unmistakable. The gurgling voice of a little baby.

And it was laughing.

11. Now.

Marla doesn't hear from the junk man or his daughter for weeks after the bird incident.

No one mentions what happened at church that day. They talk about the weather. They talk about the increased hours at the factory. They talk about grandbabies and funerals and whether they should plant corn or soybeans this year.

All the while, in the silent spaces between neighbor and

neighbor—*the bird, the bird, the bird.* It rings and spins and rico-chets between mouth and mouth, heart and heart, eye and eye, though all in silence. A storm is mentioned—*the bird!* A wed-ding is announced—*the bird!* A potluck is planned—*the bird, the bird, the bird!* That foul-tempered cancer-bird haunts darkened corners and hidden alleys and littered streets. It is everywhere, and it is silent. No one mentions the bird. Everyone thinks about the bird.

But, bird or no bird, one thing is for sure: Martina Strange is healed. *Healed.* For the first time in her life she breathes and breathes without hack or hesitation or wheeze. Her cheeks are pink, her eyes bright, and, perhaps most weirdly, her seven missing teeth have suddenly re-erupted in her mouth—straight and white and shining. She walks back and forth between her hovel of a house to her job as a charge-packer at the munitions factory with a gravity of bearing, an integrated sense of deep joy. She walks like a prophet, a sage, a queen.

Marla the egg woman doesn't know what to make of it. And she worries.

Because under her feet she can feel it.

A buzz.

A rumble.

Getting bigger every day.

"My Sparrow, my Sparrow, my Sparrow," she whispers. "What are you planning?"

Except her heart does not say, *what are you planning?* Her heart says, *don't leave me.*

And it does not say *my Sparrow.* Her heart says, *my child.*

12. Then.

There was a time, so long ago the Minister could hardly remember it, that he was a boy. A *child*. There was a memory that he treasured above all others, of standing with his mother in a field and looking up at the stars.

There, his mother said, *a planet.*

And there, she pointed high above, *the largest of all known stars.*

And there, she tracked her finger across the sky, *a bit of magic. If you can find where it lands, then none of us will ever die. Not me. Not your father. Not you. We will live forever.*

In his memory of that moment, his mother's face was young and beautiful, made more so by the long thin scar that began at her left temple and arced prettily down her cheek, hooking over the curve of her jaw and ending at the center of her windpipe. The Minister, as a boy, loved that scar, and he tracked its trajectory every night with his index finger, just as his mother tracked the falling star.

When he was young enough to assume that his hopes were powerful enough to true themselves upon the face of the world, and old enough to understand loss, both his parents donned their uniforms and marched off with most of the other parents of his acquaintance and headed into war. He had no idea what *war* was, and assumed it was similar to the wars that he fought with the other children in the neighborhood, in which the only casualties were the occasional broken arm and a few tortured pet dogs that were not to be mentioned later.

His mother was so beautiful in her high boots and fatigues. The moment before they marched away, both his parents gathered him in their arms and kissed him. The Minister sat on his grandfather's lap and waved and waved and counted the days until his parents would return and life would become normal once again.

It did not, alas. His mother, thanks to an inopportune step, had been blown to bits. There was nothing to bury. Only his father came back. The Minister never forgave him.

In the ensuing years, the Minister spent most nights in the backyard, looking up at the stars. He couldn't bear to be under the same roof as his father, who couldn't bear to look upon the face of his son. War had become commonplace in those days, and blackouts were a way of life. The roof of the night sky, therefore, was unspoiled by leaking lights or passing cars. While his neighbors crouched and shivered in the darkness, the boy Minister watched the workings of the heavens on full display before him—each glittering body smartly following their courses like soldiers. He kept records and drew maps. He delighted in their punctual grace. Each time an asteroid fell, he traced it with his finger along the curve of the sky, and thought of his mother.

There, her voice in his mind, *a bit of magic.*

And the Minister became convinced that his mother's words were true. And he became convinced that perhaps he *should* have found the place where the falling star fell, and perhaps if he *had*, he might have been able to save her.

And perhaps there was a way to prevent *himself* from ever dying. It was a thing worth wishing for, after all. Freedom from death. From erasure. From oblivion. And once he thought it, he began to want it. And then it was all he wanted. Well, almost all. He held his finger in the darkness before him, and traced the curve of his mother's scar. He would never forget it. It haunted his dreams.

And maybe I can bring her back.

13. Now.

They are two towns over, the Sparrow and her father, and they are wet through, and chilled to the bone.

"How can there be no whiskey," the junk man moans. "There is always whiskey."

And it's true. There is always whiskey. Or at least there has been whiskey in abundance for the last fifteen years. There have been many things in abundance for the last fifteen years. The junk man has theories about this. He has memories of a miraculous baby. But they are faded and fuzzy, as wobbly and patched-together as his own dear cart. He puts his arm around his daughter, who wraps her arms around his middle. She is the only thing that's real.

The rain pours harder. The Sparrow pulls her father close, helping him scoot further into the lee of the wagon, their backs curving under the edge. Surely it will stop soon. Four identical chickens—all Most Remarkable Hens, and all named Midge— peck at the ground under the cart. From time to time, they touch the tops of their heads to the girl's back, as though reminding themselves that she is still there.

They love her. *So much.*

The face of the Minister gazes over the town from massive billboards. They are everywhere. The Minister's smile is practiced, his skin is slick as resin. Even from here, the Sparrow can smell the formaldehyde and camphor on his breath.

The billboards will be useful. The junk man's daughter has a plan. *But not yet*, her heart pleads. *I'm not ready.* She leans her cheek on the bony angles of her father's shoulders and tries to breathe him in. She cannot leave him yet.

People rush by with their homemade umbrellas or their oil-cloths or their remnants of old plastic sheets. They see the junk man, but they do not greet him. They do not offer shelter. They have heard the stories. They have considered writing reports, but they fear incriminating themselves. After all, the junk man has been selling his wares in their jurisdiction for years. *Years.*

A troop of soldiers—twelve in all—marches by, their boots splattering mud. Their original faces are covered. No one knows what they looked like before. On the day of their initiation, their bright Interfaces are fused to their cheekbones and linked to their eyes—allowing everything they hear, smell, see, and think to be uploaded, searchable by the Minister himself. Each Interface has a scar, starting at the temple, arcing prettily across the cheek, and hooking under the limit of the jaw.

The Interfaces look ever so much like the Minister's mother. No one knows this. No one except for the Sparrow. It only makes her love him the more.

"I just don't understand it," the junk man says, shivering again. "How can it be *gone?*"

"It's a mystery, Papa," the Sparrow says, but it's not. In truth, she dumped it out. It's an experiment—one that currently is going poorly. "You'll adjust to its absence in a bit I'm sure."

It has been thirty-two hours exactly since the junk man's last drink. He is not adjusting well. He is yellow and gray and woozy. A shadow of himself. He shakes and groans and sweats and shivers. He cannot hold water. His heart strains in his chest.

"Just hold on." *You need to be okay if I am not here,* her heart pleads with him.

Not if, says a voice deep in her soul. *When.*

"I am so hot, my child. And yet I am cold. I am dying, or perhaps I am dead."

"If so," she squeezes harder, "perhaps it is temporary." She smiles at him. She is not a particularly pretty girl, but he loves her face—its over-wide forehead and over-small nose. He loves each freckle and those black, beady, glittering eyes.

"Temporarily dead," he muses. "I remember . . ." He holds his breath. He presses his hand to his chest.

And the junk man's daughter feels an opening in her heart. It is made of light. It is not death she fears—indeed, why should she?—but it is the thought of her own oblivion that keeps her up at night. There are so few people who see her, who notice her, and most that do forget her within a moment.

To be remembered by somebody.

To be longed-for.

To be missed.

This is her hope. It is all she wants.

"Come on, Papa," she whispers. "Temporarily dead. There is more to the story. It's in there somewhere. You can do it."

And in a flash, the junk man remembers. He remembers everything.

14. Then.

The Constable sent Marla the egg woman to see to the mother of the dead baby.

"I won't do it," Marla said.

"She won't see me, that's for damn sure," the Constable said. "And someone needs to look after her. After all, considering your history—"

Marla slapped him as hard as she could across his right cheek. And then she slugged him in his belly. The Constable wrapped his arms around his middle and doubled over.

No wonder no one wanted this stupid job, he thought.

Marla sighed. "Fine," she said. "I'll do it. Never mention my history again."

And she walked away.

People didn't mention Marla's history. It was too sad.

The mother of the dead child had taken no food or drink, save liquor, for over a week. When Marla arrived, the woman was in bed. The room reeked of sweat and sick and an overripe chamber pot. The husband had given up days ago, opting to drown his grief in the company of men at the tavern, rather than increase it in the presence of his raving wife.

Marla took the pitcher to the pump and filled it. She emptied the chamber pot and changed the sheets and opened the windows to let in the day. The mother of the dead child scowled and howled and made a feeble attempt at fighting, but she was too weak.

And anyway, no one could best Marla in a fight. No woman, no man, no soldier. No one.

Finally, when the grieving mother was in a clean gown on

clean sheets, Marla propped her up on a pillow and started spoon-feeding a soup with eggs and chicken and chervil. Easy to digest. Good for the soul.

The mother sipped it dutifully.

Finally: "You had one, didn't you?" the mother said. "A magic child."

Marla took a long breath through her nose. Her face was stone. She didn't answer.

"How old were you?" the mother said.

Marla closed her eyes. "Fifteen," she said. "I was fifteen."

The woman's eyes were red and damp. "Hell of a thing," she said, and Marla nodded. "Yours still alive?"

Marla stood. She needed to get out. Right now. She forced herself to stay. Turning to the woman in the bed, she held her eyes for a long time. "There's no way to know. They don't exist, remember?" But the woman's face was pleading. And insistent. Marla sighed. "Probably not."

She filled up the water jug one more time, and hid the whiskey and made sure there were enough foodstuffs nearby. She kissed the mother on each cheek and told her that every day would be a little easier.

A lie, of course.

She left without another word.

She did not tell her that her breasts still leaked for a child who went away forever.

She did not tell her that her heart, once big and passionate and full of heat, was now a tight, tiny stone, rattling in her cold, empty chest.

She did not tell her that every night she saw her girl, her taken girl—pale lips, milky eyes—at the top of a dark tower, flung out against the spangle of stars in a limitless sky.

She did not tell her that every night she dreamed of flowers. Red flowers, red flowers, red, red, red, red.

15. Now.

The junk man's daughter slides along the back of the low, one-roomed building that houses the Constable's office. The alley lights are out again—energy crisis. It is always an energy crisis. She appreciates the dark. Pressing her hands against the wall, she curls her fingers into the bricks. The sun is down and the moon isn't up yet. The night air is a puckering cold, but the wall is still warm, and so are her hands. She can hear the Constable inside, explaining things to the Inquisitor.

"I don't care what you think you've heard, sonny," she hears the old man say, "there ain't been a whiff of magic anywhere in the county since the last batch of those babies, and we both know full well what happened to 'em, don't you dare think I don't remember. You can't make a stone bleed and you can't make an ox lay eggs and you sure as hell can't find magic where it's not. Now you can write that down on your report and send it on up to your superiors. You got bad information is all. And not the first time, neither."

A scribble of pen on paper.

An old man's harrumph.

The junk man's daughter leans her cheek against the radiant bricks and inhales the scent of sun and clay and smoke. Dust from the stockyards. The oily belch of the munitions factory down the road. The bricks keep a record of the town's life in smells. The girl smiles. She loves her home. She loves it *so much*. Despite everything. She bounces a couple times to steady herself, and then she begins to climb.

The Minister's many faces loom on the top of every building—paper eyes, paper lips. They are large, faded, and garishly lit, as though watching the town. The Minister is always watching, with his smooth face and his white teeth and his rigid smile. There are only eighteen buildings in town, and thus there are also eighteen Ministers of varying sizes, the largest of which sits atop the Constable's office.

It is terribly large.

And in this, the largest of the Minister's faces, the dear leader does not smile. He does not show his teeth. His eyes are wide. His lips curl in. He is frightened, she thinks. Or angry. He is a child lost in the wood, a supplicant at the feet of a cruel and unfeeling god. The rims of his eyes are wet. His prominent cheekbones have a greenish pallor. She closes her eyes as she climbs and feels her heart skip a beat.

The junk man's daughter loves this billboard best. And she loves the Minister, though he does not know it. She shinnies up the bracework behind the Minister's face, as clever as a spider, and hooks around to the catwalk along the bottom rim.

"There were only two babies in this county born with the mark last time 'round, and one of them died before it took its first breath. You know it. You saw 'em. You held that dead baby in your own two hands and you made me throw it in the trash heap to be burned." The girl hears the smash of a fist on a desk. She hears mugs and paperclips rattle and fall. The Constable's voice is loud. Rageful. The Inquisitor says nothing. He only scratches his pen on the paper. "You think I don't remember? I was there, damnit. You took the pictures and ran the tests and filled out your goddamned forms, and that was that." Each word is an accusation. "And now you're wasting my time on rumors? Please. It's a lot of old nonsense, and you know it."

She can hear the worry in the Constable's voice, hiding under the righteous anger and indignation, and she knows it is for her. The Constable's one for secrets, that's for sure. And he's one of a precious few that gives a rat's nethers over whether she lives or dies. Which is why she feels a great sorrow for what she is about to do. She has never wanted anyone to get in trouble.

She closes her eyes and takes a deep breath.

"You can interview the whole damn town if you want to," says the Constable's voice. It is heightened now. And even louder than before. He is a man to be reckoned with, even when he is lying. "But it's the same. You'll find nothin' when there's nothin' to find. Unlicensed magician, my *eye*."

The junk man's daughter feels it first in her ankle bones. A buzz and heat. She removes four strands of hair from her head and, with loops and skillful knots, ties them into the shape of a butterfly. The buzzing sensation crawls its way through her bones. It is in her knees, then her hips. It inches up her spine. The butterfly made of hair is motionless in her hand. The buzz reaches her shoulders and down her arms, and spreads upward into her skull. It is in her fingers, her jaw, her teeth. She blinks bright floaters out of her eyes. Her eyelashes begin to singe.

She places the butterfly made of hair on her tongue and gently presses her lips together. She puffs out her cheeks and closes her eyes, and feels that unpleasant buzz heat its way through her muscles and organs. She feels it crawl across her skin like the scuttle of a thousand ants. She is covered. She is burning. She is so alive.

She opens her mouth wide and sticks out her tongue. And it begins.

The butterflies shoot out in threes. They are large, luridly colored, and glowing. They have bright eyes, hot antennae, wings that could heat a kitchen on a winter morning.

Fifteen butterflies. Eighteen. Twenty-one.

Her body shudders and shakes. Her eyes water and weep.

Thirty-six. Thirty-nine. Forty-two.

Her skin burns, her teeth burn, her tongue may never be the same.

One hundred and two. One hundred and five.

The butterflies hover over her head in a bright cloud. They shake the air. By the time the three-hundredth butterfly (the largest of them all, with electric-blue wings) emerges from her choking throat, she slumps onto the slats, utterly spent.

The butterflies await their orders.

"The eyes," she gasps, her voice barely a whisper. "Infect the eyes."

The butterflies need no other encouragement. They fly fast as missiles into the open eyes of each billboard Minister, disappearing into the depths of ink and paper.

"Well," she hears the Inquisitor say. "Thank you for your time."

"Make sure you stop at the baker's before you go. Bring a pie home for the missus. You won't regret it."

The eyes of each Minister burn black as coal. They glow red. Then gold. Then purple. They pulse and swell.

"I'll be sure to make a note of your cooperation in my report."

"I'd appreciate that. We all serve at the Minister's pleasure."

The largest butterfly stays with the girl. It rests on her chest, wrapping its wings over her body like a blanket. She shivers and heaves. Above her, the eyes of the Ministers brighten and beam. She can feel the vibration worming through the air.

And though she is weak, she smiles. She lets her left hand drift over the luminous body of the butterfly, stroking it tenderly. *It's working*, she thinks. *I knew it.*

The Inquisitor wears his visor and keeps his eyes on the papers secured on his clipboard. He fusses over forms signed in triplicate, over figures and diagrams and proper terminology. He knows that careers are made, stagnated, and destroyed by words, that a single misplaced comma can hang a man. Indeed, it happens all the time. He remembers his less careful colleagues with a shudder. He is fastidious for a reason. He has held this job now for eighteen years. Almost a record. The Inquisitor jabs his last period with a flourish and does not look up. Instead he exits the building, slides into the backseat of the long, black car waiting for him outside the Constable's office, and raps on the glass separating the driver from her passenger. The driver clicks the car into gear and allows its girth to glide silently down the quiet street.

The Inquisitor does not stop for pie.

The Constable follows the Inquisitor out of the building, crosses his arms, and watches the silent car disappear into the dark. He draws in a long slow breath of cold night air and looks up at the glowing eyes of the Ministers. He sees a growing brightness, and then a burst of energy shooting across the quiet street from eye to eye to eye, making a multipointed web over his head. He sighs deeply, rubbing his arthritic hand over the loosening folds of his face. He needs a shave. He always needs a shave. He looks back up and sees the slumped figure of the girl on the catwalk, her butterfly still wrapped protectively around her chest. He shakes his head and goes inside to place a phone call.

The telephone on the wall is an ancient thing—heavy black plastic, with a twirling wire that attracts dust. He dials the number he knows by heart and braces himself.

"Yep," he says. "Got a little sparrow on the roof." He waits. "There's been a development." He holds his breath and nods. "She did indeed." Listens to the other line. Holds the receiver away from his ear for a bit, wincing. "Well, there's no call for that kind of language," he says. "Channel was already open, and we both knew it. Been open for a long time. She just opened it more. Well. A lot more. Fool girl. Don't matter either way. Secret's out. Someone blabbed. Don't know who, but someone did, no mistake. And now we've got a whole mess of trouble coming our way." He waits a bit more. Rests his forehead against the wall. He's getting too old for this sort of thing. "Yep. I'll get her down. Why don't you come and collect her when you can. Bring the other fool too, assuming he's sober enough to stand."

Outside, the light emanating from the eyes of the Ministers is so bright that he can't see the stars. It's a pity. A little starlight might clear his head or soothe his soul. It usually does. He shrugs, rears back, and with more agility than would seem possible for a man of his age, leaps halfway up the building and clings like an insect to the bricks. He scuttles the rest of the way, scoops up the girl and her butterfly in one arm, and rappels back down, leap after downward leap, gripping the bricks with both feet and one hand. He lands on the ground, as light and soundless as dust. He brings her inside, locking the door behind him, and lays her gently on the cot in his office, crossing the room to put the kettle on.

"Huh," he says.

The Constable stares at his hands, utterly amazed. He curls his fingers into tight fists and stretches them out as far as they will go. His arthritis is gone. His joints are unswollen and loose for the first time in twenty years. And his performance on the side of the building is a thing he never has been able to do—even when he was young and strong.

And what's more, he hadn't even *thought* about it. His body knew what it could do before he did. He removes his eyeglasses and scans the room, blinking all the while. Crisp, sharp lines; details standing in stark relief. He slides the spectacles into a drawer, closing it with a decisive click, wondering if he will ever need them again.

"Good god, girl," he whispers to the sleeping child on the cot. "What did you go and do?"

16. Then.

On the morning after the Boro comet finally vanished from the night sky, not to return for another quarter century, the junk man—the man with the wobbly cart and the hand-patched boots, who smelled always of grave mold and vomit and whiskey and piss, the man who came through town every Saturday from the West Road and left every Monday by the East—found the dead child lying on the rubbish heap. The child with the magic mark.

The junk man wasn't looking for a child—living or dead— nor did he trouble himself with the national frenzy over the Boro comet, whose arrival always meant trouble. Whose presence in the sky, moreover, caused certain . . . anomalies in some children. He had better things to do.

The junk man had begun searching the rubbish heap, picking up treasures as he went. A possibly gold chain. A perfectly good shoe. A solicitor's briefcase, likely taken before the gentleman in question was thrown into the river with stones tied to his ankles. It was a dangerous profession these days, soliciting.

There were fliers. Signs. Banners. All regarding that troublesome Boro comet with its foolishness and woe. The junk man kicked a banner with his hand-patched boot.

He sang as he picked through the heap. His feet quivered with a bit of a suppressed jig and his fingers began to itch. He loved the rubbish heap. He never knew what he might find in there. Once he found a ring so valuable, it kept him in butter and beef for over a year. He had found the deed to the land where his shack now stands on the heap. Tools. Outlawed books. Loose change. Mostly operational eyeglasses. A set of false teeth.

And now a baby. When he first came across it, it was shocking, of course (though not, it should be noted, as shocking as all that, times being what they are). But there was no denying the fact that the poor thing was as dead as can be. A days-old corpse, to be clear about it, its eyes pecked out by ravens, its body gray and foul and leaking.

And then, without warning, the child curled its lips. It stuck out its putrified tongue and crinkled its cheeks. It began to whimper. Then cry. It blinked and blinked, raking its eyelids across the fleshy sockets until two bright eyes suddenly appeared, as shiny as new pennies. Its cheeks plumped and pinked, their skin suddenly glowing with good health and vitality. The child breathed. Blew bubbles. A rosebud mouth sought a nipple, and four tiny limbs kicked and flailed with hunger and cold and rage.

It was warm, ruddy, and *alive*.

Impossible.

The junk man fell to his knees, clutched his heart. His first thought was to dash the child's head against the rock. Surely it was possessed. Or it was a demon. Or it was an apparition dreamed up by some wronged customer to cause him to lose his mind before losing his life. Clearly it would devour his flesh, suck his brain, and go carousing through the countryside finding innocents to maul.

He approached the child cautiously. He rubbed his mouth with the back of his hand and sank into a crouch, resting his bottom on the heels of his boots. He settled his face into a suspicious stare. The baby, hardly noticing him, began to wail.

It sounded like a baby.

It smelled like a baby.

The baby was naked. A girl. She hiccupped in her loneliness and grief. The magic mark curled out like a snail's shell from her navel. It gave off a pale glow. The baby girl brought her fist to her mouth and sucked it desperately.

And oh! She was terribly alone. The junk man cupped his hand over the top of her fragile skull, and felt the gentle pulse of her fontanels, like the wing of a bird.

And the junk man felt something stir within him. The heart that he did not know he possessed eased into an unused groove and clicked neatly into place, like a coin into a slot. His eyes sprang wide. He shuddered and gasped. He was alive in a way he never knew before. He pressed his index finger to her palm, and felt the pincer grip of those tiny digits. The tendrils growing around his heart, holding it in place, pulled in tight. And everything was plain.

He cleared his throat and looked levelly at the child. He had never spoken to a baby before and was unsure how to begin.

"Good god, girl," he said. "It's not every day that you meet a body what can outwit a pack of soldiers. Good for you." He shook the child's hand solemnly and looked behind him to see if he was observed.

There was no one on the rubbish heap—save for a mostly drunk junk man and a recently dead baby. He found an old bedsheet and tore it into strips, binding the baby to his body. The child calmed. She abandoned her fist, opting to suck on his filthy shirt instead. Buttoning his coat over the baby, the junk man took a deep breath and pushed his cart down the road.

The child squawked twice. He began to walk with a bit of a sway, rocking her with the swish of his body. "Hush now, little sparrow," he said. "I'll get you fed soon enough. That or you'll feed the buzzards again. We'll see."

He headed to the far side of town and down the path into a thicket of wood toward the egg woman's house. She would know what to do. She usually did.

17. Now.

The egg woman and the junk man arrive at the Constable's office just before midnight. He is pushing his wobbly cart, emptied of its usual cargo.

He grumbles. She pays him no mind. He grumbles louder.

"Had it all arranged just so," he says. "Just how I liked it."

"Stuff it, old man," the egg woman says without turning around. "This is all your fault." She looks up and sighs. She is being unfair, and she knows it. Someone else is at fault. She glances up and gives the lurid billboards atop each building a hard look. The bright web linking the eyes of the Ministers is starting to fade a bit, but she can feel it all the same. An electric hum in the air. Pricks in the skin. Something bubbling underground. Like as not, everyone in town can feel it too. It's only a matter of time before things start happening.

Not that they hadn't been happening already.

The Constable's office is dark; she knocks anyway. The old

man's face appears in the window, lit by a candle. He grunts, fusses with the chain, and ushers them inside.

"Marla," he says to the egg woman with a respectful bow. "Sonny," he says to the junk man with his usual derision. The Constable calls all men younger than himself "sonny," but he reserves a special bit of extra scorn for the junk man, *on principle.*

"Who brought the bug?" the junk man slurs, squinching his face at the luminescent butterfly still resting on the girl's chest as he sways back and forth like a boat in a ceaseless gale. He shakes himself to clear the drink. It doesn't work. He feels light-headed and buoyant, as though his feet are only barely touching the earth.

(Which, incidentally, they aren't.)

"Please don't speak unless you can find a way to make yourself less of an idiot, Simon," Marla says. She turns to the Constable. "Has it started?" She doesn't know why she asks this. It has clearly started.

"She's done this to me before," the Constable says. "Sudden bursts of strength. Wholeness. But never like this, and never for this long. I went up and down the side of the building with my bare hands and picked that girl up like she was a bag of feathers. And now, I been leaning down and tying and retying my own shoes. Opening jars without pain. Push-ups. Handstands. Flying leaps. The whole bit. I even lifted my desk over my head without strain. And that thing is heavier than a truck." He says this in the same flat way that he describes the details of a crime scene. He will have time to be astonished later.

"I see," Marla says, closing her eyes.

The junk man walks (floats?) to the sleeping girl. He tries

to wipe the drunkenness away from his face. The whiskey stink pours from him in a cloud, and, suddenly, he feels ashamed. He lays his hand on her forehead, sliding his fingers onto her cheek as though she was still a little child. In his heart, she is always a little child. She feels hot and dry. "She's sick," he says.

"It'll pass," the egg woman says firmly.

"You don't know that," the Constable says. "And you don't know what'll happen next. Us three've been protecting her all these years. And now . . ." He raises his eyes to the ceiling. "The thought of government soldiers marching into my town is a thing that has kept me up at night ever since the two of you pulled me into this business. In any case, this is where they'll come first, so this is where she needs *not* to be. Get her back to the farm. And maybe get her out of town."

The junk man curls his arms around the sleeping girl. Her body feels lighter than it should, as though she had been filled up with helium. He pulls her to his chest and cradles her like he did when she was a baby. "Little Sparrow," he croons. "My precious little bird." Though he is unsteady, he doesn't drop her. Marla gives him a look—hard and exasperated and forgiving all at once. She follows him out the door.

Outside, as they laid the girl and her butterfly in the cart, Marla reaches into her basket and hands three eggs to the Constable. He tries to decline.

"I couldn't possibly. *Three?* Not during a food shortage."

"You'll eat them and you'll be grateful for it. One's for strength and one's for luck." She nods and turns down the road. The Constable stares at his three eggs.

"What's the third one for?" he calls after her.

"Lunacy," the egg woman says without turning around. "It might be our only hope."

18. Then.

At first, the junk man didn't notice anything strange about the recently dead baby. Besides, of course, its de-corpsification.

That, he allowed, was *odd*. And was a thing best not thought about.

In any case, he was the last person to get judgmental or *holier than thou*. Live and let live, that was his philosophy, his heart giving a little thrill at the word *live*.

Live, live, live. He nearly sang it.

And besides, despite the fact that he had seen it with his own eyes, he had difficulty accepting the whole business as fact. *Not really.* She was too alive, too . . . *wonderful*. It was as though she was only dead *in theory*. A clever trick by a clever girl.

Without meaning to, he leaned in and kissed the wobbly, delicate top of her tiny head. She smelled so good, it made him weak inside. And yet *strong* too. As though he had the strength to do bare-handed battle with legions of soldiers-of-fortune just to protect her. He wanted to do harm to any who might try to harm her. He wanted to find the individuals responsible for throwing a baby—*a baby, for god's sake!*—onto a rubbish heap. As though she were, well, *rubbish*.

The very idea!

It enraged him just thinking about it. He wanted to tear out their hearts and rip off their heads and spit upon their graves. He wanted their reputations slandered, their good deeds questioned, their names forgotten by history. He wanted *their* corpses thrown on rubbish heaps. Let them see how they liked it! Actually, no. He enjoyed rubbish heaps as a general rule. Best not pollute them.

The child whimpered. She was *so* hungry.

"Soon, my sweet," the junk man said. "Soon my little sparrow. You will eat and eat until your blood runs sweet. Sweet in the mouth, sweet in the eyes, sweet in your tiny heart."

(Where was this coming from? Poetry? Crooning? Great heavens. He had never been a sentimental man. What other strange magic did this child possess?)

He wasn't sure what infants ate when there wasn't a mother to do the job. Milk seemed a reasonable option, but milk from a cow or milk from a goat? Or perhaps a sheep? He had no idea. But the child was hungry, and she must be fed. He worried about her crying—what if someone alerted the authorities? What if someone handed her off to the same soldiers who threw her away? His fear was hot and cold at once. He curled his arm around his precious bundle and walked faster.

He didn't know what family she originally belonged to— most of the pregnant women had been rounded up and stored in an asylum until their due dates came. He could ask around, but not many people in town wanted to talk to the junk man— or anyone, really—about such things. You never did know who might be a spy for the government. He skirted the main road and went along the back byways. He shot furtive glances at people who did not glance back. If they heard the child crying, they did not show it.

In her little carrier under his shirt, she squawked and kicked and sucked, just like a normal baby. So he sang as he walked, bowing his arms out slightly as he pushed his cart down the ragged road through town.

And out of town.

And into that little diagonal trail into the woods that few people knew about. Marla the egg woman liked her privacy and didn't advertise her address. But he and Marla had a history, didn't they? Surely she would be willing to offer advice at the very least.

The egg woman was just exiting the coop when he arrived. She was covered in dust and feathers.

She set her basket of eggs gently on the ground and glared at the junk man. She curled her meaty hands into fists and took a long, slow breath in through her nose. He had been worried this might happen.

"Marla," he said. "You are a sight for sore eyes." He meant it, too. (He loved her, once, after all. And once he had a chance to make her happy, and to be made happy in return. But he loved the drink more. And she hated drunks. So it goes.)

"What do you want?" she said, as she brushed the chicken debris from her overalls and hair.

"Found something on the rubbish heap today," he said. He was breathless. He was worried. He wanted to show her the child, to have her inspect and evaluate and *love* her. And yet, *not*. At the same time. What if she wanted to take the child from him? What then? He felt a sob bloom in the depths of his throat.

"I'm not interested." She arched her back to crack the kinks out of her spine and tilted her head to the sky. As if just talking to the junk man required divine intervention. She picked up her basket and walked toward the front porch.

"Marla—" he began. The baby's whimper increased to a full wail. The egg woman didn't seem to notice.

"That's enough with the familiarity, thanks. You know the rules." It had been like this for years. Her voice was a brick wall with him. And he was a broken bottle. This is why they never spoke.

"The soldiers," he insisted. "The ones that took the baby with the mark."

"Don't talk about that," she said. "It's too sad."

The baby squawked again. Marla didn't seem to notice.

"Please—um, Madame Egg Gatherer. I really and truly need your help. The baby—" The baby raised her voice to a wail. Still Marla did not notice.

"I will be setting the dogs out soon," she said. "You would be wise to be gone." She disappeared into the house. The junk man stood on the porch, his head muddled by confusion and drink, and further addled by the loudening wails of the hunger-panicked baby.

He sighed, ran his hand over his face, and shook his head to dislodge the clouds in his brain. He unbuttoned his coat and laid it on the ground. Untying the baby's wrappings, he realized one reason for her growing discomfort.

"Poor little thing," he said, "sitting around in your own poo. Unfortunately I know the feeling." He wiped her off with the torn-up sheet and laid her on the coat. She spread out her hands and waved her fists, and kicked vigorously with untamped rage.

"Marla!" he called.

"Don't call me that, Simon. I have been very clear."

"What kind of milk do you give to a baby?"

"Why on earth do you want to know that?"

"Whatever the best kind is, I'd like to buy it. You sell it don't you?"

"The dogs are coming out right now, Simon. I would be terribly sad if they ripped your face off, despite everything. But I will comfort myself in knowing that you brought it on yourself." She opened the door and three large dogs came tumbling onto the porch, snarling and snapping.

The junk man rubbed his thumbs on the soles of the baby's feet and moved her legs back and forth. She calmed a bit, hiccupped, and launched a spray of urine straight down onto his bended knee. She smiled.

"Atta girl," the junk man said, utterly delighted.

The dogs stopped their snarling and tilted their heads. The largest of the three leaned down and sniffed the head of the baby. It wagged its tail and whined a bit.

"What on earth?" the egg woman said.

"I told you. It's a baby. Your dogs know better than to attack an infant, thank god. I think I'll keep her around."

Marla slid out the screen door and skirted the sniffing dogs. She glared at the junk man hunched over the coat. "There is nothing on that coat, Simon," she said.

"Close your eyes," the junk man whispered. "Close your eyes and *smell*."

Knees cracking, the egg woman folded her legs, sitting primly on her heels. She rested her elbows on her thighs and closed her eyes, breathing deeply through her nose.

"Oh!" she whispered.

"You see?" the junk man said.

"But . . ." She opened her eyes. *"Oh!"* A gasp, a shudder, a sigh. And she *saw*. He could tell. Hesitating slightly, she extended her right hand to the magic mark curling from the child's navel. She let her fingers linger there for a moment, each breath shuddering in and out, in and out. She pulled away, pressed her hands to her mouth, and tears leaked into the crinkles around her eyes. *"The poor little thing!"*

The junk man gathered the child into the crook of his arm and looked imploringly at the egg woman. "Will you help us?"

The magic mark glittered and glowed. The child sucked madly on her fist.

"Please." He placed his hand on Marla's strong shoulder. He hung on for dear life. She didn't bat his hand away.

She felt her heart start to swell.

19. Now.

After three days of profound, dreamless sleep, the Sparrow emerges from her nest. Her hair is matted and her mouth is raw. There are burn marks on her throat and tongue, and deep cracks in her lips.

She remembers the buzz.

She remembers the butterflies.

She remembers a burning web and an open door and the shiver in her bones telling her that she wasn't alone anymore. Well. *This should be interesting.*

They are at the egg woman's house—she knows it well. She is in the loft. It is a comfortable place—thick quilts and a hand-woven rug and wood walls and a view through the roof-peak window that is shaped like an eye. She knows that Marla is not her mother (her birth mother is the woman with the hollow eyes and the early gray hair, and the face marked by munitions grease and too much drinking and not enough sleep and too much sorrow for anyone to bear—the Sparrow knew her instantly, and saw her story etched on her face, as clear as any map. Her mother can't see her. The Sparrow thinks this might be a blessing), but Marla has served as her mother—enough for as long as the girl can remember, and will continue to do so for now.

Many things will do for now.

(But not for much longer.)

Her butterfly clings to the far wall, its luminescent wings folded against one another, showing their dusty undersides. It is, she suspects, the only one that survived, and she does not know how long it will live, or whether it grieves its brethren, or whether it will stay with her at all.

She only knows what she *hopes.*

She sits up. She is, she realizes, naked under her sheets, and bathed. There is a bowl of water with lemons and mint floating on its surface and a dish with a small, clean sponge resting in its center. She runs her tongue over the injured inside of her mouth. It tastes slightly of lemons.

How long have I been sleeping, she wonders. She knows that she has been dead once, though she does not remember it. Did she die again? Is her borrowed time nearly gone? She suspects it may be, which is why she feels she must help people while she still breathes. As many as she can.

Which is to say, *everyone.*

There is a flowered dress draped on the chair, and a brush and a pitcher of water and a wash bowl on the dresser. There is a pair of soft shoes as well, but those she does not put on. She has never been one for shoes, despite the egg woman's best efforts. She slides over to the ladder and pads downstairs, her butterfly fluttering behind her.

Marla is nowhere to be found. The junk man sprawls his skinny limbs across the couch, his mouth wide open and snoring. The egg woman's dogs have opted to remain in the house, and are sitting at attention, watching the junk man intently, their ears pricked up and their eyes narrowed to slits. As though he is a dangerous creature who might need to be subdued at any moment. Or torn to shreds.

"Papa," the girl says, her voice a ragged husk of itself.

The dogs whine and thump their tails on the ground. They love the girl—always have. They are old dogs now, impossibly old, but still strong and bright-eyed and spry. It isn't magic. Of course it isn't. Magic is illegal. Still, whenever she is near them, she can feel her navel glow and heat, and she knows that when the time comes for her to leave town, the dogs will not likely live to see her return. She has accepted this. In a unified motion, all three dogs slide to their feet and stalk next to the girl, lowering their heads toward the junk man and showing their teeth. He wakes with a start. He stares blearily at the girl and blinks.

He does not smell of whiskey. He smells instead of pickles and mustard plaster and rosemary tea. Marla has laid down the law. Again. The Sparrow finds herself wondering how long it will last.

The junk man coughs. "You're not dead." There is a sob hiding in his voice. The Sparrow has one too. She knows the ferocity of his love for her, and she reciprocates it.

"No, Papa," she says. "I am not dead. Not yet. Where's Marla?"

"Town." He sits, rests his spindly elbows on his bony knees. His fingers are long and delicate as willow twigs, though his knuckles are red and raw from the careless gnaw of his teeth. What is left of his teeth.

"I'm going to follow her. I need to tell her something."

"She told me to tell you to stay put. She made me *promise*." His eyes are red too. Bloodshot and red. And it is not from missing the drink. He has been weeping. He will weep again. The girl knows this for sure.

"She will forgive you. Anyway, there is something I need to take care of."

"My bird, my bird. What do you think you're doing?"

She smiles. He presses his hands to his heart. She crinkles her eyes to keep her tears at bay.

"The right thing, Papa. I only ever try to do the right thing."

She kisses the top of his head and slips out of the room without another word, her butterfly clinging to her back. The dogs follow at her heels.

20. *Then.*

Despite the egg woman's protestations, the junk man insisted on bringing the girl wherever he went. Their nation was formed in the shape of a dandelion gone to seed—each province made up of several small towns connected on one circular road, largely left to their own devices (most of the time), and connected to the capital by the main road, which was heavily guarded and maintained. There was no communication between provinces, and there was no travel to the capital except by express permission of the Minister. There were rumors that it wasn't always so, but no one could say for sure. No one had actually read a history book, after all.

History was another banned subject.

Within the towns of their province, the junk man enjoyed total freedom of movement. He reported to no one, served no one, needed no one, and slept each night under the stars. With the addition of the baby into his life, only the last bit remained true.

"What if it rains?" Marla protested.

"Then it will rain. And we will be clean," the junk man said, dandling the babe on his knee. He made a carrier that could attach to his back or his front or his hip, depending on what made the child happy. He also built a swing to hover over the cart and a shade to keep her from the cruelties of the sun.

"What if the soldiers come?"

"Let them come," he said with more conviction than he actually felt. "They can't see her anyway." This had largely been true. While the dogs were aware of the child from the moment they encountered her, no one else seemed to notice that she was there. Both the junk man and the egg woman had tested this, taking the child to the market, to the well, to the monthly census, and to the required church services, and the results were the same: no one noticed the baby. Not even when she cried. She was invisible, inaudible, a cipher.

All's the better, the junk man thought.

But Marla worried. *For what purpose?* she wondered. *And for how long?* At Marla's insistence, the junk man agreed to have the girl stay with the egg woman for one week per month.

"Because someone has to teach her how to keep herself clean and whole," Marla explained. "Someone will have to teach her to read and write and reason. How to mend a sock and make a jacket and keep the wind out and make stew. Someone will have to show her how to take care of her lady bits when they change and how to shoo the boys away when they come sniffing around. Someone will have to teach her how to protect herself."

The idea that there might, some day, be any lady bits to manage or any wooing boys crossing his path was more than the junk man could bear, and he agreed to the situation.

(Besides, he reasoned, while he could get reasonably drunk with a baby in tow, he couldn't get *good and drunk*, and the thought of saying farewell to his periodic blackouts was a devastating one. Now, he could limit his benders to the first week of the month.)

Marla, of course, had come to a similar conclusion, which is why she suggested the situation in the first place. She knew how much he loved the inside of a bottle.

But most of all, Marla thought of her own taken child (dead now, most likely. Worked to death. *Pale lips. Milky eyes. Red flowers, red flowers, red, red, red*) and how to protect the Sparrow. How to hide the curious curl in her navel. Hide the oddness of her birth. And her death. And her un-death. Hide everything. Marla worked twice as hard and sold what she could and bought fabric for the girl's clothes and leather for her shoes and traveling gear, should they ever need to leave her beloved home at a run, and live out their lives in hiding.

(*Where would they go?* her heart asked her.)

(Marla told her heart to hush.)

And Marla hoped that the magic inside the girl—untapped, unknown, unnamed—would remain inside. That if she didn't *know* about the magic, then she would not *use* the magic, and thus no laws would be broken and no unlicensed magic children would be repossessed by the heartless soldiers of the Minister's personal guard. She would be raised as a regular child—hidden, yes, unconventional in terms of lifestyle, clearly, but fundamentally a *regular child*.

It was a good plan, Marla decided. And it would work. She decided *that* too.

But then, odd things started happening. Things the girl did not initiate or intend. It was as though *the magic itself was leaking out.*

The stick that became a snake.

The pebble that became a beetle.

The withered apple tree that, after a single touch, became heavy with apples the size of watermelons.

But surely those could be explained away. The snake was just a trick of the light. The beetle must have been there the whole time. And don't fruit trees always surprise a person—coming back just when you think all is lost? They are the phoenixes of the plant world—though she couldn't quite remember how she knew what a phoenix was. She certainly had never encountered one in a book. Still, everything was explained. Rationalized. Forgotten.

For a while.

The Sparrow turned five on a Tuesday. It was the first week of the month, so Marla had sent the junk man packing (he had several bottles rattling around the cart in anticipation of his weeklong bender), and had brought the little girl with her to the chicken coop.

Sparrow, then as now, delighted in the populations of multicolored birds living in the chicken coop, but saved the majority of her love for a Blue Speckled by the name of Midge—a fat, fine princess of a chicken, with a tall, proud comb atop her head, and two deep red wattles adorning each side of her face like rubies. On the way to the coop that day, Sparrow jumped off the porch in a high, clean arc, going much higher and much more slowly than seemed possible (*a trick of the light*, Marla told herself). She landed daintily on the very tips of her toes.

"Well, look at you," Marla said. "A ballerina."

The word stopped her cold.

She had no idea what a ballerina was. She had never seen one, nor had she seen a picture of one, nor had she heard the word before in her life. And yet, there it was. In her mouth. In her memory. *Ballerina*. And not just the word, but the essence of the word as well. In her head was the swell of violins (*what on earth are violins?*), the toes like grace notes on a polished wood floor, the ribbon-wrapped ankles, the long, oiled hair tied back in a hard, round knot. She saw a feathered woman who was both princess and swan, a toy who would be king, a red bird with jeweled eyes (the downfall of tyrants, that bird, and *oh! To have such a bird!*). It was as clear as water, this meaning. As true as the breath in the lungs. *Ballerina. Ballerina. Ballerina.* The Sparrow looked at Marla and smiled.

"Yes," the girl said. "A ballerina. See?" And she twirled on one toe, arms extended like wings.

The egg woman felt her heart sink—a heavy stone in a dark, murky pool.

Seeing things I got no right to see, knowing things I never heard of. She shook her head. What other tricks was that girl up to?

When they opened the chicken coop, they saw Midge lying on her side on the packed earth floor, her upper eye muddy and opaque, and gazing at nothing.

"No, no," the child cried. She ran to the far side and skidded to her knees. She paused and held her hands outward as though blessing the bird, great tears streaking down her cheeks and falling onto the chicken's beautiful feathers like rain. She scooped Midge into her arms.

"No, Sparrow," Marla said. "It's too dirty. You'll need another bath. And how many baths can one girl have, really?"

But the girl didn't listen. She buried her face in the stiff breast of the dead hen and couldn't speak for sobbing. Marla sighed.

"There, there, child," Marla said. "Things live and then they die. There's no use in crying over what can't be helped."

The girl wailed louder. She sprang to her feet, clutched her dead chicken, and ran from the coop in a rage. The dogs followed her, as always. They never liked to have the child out of their sight.

Marla shook her head. She let the child go. She swept the coop and fed the chickens and fixed the wobbly bits on the fence, and stripped and squatted on the ground to urinate at the four corners as a deterrent for foxes and stoats. When she was finished, she walked around to the far side of the house and saw the dogs watching the girl as she played with the hen.

The hen!

It was, as before, fat and hale and shining. A princess among hens.

"My Midge," the girl sang. "My Midge, my Midge, my Midge."

The once-dead hen clucked and preened. It was a thing of beauty. It loved the girl. Of course it did. Everything loved the girl. Marla snatched Sparrow around her waist and hauled her, screaming, inside.

She fed the girl, bathed the girl, and distracted the girl. She told her stories. She looked out the window to make sure Midge was gone. But Midge wasn't gone. And what's more, there was Midge and an identical Midge strutting through the grass, looking for tasty bugs to catch. Marla closed the curtains and convinced the girl to play in the basement.

By lunch there were five Midges in the yard. Two of them had laid eggs—fat and speckled and gorgeous, nestled in the grass. Marla locked the door.

By supper there were fifteen (though there would have been seventeen—a hawk made off with one and another made a fine supper for a passing feral cat).

Marla sighed, and let the girl outside.

"My Midge," the girl sang happily as she frolicked among the flock of identical chickens. "My Midge, my Midge, my Midge." And she kissed each one on its ruby wattle and was, by all reckoning, the happiest girl alive.

Marla sighed. *Fine*, she thought.

That night, Marla told the Sparrow the story of the magic children. And the Boro comet—the source of all this nonsense. She told her how frightened the nation's mothers were each time the Boro comet appeared in the sky. She told of the children born with the magic marks. Of the soldiers who took those children away. Of what happened to them.

She told her about the day the junk man found her.

She told her about the Minister. He was old, that Minister. And yet, *young*. Maintained by magic. Hungry for magic. *So hungry*. How he lived alone in that strange fortress stretching up to the sky.

She even told her about her own dear baby. Marked. Taken. Lost forever.

(*Red flowers, red flowers, red, red, red.*)

The girl listened for a long time, her large brown eyes sober and serious, a thin slick of tears at the bottom edge.

"Does my junk man know?" the girl asked gravely. "For real, I mean. Does my papa know he is not my papa? It seems like he might not know."

"I know what you mean, love," Marla said. "Your papa lives in a world of his own making. He was there, though, and he knows. But you are wrong in your thinking. It isn't blood that makes a papa, a papa. Love does that. Simon's love for you is limitless.

Your papa is more papa to you than most can claim." There was a note of bitterness in her mouth. Her own father had turned her out, years ago, when her teenage waist began to swell, and did not welcome her back when the soldiers took her baby away (though he was happy to relieve her of the hefty payment—and she didn't argue. She didn't want it anyway. Blood money, she said). He later died in a brawl, and Marla never mourned him. "Your papa is what he is, and he is doing as fine a job as he can, and he loves you *so very much*. More than you will ever know." And, for the first time, Marla knew it was true. What's more, she could *feel* it too.

"Me too," the girl said.

"Not everyone can see you, my darling," Marla said. "But I don't know how long that will last. And you are not safe. And you need to be safe. Your papa needs you to be safe." She closed her eyes and closed her fingers around the girl's soft, pliable hands. "*I need you to be safe.*"

And so, as the sun went down, and in the quiet of the loft, surrounded by quilts and candles and safe arms and hushed voices, the girl and her Marla began to make a plan.

The army of blue speckled hens—nearly a hundred of them now—stood guard on the fence, their bright black eyes beading into the night.

21. Now.

The butterfly takes notice of the flowers along the trail leading to the town, and releases itself from the girl's back in order to gorge itself on pollen. The dogs whine a bit. They don't like that butterfly. Too bright. Too big. Too unpredictable. They don't like how it clings to the girl, how it refuses to walk on the ground. They whine and growl, but they do not snap. The girl lets her fingers linger on their heads, and they calm.

They are *so old*, these dogs. And they love her so much, they feel that they will die without her. (Which, the junk man's daughter knows in her heart, is likely true. *I will miss you*, she thinks.)

She reaches the fork in the trail, where one branch goes to town and the other branch wanders up to the top of a rocky knoll. There are seven standing stones at the top of the knoll—remnants, she's heard, of another time, another people, another way of thinking. Gone now. No one knows where or why or when. History is banned, after all. There is only now. There is only the Minister. That is all they ever need know.

The girl smiles. *The Minister.* He has haunted her dreams for as long as she can remember. His damp eyes. His receding hair. The delicate lobes on his ears, fragile and soft between her finger and her thumb. She has not touched the Minister. She has not laid eyes on him. But she knows him, even so. She knows him from the inside out.

She summits the knoll and climbs the tallest of the standing stones and sits, cross-legged, at the top. She cups her hands around her eyes. The Minister's fortress is too far away to see—miles and miles and miles away. And yet she can see it all the same. Its happenstance form. Its blackened windows. Its terrible height. Its dark stones, each one groaning with the souls of magic children. She can see the Minister too, sitting cross-legged atop his own standing stone, perched on the roof of his impossibly tall tower. Every quarter century, the tower gets taller. Every quarter century, it is imbued with more magic. Every quarter century, it brings him closer to the thing he desires most of all.

The Boro comet.

Its strangeness.

Its miracles.

Its curses.

She plucks another hair from her head and weaves it into a pentagram. She curls her fingers into its center and pulls, stretching it larger and larger and larger. And as she pulls, the fibers of the pentagram thicken and strengthen. They are rope. They are wire. They are rod-iron. It is a trinket, then a mirror, then a window. She holds it in front of her as though she is hanging a picture on the wall. She jiggles until it feels secure, and lets her hands drift down to her sides. The pentagram floats in front of her, its center shimmering like the moon on a quiet lake.

And she sees him. The Minister. And he sees her. The junk man's daughter. She smiles. He is terrified. She waves. He does not wave back. His mouth opens and closes, but nothing comes out. He looks exactly as she imagined him, though his skin is more dull than his billboards lead a person to expect. Age, perhaps. Or stasis. Or an overindulgence of magic.

Not that she knows anything about magic. She doesn't. How could she?

She stands. Slides her arms out of her sleeves. Peels her dress from her shoulders, her chest, her belly. She is before him, in the window of the pentagram, naked to the hips, the strange mark on her stomach curling from her navel, glowing so bright to make him squint. There are tears in his eyes.

"You!" the Minister says.

"Me," she says. Her eyes glitter. Her teeth flash.

"You're dead!"

"Am I?"

"I need you."

"I know."

"I've always needed you."

"I know."

She loves him. So much. She can't help it. He is broken. And the world broke with him. She rears back and kicks the pentagram—a quick, sure force. It goes flying away. She can hear him screaming for her to come back, screaming for the guards, screaming for his mother. Screaming, screaming, screaming. And then the pentagram hits the ground, unravels, and his voice is gone.

The dogs wait at the bottom of the standing stone. The butterfly has rested on the head of a Labrador. It is not amused, but it does not fuss at the butterfly.

The girl jumps, and lands lightly on her toes. The dogs whine.

"I know," she says. "It's not too much longer."

And they head toward town.

22. Then.

The chickens were just the beginning.

Marla had to build eight new coops to house them all. Fortunately, one of the Midges turned out to be male (Marla was unsurprised by this—it stood to reason, knowing Midge). And what a male he was! Her entire chicken population—from the bitter leafs to the argonites to the peppershells to the reds—started to wriggle and swoon in his presence. They preened and clucked and presented their bottoms with a saucy swish. The rooster-Midge only had to turn his head and an entire coop would be sent into a tizzy. Their laying quadrupled overnight. And *what eggs!* They had shimmer and heft. They caused a shiver up the spine at just the touch of them.

Marla came home from her first day in the marketplace selling those eggs with a smile on her face. She bought real beef and shared it with the dogs. She bought a coat for the girl (she told people it was for a country family she knew on hard times). She even bought a new hat for the junk man.

It wasn't until she waved good-bye to the girl and her papa in their handmade cart that she started to worry.

Because *those eggs.*

They did things, those eggs.

Cured illness.

Eased pain.

Repaired marriages.

Within two weeks six young wives of her acquaintance grew green about the gills. Dark circles around the eyes. A glow on the cheeks. They had been trying to get pregnant for several years, and suddenly all six were pregnant at once.

Word got around. But no one said "magic." They didn't dare.

Then there was the herb garden. And the vegetable patch. (Both, of course, were fed with the manure from the chicken coops—now providing the plants with more than simply nitrogen.)

And then it was the cow. Her butter could remove scars,

regrow hair, whiten teeth, and cure arthritis. Her cream cured gout. No one mentioned this—they just bought Marla's wares without making eye contact, and hurried home like the devil was after them.

And Marla worried.

Meanwhile, the junk man, with the help of his daughter, was finding more and more curious things in the rubbish heaps. A pair of eyeglasses that allowed the wearer to see in the dark. A pen that never ran out of ink. A picture frame that would show the face of the person the holder missed most. The Sparrow helped the junk man to identify these curious objects, and then connect them to the person who needed them most. The Sparrow had a keen eye for people. She could read them like stories. They didn't see her— not usually, anyway—but she could see them from the inside out. And she loved them.

These objects were few and far between—often they would find only one during the space of a month, and some months would come up empty. Still, as the years passed and as the girl grew, the objects began to proliferate.

Shoes that would allow the wearer to run and run and never tire.

A pot that was always filled with soup.

A blanket that would calm even the fussiest baby.

When the Sparrow was nine, Marla stood in her stall at the market, selling her eggs by the basketful. She saw the Sparrow and the junk man perched on the cart, selling god-knows-what to god-knows-who. She saw the church pastor examining a small, leather-bound volume. She saw how his eyes lit up. He stuffed some money in the junk man's hands, tipped his hat to the Sparrow, and hurried away.

The pastor tipped his hat. To the Sparrow. He saw her, noticed her, greeted her. *Not good*, Marla thought. *Not good at all.*

And then a little boy waved at her.

And a matron looked the girl up and down, crinkled her nose, gave her a harumph.

Marla sold her last egg, wrapped up a bundle of cookies, and walked across the square.

The Constable sat on a folding chair, under a banner that said, "See Lest Ye Be Seen." It was highly produced and shiny. Made in the capital.

"Hello, Henry," the egg woman said.

The Constable started. No one had used his name since he became the Constable. He had almost forgotten that he had one to begin with.

"Marla," he said. He gritted his teeth. He remembered the punch. He hoped Marla wasn't mad at him. "Do you have an observation to share?"

"No. An invitation. There is something that I would like you to see. And something that I feel that you should understand. Can you find your way to my house?"

"I do believe I can." He gazed at the egg woman under the shade of his regulation hat. Her arms were crossed over her ample bosom, and her face was set. Of course he knew where she lived. He also had a history with Marla. And not a happy one.

"Be there at sundown. Bring a toothbrush."

And she walked away.

The Constable could have made his way blindfolded.

There was a trick, he had learned, to the constable business. An eye that fluctuated between the blind and the keen. A show of fairness, with an open hand toward those who were able to come and go between the province and the capital with ease—factory owners, bureaucrats, and the like (he never had to worry about over-expectations; aside from the Inquisitor, none of them lasted very long). And a gruff presence, which gave the impression of a stricter fist than he actually possessed. (There was, he grudgingly allowed, something to be said for maintaining order in a population so weighted by worry and work and weariness that they didn't have time to fool with crime or sedition or independent thinking. The Minister, when it came down to it, knew what he was doing. All hail the Minister.)

The Constable loved his home. And he hated the capital. And so he stayed, protected his own. (Not like he had much choice in the matter. There weren't a lot of retired constables around. They had a tendency to disappear. No one had ever lasted as long as he did. He wasn't going anywhere. He had decided as much.)

He arrived at Marla's tiny farm shortly before sunset. The chickens were just settling into their coops. And there were *so many of them*. Hen after hen after identical hen, all murmuring their goodnights to one another. He pulled a cheroot from his pocket and chewed on it thoughtfully. He didn't turn when Marla approached from behind.

"I wouldn't want to have to report an illegal breeding operation, Marla," he said.

"Fortunately, you won't have to," Marla said.

"Marla, I turn a blind eye to a lot, but this? The Ag Czar is going to—"

"These are not bred birds," Marla said. "They're made."

"What's the difference?"

"They're all the same hen. Midge. They're all Midge."

The Constable peered into the coop. The chickens all turned their beaks in unison toward the left. They shivered as one. They blinked as one. He looked carefully from hen to hen, and couldn't find a speck of difference. They weren't just the same breed. They were the *same*.

His mouth went dry. "What are they looking at?"

"I'm getting to that in a minute. First I want to tell you a story. About a baby."

23. Now.

Jonah kneels in the backyard with his spyscope, gazing up. The ground is damp and the wet soaks the knees of his trousers. He doesn't care. The sky is darkening by degrees, but it still isn't dark *enough* for good stargazing. He doesn't care about *that* either. The night, after all, is long. There is plenty of time.

As he waits for the fullness of dark, Jonah enjoys watching the alterations of light—the decay of color, the way the day strips itself from the surface of the sky. He likes things in *flux*.

There is an object that he hopes to see. A star, perhaps. Or a galaxy. It behaves oddly, appearing and disappearing at will. Lately, the object has been coming closer and closer to a star known locally as the Eye of Ashra, though it has a different name in different towns—his favorite star—approaching, vanishing, approaching, vanishing. He has tracked the odd object's movements. He has documented the quality of its light. He has scratched through equations and theorems. He has an idea. It is too stupid to even write down.

The dew clings to his clothes. He shivers. He has a locket around his neck. His hand grips it absently. Most days, he has forgotten that he has it.

His spyglass is of his own design—a polished wood casing, cast-brass hardware that he poured himself in the hidden workshop in the barn. The glass was tricky—it took him years harvesting the broken glass windows from the munitions factory, the patient and precise work of grinding lenses and convex mirrors, experimenting with thickness and curve until landing on the right combination, polishing each piece until it gleamed. There was one particularly excellent piece of glass that he snatched from a landship. He was never caught. If it was ever found, he would have surely been killed.

He gives the outer lens of the spyglass a wipe with the chamois in his pocket, clearing off the damp. He positions his face against the eyepiece and waits.

The Sparrow approaches from behind. Her feet are silent on the dampening ground. The dogs and the butterfly are waiting for her in the shadows. They will not come until they are called. They hold watch and do not move.

"Are you real?" Jonah asks. He does not pull away from the eyepiece. He keeps his gaze upon the stars.

The Sparrow says nothing. She is right behind him, so close

she can feel the heat from his body, so close she could let her fingers drift in the soft clouds of his breath. So close she could kiss him if she wanted to.

"I think you're real," he says, adjusting the second lens. Tipping the whole of the spyglass slightly upward on its hinged tripod.

"How do you know?" the girl whispers.

Jonah yelps in surprise, and scrambles to his feet. He faces the Sparrow, breathing hard. He opens his mouth. Closes it. Opens it again. He reaches his hand toward her, but thinks better of it, and shoves both hands into the mop of his hair, hanging on tight.

The Sparrow feels her heart in her throat. She smiles. Her body feels more discombobulated than usual. As though each particle is only barely hanging on to the others. As though she may fly apart at any moment. She is hot. She is cold. She shivers all over.

"You're shaking," the boy says. "Are you cold?"

"Yes," she whispers. Her voice wobbles. It is a dry leaf on a windy day. She pinches her face and shakes her head. "No," she corrects herself.

"You are real," the boy says. "Aren't you? You've been real this whole time."

She says nothing. Her skin is heat and light and sweat and goosebumps. Her face is tight with hope.

He stands. Brushes the grass and damp from his knees. There will be no moon tonight. The sky will be so dark it will hurt to look at it. The stars will stab the eye. The girl is beautiful in the fading light. She is the most beautiful thing he has ever seen. Her skin glows orange and pink and damp gray. She is an opal in the gloom. He is dizzy. He wants to touch her but he doesn't.

He has seen her before. He has talked to her before—and she to him. He remembers it now, standing in front of her. He remembers it all. He remembers that each time he sees her, he has a similar flood of remembering—that each meeting vanishes when she vanishes, and unfolds again before him when she returns. That her presence opens his mind like a map. And when she leaves it flutters away, as though snatched by a strong wind.

He knows that the last time he saw her, he nearly kissed her. Nearly.

"Will I forget you this time?" he asks, a sob hiding in his throat. He feels a needle in his heart, and he sees her wince.

Is it the same needle? he wonders. *Is it the same thread, pulling at my heart and her heart?* He does not say it out loud. She takes a step closer.

"I don't know," she says. There is too much breath in her voice. As though she is already fading. He reaches out his hand, palm up. An invitation. She accepts, lays her palm on his, as light and hot as ash. He nearly blisters from the heat of it.

"Are you sick?" he asks.

"I am," she says. "But not for long. Soon I will never be sick again—but I need you to help me."

"What can I do?" His breath comes in quick, short gasps, his soul escaping in sigh after sigh after sigh. He doesn't blink. He doesn't want to miss her for a second. With everything in him, he tries to stitch her in place in his mind.

"Leave a note for your mother. Tell her you'll be back when everything changes. And tell her to cover for you."

The Sparrow waits for a long time in the growing dark. She lays her hand on the homemade spyglass. She knows that Jonah had a brother, two years younger than he, who was taken away by soldiers on the day that she was left on the trash heap. She knows that his family does not talk about the lost boy—worked and squeezed away to nothing by now. Drained. The Sparrow has no idea what happened to the children like her—not *really*—but she has always suspected the worst. Even in her situation, even after her lifelong attempt to suppress the magic welling up inside her, she knows she can't last long. Already, she can feel her body yearning to disassemble, fly apart, scatter across the landscape like mist. It doesn't frighten her, this thought of her own dissolution. She only wants to make it *matter*.

All this magic, pulled up by the comet. It's too much for one person. *Spread it around*, she thinks. *Bless the land and the people on it.*

The minutes tick by. The wind picks up. The stars keep their rigid courses in the dark sky. She crouches down and hangs on to her knees with her jacketed arms.

"Come," she calls, and the dogs and the butterfly come. The dogs take posts on either side of her, while the butterfly alights on her back.

The boy comes too, carrying food in a satchel. He has been well brought up. His parents have taught him to plan for the future, to provide for himself and others. They have raised him to be a good person—and he is. The Sparrow stands. The dogs growl. The boy hands her a bit of homemade bread and honey. She eats it gratefully.

"Where are we going?" he asks. And she knows he will follow her anywhere.

"We are going to meet the Minister," she says with her mouth full. "But we don't have to go far. He will be coming to us."

24. Then.

The day after Marla told him about the baby—not a baby anymore, obviously. She'd been a girl for a while—the Constable put a sign on the door of his office. THE CONSTABLE IS ILL TODAY. PLEASE REFRAIN FROM COMMITTING CRIMES UNTIL TOMORROW.

It was not the first time he used that sign—indeed it was heavily wrinkled and ragged around the edges. Rain-blotched. And oddly effective. Every time he had actually *been* out ill, the town residents who might normally bend toward rule breaking followed the sign to the letter. Bar fights ceased, petty thievery vanished, employee insubordination all but evaporated, and domestic disturbances were blissfully unavailable.

There were times when the Constable put the sign up just to give everyone a break from themselves.

On this day, though, he locked himself in the back room of the Constable's office—the room with no windows and one door and one lock to which he had the only key—and did not come out no matter how hard the egg woman knocked.

He had a jug of Special Occasion Whiskey, one that he received as a gift from his mother the day he was appointed to his position (a bald-faced attempt at brownnosing, the Constable knew, but he appreciated it all the same). He'd never touched it in all those years, but he would do so now.

That baby!

He took out his notes and files—illegal, probably—on the birth of the stillborn magic child, of its mother's eventual unraveling, of its days in the box on his desk, of the sounds (oh, god, that laughing) that came from . . . *somewhere.* He couldn't say where. Indeed he did not want to.

Whiskey, in the end, tastes no better in the dark than in the light, and it certainly is not improved with lack of sleep, or a hot morning mouth, or a belly raging for some kind of food.

He threw that child on the rubbish heap. A baby, for god's sake. And by some miracle . . . He shook his head. He couldn't even *think* it.

The cardboard box haunted his dreams.

The sound of a laughing baby, from that day to this, *any* baby, made him shiver and quake.

And he hated the Minister. *Hated* him.

The egg woman gave him three days to think—or in this case, *drink*—on it before she came in with her tools and her grim silence.

Working quickly, she removed the door from the wall, hoisted up the mostly unconscious Constable onto her shoulders, and heaved him into the back alley where she could wet him efficiently with the cistern hose. He stood there under the back awning, dripping and cold, his nose and eyes running with old rainwater and old regrets and new sorrow. He let out one long, lonely wail, and let it die in his throat. He closed his mouth and shivered in silence.

Marla let the hose fall to the ground. "Are you quite through?" she said.

The Constable nodded.

She offered a curt, grim nod in return. "Very good. Now, if you wouldn't mind putting on dry clothes and following me, there are things that I would like to discuss. And it wouldn't do to have such conversations on government property."

The Constable did as he was told. He made a stop at the shower, cleaned the stink of the last few days off his skin, and slid into clean clothes. He slumped his shoulders and bowed his head and went outside next to the egg woman, and allowed her to lead him.

The junk man and the girl were camped on a small hillock just outside of town. It was one of their favorite spots. Three of the Midges had escaped the coop, opting to follow both junk man and girl for the last several days, and were having the time of their lives hunting for bugs in the grass. The girl sat in the branches of one of the trees, encouraging a nest full of baby birds to crawl onto her dress, as the mama bird looked on indulgently.

The junk man squatted by the fire, roasting fat, greasy sausages on sticks.

"I hope you're hungry, my bird," he called up to the girl in the tree.

"Simon," Marla said sharply. The junk man looked up and nearly fell onto the ground. He pointed an accusatory finger at the egg woman.

"TRAITOR!" he shouted.

"I am no such thing. I have brought us an ally. Sit."

And the girl listened as the three adults discussed her future. They said things like *escape plans* and *protective custody* and *worst-case scenario*. She could hear their worry and their fear. She could hear the echoes of loss.

They spoke of the Minister. Their voices trembled with fear. And hatred.

"He can't have her," the junk man said, his voice dangerous— the rusty edge of an old tin can. "I'd die first."

"Yup," the Constable said, rubbing his face. "She does seem to have that effect. Did when she was a baby too. Or a dead baby. In any case, I pretty much feel the same way. The exact same way. The Minister takes too much. And enough is enough."

The girl listened intently. The mother bird flew away to find food, and the babies had been replaced in the nest. They cried out—not for their mother, but for the junk man's daughter. She frowned.

She didn't understand everything that the adults said. She did not fear as they feared; she did not hate as they hated. But she knew this: She had something inside her. Something special. And a bad man wanted it.

(Or a good man; or a bad man who could change; a human being deserving of love, and *oh! How she loved!* How she loved everyone.)

She looked up at the sky. The sun hovered over the horizon, fat and lurid. A delight of color. And it was for everyone. It shone equally on Minister and junk man, on soldier and egg woman, on dogs and hens and bugs. It could not be claimed by a single individual—it shone for all.

Well, she thought. *What if I did what the sun does? What if the Minister came and the magic was gone? What if I gave it to everyone else instead?*

And, as she drifted to sleep, she dreamed of a wave, swelling up beneath her feet. She smelled foam and wind and salt. Yellow coins. Red flowers. A dead child. A child that lived. A particularly fine hen. And she felt herself lift, bubble, dissolve. She felt the wave cover the world.

And she disappeared.

25. Now.

The Inquisitor, in the end, did not make the customary stop in the baker's shop, and he did not purchase a pie for his wife. (And more's the pity. One slice would have saved his marriage, cured his gout, straightened his back, ended his impotence, ensured his raise, and set his career on a more prosperous track; the apples, after all, came from Marla's farm. They were not to be trifled with.) Despite the dark that night, despite the jittering fear that chokes the town every time someone from the capital comes calling, everyone living along that dark street peeked through drawn curtains and watched that black car as it slid to the Constable's office. They held their breath as it slid away.

The Inquisitor, people whispered. *Here?* They wondered and fussed, but they did not look up. They shut their curtains and counted their children and looked around their houses for anything incriminating.

Not a soul in town slept a wink that night.

And now, the next day, everyone continues to whisper. They

continue to fuss. They confer and collect and collude. A crowd forms in the square. They speak of nothing else. *First the Inquisitor. Now what?*

It's not so much the visit, they think but do not say, *but what comes after.* Soldiers, maybe. Re-Educators. Overseers. There were rumors of labor camps. And family splitting.

There's no concrete proof of that, people whisper. *You're being ridiculous.*

They have heard of whole towns simply wiped from the map in earlier generations. Well. No one can be sure. It's not as though a thing like that would be included in a book.

Inquisitors don't just visit towns for their health. And the Minister's eye doesn't stray on communities by accident.

That thing that no one talks about.

That thing that no one *says*.

Well. Someone blabbed.

But who? Who is the blabbermouth? The mayor? Surely not. Not the Constable, neither. Constable's got everyone's back—that's well known. Maybe the tax collector? Or the orphan matron. Or the junk man.

Yes, the preacher nods. The junk man. That's who told. Must have been.

"Heard it from his own lips," the preacher says. "Junk man told me just before he sold me this here watch. I mean Bible."

He clears his throat, gives his fist a quick shake, and the gold watch in his palm vanishes. In its place is a Bible—dusty, well worn, lovingly thumbed. The preacher smiles. If he decides to shake it again, it will become a glass tumbler of good whiskey, served neat. Beautiful thing. God bless the junk man. Despite the unpleasant aroma, the gentleman knows his business, that's for sure—links the right product to the right customer, always. And this little beauty, thinks the preacher, is the rightest of them all. He licks his lips and grips his Bible tight. *Soon,* he tells himself. Once he has left his insufferable flock for a blessed minute alone. He gazes out at his community with what he hopes is a beatific and forgiving expression. "But the junk man only reports rumors, and does not participate in vice. Remember this, my friends. Let us not judge—"

"Nah," a neighbor interrupts. "The junk man never knows nuthin'. It was the egg woman. The egg woman knew it first. Heard it from her last week, and that's a fact."

"You never did," Marla, the egg woman, says. She had been standing in the shadows, listening. How strange that no one noticed her. *Very strange.* She gives the man a swat on the backside of his head. The man rubs the injury, mutters something that sounds like *didn't see you there,* and stares at the ground. Marla gives him a hard look. (She is also agitated, some notice. She scans the crowd, and beyond the crowd. She searches the sky. She is looking for something.) "I only heard it just now. Just like you." She says it like she means it.

And it's true enough. They all *just know.* That's why they're talking in the first place. But who knew *first?* This is important. Lives might be at stake. And the crowd is divided.

"The schoolteacher," says another neighbor. "Musta been. She has that look on her."

"Or the men at the Soldiers' Home."

"I think it was the undertaker."

"No! The butcher. Pretty sure."

"Or the washerwomen."

"Or the miller."

"Or the miller's shiftless sons."

"The children told me," says another. "It is always the children who know."

"By the way, has anyone seen my son? He left before we woke."

Everyone's children left before dawn. School project, their notes said. Odd. But no matter. There are more important things to be dealt with. Not getting arrested, for starters.

The town murmurs and frets. They practice their excuses and alibis until they know them by heart. They imagine what they will say to the constables, or the soldiers, or the inquisitors. They pick at their teeth and rub at their beards and shoot worried glances at the road.

An unlicensed magician, people whisper. *Here. Of all places.* They shake their heads, carefully layering incredulity into their voices. *Well. My stars.*

Marla, the egg woman, listens to the conversation for as long as she can tolerate. She lives, she knows, in a village of idiots situated at the edge of a nation of morons. There are worse things, of course.

Though, in truth, not many.

She clutches her basket as though it is a raft in a stormy sea.

No one knows for sure, of course, what a magician looks

like—unlicensed or not. Who had met a magician, after all? One that wasn't a baby, that is. The only thing for sure is that magic belongs to the government, which is to say that it is given, freely and forever, to the Beloved Minister, and him alone. The unlicensed practice of magic? Well. There are punishments for that sort of thing.

Harsh punishments.

No one knows what those are, and indeed the idea that anyone could even attempt at magic is a bit of a head-scratcher. It's not like there are any books on the subject. Or stories. Magic is a banned subject, after all.

Clearly, the town decides, they are all blameless. One by one they excuse themselves. One by one they hurry home. They whistle as they lock up their apple-producing bowls and their bottomless liquor bottles and their baby-soothing blankets.

Marla the egg woman sits on the stone edge of the fountain. She presses her basket to her ample bosom, and waits.

By noon, the junk man arrives. He sits next to her. He hesitates, swallows nervously, then lets his bony arm drape across Marla's shoulders. She doesn't shrug him away. Their eyes are red. Their noses are red. Their cheeks are the color of ash.

At mid-afternoon, the Constable sits down as well. He feels he should offer them something. He has nothing to give.

"Where is our child?" the egg woman asks.

"What has she done?" the junk man sighs.

They do not move from that spot. By late afternoon, the first landship arrives. And another. And another. They encircle the town, like a noose.

26. *Now.*

They spend the night together, the Sparrow and Jonah, going from house to house, holding tightly to one another's hands as they run through the town. Rapping on windows. Crying through the locks.

"Come," they say. "Come with us."

And they do come. As young as five, and as old as twenty. They rub the sleep from their eyes, and throw homemade woolens over their nightclothes. They tramp silently into the dewy starlight.

"Okay," they say. "We'll come. We'll follow you anywhere."

They can see the Sparrow. They can't remember *not* seeing her. And they love her. And she loves them. *So much.*

The butterfly clings to the Sparrow's back, making her look as though she has luminescent wings—which is helpful for spotting her in the dark. The dogs lope along the sides of the growing crowd, herding the stragglers back to the group.

"This way," the Sparrow calls. "To the rubbish heap. It's where things start."

None of the children have ever been to the rubbish heap—indeed, they've been warned away from it. Rumors insist that it is haunted by ghosts. And if not ghosts, the junk man, who is just as bad. The way he talks to himself. The way he has conversations with people who are not there.

"Trust me," the Sparrow says. And they do.

Jonah refuses to let go of her hand, even though his hand has begun to ooze. His blisters now have blisters. He won't be able to use that hand for a month. But it's worth it. He will hang on to the girl with the butterfly wings until he cannot.

The Sparrow is barely there. She can feel each cell, each molecule, each electron cloud—the bonds between every speck begin to shiver and moan. She is a thing in flux. Not particle, not wave. Something else.

"The Boro comet," she tells the children, "does not cause the magic. I was born under the comet's influence, but it is not the comet that made me what I am. The comet *draws*. It doesn't *make*. There is an ocean underground—an ocean that swirls and swells. There is a tsunami under our feet, and we are going to let it loose. Let it cover the world."

"But the Minister—"

"If we are all blessed, then we are all empowered. If we are all enhanced, then we are all protected. And if the magic is diluted, then there will be nothing for the Minister to mine."

"How will it happen?"

"It is already happening. You feel it, don't you?"

And they do. The buzz in their anklebones. The crackle in the air. The slightly wobbly feeling, as though the ground under their feet was about to give way.

"Hold hands," the Sparrow says. "The first wave is about to hit."

27. Now.

Soldiers flank the landships and move in procession into the town, marching by twos along the West Road, their faces hidden behind the perpetual grins of their metal masks, the required iron rings welded around their throats.

Once a soldier, always a soldier, whisper the townspeople as they pass. *Poor things.*

The soldiers' boots are polished to a high gleam. Each smart stride leaves the smile of their heels pressed into the ooze of the road. Their knees snap; their wool-clad thighs whip forward; their electric eyes do not drift to the right or the left, and they betray no feeling or thought.

The junk man hails them as they march by.

"Welcome misters," he says with a toothless grin. The egg woman elbows him in the ribs. Her hair stands on end. Her eyelashes have begun to singe. There is something coming. It is underground. It is in the air. It is all around them.

28. Now.

The children head into town at a run. They are sun and water and wave. Kinetic energy. They are comet and star and nebula. The vacuum of space. The multilayered folds of time. They are all these things at once.

Frogs appear in their pockets. Birds appear overhead. The children have cats' ears or lizards' tails or wings. They are giants, then elves, then nothing at all. Another wave hits. They change again.

The butterfly clings to the Sparrow's back, lifting her above the crowd. Jonah runs below her, keeping the girl in view. His hand is burned. It will scar. He does not care.

The Sparrow sees the landships surrounding the town. She sees the soldiers crowding the streets. She laughs.

"That's not a landship," she says. The children below her agree.

"It's a bunny," one of the smaller children says. And indeed, the landship *is* a bunny. It was always a bunny. It has a bow around its neck. "And that one is a cow," another child says, pointing at the next landship.

"And that one is an ice-cream cart."

"And that one is my mom."

As landship after landship transforms, their occupants go tumbling out onto the ground. Soldiers. They are flabbergasted.

The Sparrow blows a kiss at a soldier. His mask transforms into a butterfly and flutters away. His eyes flood with tears. He falls to his knees.

"An angel," he cries, as another soldier is freed.

"A god," cries the next.

The soldiers stumble and scatter. They blink their flesh eyes again and again, seeing as a baby sees.

The children don't stop. They weave through the astonished soldiers and speed past the abandoned landships. They run faster.

"The fountain!" the Sparrow calls. "Run to the fountain!"

The Minister is waiting for them. His personal landship has parked in the center of the square, which is deserted, except for a bone-thin man and a boulder-thick woman and a man in a constable's uniform, sitting side by side by side on the fountain wall.

The Minister looks down. The three stare blankly back.

Imbeciles, he thinks. *They must be imbeciles.*

He can feel the magic in the air. He can taste it on his tongue. He thinks of his tower—his beautiful tower. He thinks of the Boro comet, due to come in a decade. What's a decade to a man so enhanced? It's like waiting for afternoon tea! He imagines grasping the comet in his hands. He imagines devouring its magic, crunching it between his molars. He imagines becoming sated, at last.

He thinks of his mother's face. That scar curving down her cheek. He thinks of her polished boots, marching away. Magic can bring her back. He is sure of it. If only he can catch that comet. Just as she told him to, all those years ago.

He hears the sound of small feet. He hears the voices of children. He feels their breathing and their energy and their joy.

Red flowers, he thinks. *Red, red, red, red.*

The Minister presses his hands to his mouth. He falls to his knees.

He wishes he had earplugs to silence his own screams.

29. Now.

The Sparrow sees the Minister on the deck of a landship. Weeping like a child. He shivers and shakes. The Minister rests his head on his knees. He calls for his mother.

"Oh," she says, her voice echoing strangely off every surface of the town. She is a chorus, a flock of sparrows, flying away. "You poor, poor man."

The Minister looks up. He is so afraid. Still he stands. Still he tries to look the part.

"My wayward magician," he calls out. His voice squeaks. He is both enraged and embarrassed. "At last."

The Sparrow floats above him. The butterfly flutters nearby— she doesn't need it anymore. The children crowd into the square.

They are a chattering mass, surrounding the landship and the fountain. They climb trees and balance on signs and climb on top of carts.

The Sparrow glances down at the junk man and the egg woman, still sitting on the edge of the fountain.

"My baby!" the junk man says.

"My baby," the egg woman whispers.

And it's true. She is their child. The both of them. The Constable is her grandfather. Of course he is. How sorry she will be to leave them. Already, she is not solid. She is a storm cloud. An electric shock. She will strike, and then she will dissipate.

"I have come to give you a present," the Sparrow says.

"I am here to receive it," the Minister seethes. His voice is syrup. It is oil. It leaves a slick on the skin that does not wash off.

There is another wave coming. The largest yet. The Sparrow is unstable. She could blow at any minute. She turns to her mother and her father and her grandfather.

"I love you," she says. "I love you, I love you, I love you. Don't forget me."

The wave surges under the junk heap (strange new animals made of old boots and broken glass and springs scatter into the forest), under the munitions factory (each bullet becomes a blossom, each firearm a shovel, each chemical a love note to the brokenhearted), under the school (the chalk grows arms and legs, the switch sprouts wings, each desk becomes a hammock, and flowers spring from the floor). The Sparrow lands before the Minister. She holds out her hand. He lays his own upon it, palm to palm. It burns. He winces.

"Are you sick?"

"Yes," she says. "But not for long."

The wave arrives. It surges under the fountain and pours out the top. It submerges the town, the farms, the forests and the road. The neighboring provinces. The capital. The magic pours and pours and pours.

"What is this?" the Minister whispers.

"An act of love," the Sparrow whispers back. And she kisses him on the mouth.

There is heat. There is light. There is a crack in the world. There is the sound of something exploding—or something coming together. The Minister cannot tell.

The Minister sees his mother. The Minister sees stars. The Minister sees the Boro comet, hanging like a jewel around his own neck. He wraps his fingers around it. He traces his finger along the scar on his mother's face, like a meteor streaking across the sky.

"I knew it," he said.

And then there is only darkness.

And the Minister is gone.

30. Now.

There are no curtains on the window, at the junk man's request, and as the sun invades his face first thing in the morning, his first thought is his missing cart. Indeed, every single morning for the last three months, the whereabouts and well-being of his cart were his daily first thought—best, he thought, to start with the small losses. Otherwise he might never get off the couch.

(The fact of his seemingly permanent place on the couch is a new development. He is inside, even. Still, after years sleeping out of doors, there are a few things he has insisted upon. The lack of curtains, for one. And at least one open window.)

He sits up, the memory of the cart's delightful squeaking wheels echoing in his ears. He hangs on to the sound, like a touch-stone. There are reports that, due to the whimsical and chaotic nature of the magic still leaking back into the land, the cart has, apparently, grown a stag's head, and has been seen in the forest, happily munching the bark off a young maple tree. The junk man isn't sure how he feels about this. He is fairly certain that the cart itself is made from maple. Wouldn't that be cannibalism? He isn't sure, but he is worried about his cart's current moral path.

He hasn't had a drink since the wave. Not a drop. He is suddenly very worried about moral paths.

He sees to the farm while Marla is indisposed. She hasn't gotten out of bed since . . .

People called it *the Blessing*. And maybe it was. The soldiers were freed, after all. The Minister disappeared in a flash of light. And the strange things that had been leaking from the girl all those years. Well, they are everywhere now. The world is filled with sparrows. He grimaces just thinking about it. He swallows acid into his gut.

My Sparrow, my Sparrow, my Sparrow, he thinks as he pulls on his pants and slides his feet into almost new boots. Each syllable follows a heartbeat. *My Sparrow.* Each heartbeat is an elegy.

He goes into the yard to feed chickens. The red plumes, the purple bantams, the snow-white silkies. And of course, the legions of Midges, outnumbering the rest. The Midges take the longest—primarily, because there are so many, but also because they have been refusing to eat. They miss the girl. The junk man croons and cajoles, and finally persuades each Midge to eat. They do so begrudgingly. They remember how the girl loved him. They are doing it for the Sparrow. Everyone misses the girl. Even those who never laid eyes on her in their lives. They weep and mourn and rend their hair. They are desolate.

By the time the junk man goes inside, his feed bucket is empty and his egg basket is quite full. He has also gathered tomatoes and herbs and a dark purple pepper. He whips the eggs, fries the vegetables, and makes an omelet. He has never made an omelet. He has never even had one. He has never known the word *omelet* until this moment. But there it is—fluffy and delicate and perfect. A delight to the tongue.

So many things he can do now. He tells himself it is because he has given up the bottle. He knows it is because of the wave.

"Here," he says, entering Marla's room and throwing open the curtains. "Eat." He sets the tray on the bedside table. He even included a vase of flowers.

"Go away," the egg woman says. "I hate you."

"I know," the junk man says. "But I will not go away. You're all I have left. And I love you. Hell, I've loved you for most of my life."

He rests his hand on hers. They do not move. They stay that way, their grief pressing on their chests. Very slowly, she allows her fingers to interlace with his. Very slowly, she hooks him close, and hangs on tight.

31. Then.

The night Marla brought the Constable to their camp, the Sparrow woke up while everyone else was still asleep. The fire was low. The junk man had laid out blankets for the egg woman and the Constable and himself, and they curved toward its fading heat.

The Sparrow stared at the fire for a long time, until the logs blazed and a pile of glowing coals piled in the center. She watched as the bodies of the adults unraveled a bit, and relaxed. They would sleep longer if they were warm. She climbed out of her tree and ran down the darkened trail.

The Tice house slept hard in the dark. Though the Vox's harsh rattle woke other families, the Tices chose to keep their pillows unpatriotically over their ears. They slept through it. They didn't even stir.

"REMEMBER CITIZENS!" the Vox concluded as the Sparrow slid open the window. "NO ACT OF LOVE FOR OUR BELOVED MINISTER IS TOO SMALL. HE LOVES YOU. HE LOVES EVERY ONE OF YOU. WHAT WILL YOU DO TO SHOW YOUR LOVE TO OUR DEAR LEADER?"

The Sparrow stood in the living room. What *would* she do? She had an idea. She imagined the wave. She imagined it moving through her, moving through whatever she touched. *He loves magic*, she thought. *He loves it so much. And he could be a part of it forever. Dissolved. Unified. A blessing.*

He would never have enough. Not the way he was going after it. This was the only way to make him happy.

She tiptoed up the stairs, and climbed into Jonah Tice's bed.

"Wake up!" she said, cuddling close.

He smiled.

"It's you."

"It's me."

"I remember you. And then you go away. And then I don't remember you. How do you do that?"

"I don't know." The thought of it made her incredibly sad.

"I'm glad you're here now," he said. And he held her hand.

"Do you have a pocketknife?

He did. The Sparrow unwound one of her braids. She pulled out a lock of hair and cut it with the knife, tying it into a tight bow and fitting it inside a locket that she had found on the rubbish heap. She put it around Jonah's neck and secured the clasp.

"Isn't this for a girl?" he asked.

"No. It's for me to give to you, and for you to keep. One day, I will disappear. Either you will remember me, or you won't."

"I'll remember you."

"Sometimes you don't."

Jonah hung his head. It was true. And it shamed him. He imagined a needle and thread, stitching the memory of her into his soul. He felt himself bleed. He gripped the pendant. "I'll never take it off. Never."

"See that you don't. When I disappear, throw the locket into the fountain."

"And then what?"

"Maybe I'll come back. Or maybe you'll remember me, and that will be enough."

"That's not enough."

"It's enough for me. Promise. Promise you will."

"Don't go."

"Promise."

He listened to the snore of his parents, the song of crickets, the lonely cry of an owl in the dark. He hugged the Sparrow, who hugged him back.

"I promise."

They fell asleep with their arms wrapped around one another, hanging on for dear life.

When Jonah woke, the Sparrow was gone. He didn't remember her at all.

32. Now.

Jonah doesn't keep his promise at first. When the wave came, the blast from its magic sent him flying backward. He hit a streetlamp, cracking his skull. The egg woman carried him in her arms to the doctor, who wasn't sure he would make it.

And indeed, he didn't want to make it. He watched the Sparrow disappear in a burst of light. There was nothing left of her. His heart would never heal.

As it turned out, while his heart, indeed, did not heal, his skull and his brain *did*. And when he woke, his pendant was gone.

Gone.

No one remembered seeing it.

His mother gathered him home to finish his recuperation. He refused to go out. He refused to eat. He stayed indoors for months, drawing pictures of the night sky and throwing them into the fire to be burned.

Six months after the wave washed over them, Jonah wakes in the middle of the night. He hears a voice calling his name. He tiptoes downstairs, and sees that the bowl of flowers in the center of the hand-planked table is gone. In its place is a locket. His locket.

He opens it up and sees the knot of hair. He brings it to his lips. It gives him an electric shock. Grabbing his coat and slipping on his boots, he runs into the night.

There is no moon, and the stars are sharp and cold, each one a bright pin holding up the sky. Their beauty begins to break his heart.

No, he thinks, *it is already broken.*

He presses the knot of hair against his sternum. Unaccountably, his heart feels more whole than it ever has. He feels as though he is floating. (And who knows? He may well be. The world is changing, after all.)

The town sleeps. No one is out. No one but Jonah.

There is a statue of the Sparrow next to the fountain. She is holding a Most Remarkable Hen. There is a butterfly on her back. Her hair billows behind her like a storm. Red flowers grow at her feet. It is the first time he has seen it, and he nearly collapses in grief. He hardly knew her. He loves her anyway.

Throw it in the fountain. That's what she said.

And then what? is what he asked.

He doesn't stop to wonder now. He throws the locket and the

knot of hair into the fountain—a great, wild hope surging in his chest, like a wave.

"I remember you," he whispers. "I remember and remember and remember. Now and forever, I remember you."

He closes his eyes and waits.

Acknowledgments

Putting together a short story collection is a strange task. It is dizzying, frankly, to go back to fiction that has long since gone out into the world. It requires a writer to think backward and sideways and inside out all at once, holding each moment of story creation and execution like beads unleashed from their string, rolling each one over and under in the hand, trying to be both inside and outside at the same time. I feel that I have become, as Vonnegut would say, *unstuck in time.*

Except, no. That's not really it.

It feels, more, I think, a little like excavation, a little like exploration, and a little like the myriad of tasks set to the infinite number of women who came before me—saving, sorting, arranging; dusting off, polishing up, finding the shine that once was lost; gathering, protecting, clucking, preening and finally tucking everything up and herding it to bed.

I started my career as a short story writer, and will probably continue being one, despite the novels. Or maybe because of the novels. The short story requires an entirely different set of muscles to build, and uses an entirely different part of the voice. They are, hands down, far more challenging to write than a novel, which is why it's important that we write them. And read them. For those of you who are reading these words right now, it means that you have taken the time to read some, or maybe one, or maybe even all of the stories collected in this volume. And for that I thank you.

A couple more thanks are in order, though, if you wouldn't mind indulging me:

First and foremost, I need to thank both Ann VanderMeer and Jeff VanderMeer—whose giant intellects and brave spirits have lit every corner of our beloved genre. They bought the second story I ever sold and were the first stalwart champions and supporters of my work. They remain, and they will always be, a bright inspiration for my career. It would have been harder, way back then, for me to continue the heartbreaking process of creating and submitting work without their support, and I am not entirely certain that I would have. Ann and Jeff, you guys are amazing. I am grateful forever.

Also, I'd like to thank Sean Wallace, Neil Clarke, Matthew Kressel, Pete and Nicky Crowther, John Joseph Adams, Beth Wodzinski, and Mike Allen—generous and tireless and brave editors, all. There is a special place in heaven for the folks who edit short fiction, and there's an even specialer place for those who edit short fiction of a Speculative nature. O Captains, my Captains, I salute all of you, and am happy to follow wherever you may lead.

I especially need to thank Genevieve Valentine for her careful and thorough reading and analysis of *The Unlicensed Magician*, as well as "The Insect and the Astronomer: A Love Story." That she is a brilliant writer is, of course, commonly known, but perhaps you do not know that, as a reader, she is perspicacious of mind and capacious of heart. And right about everything. Thank you, Genevieve. Those pieces are better because of you.

Also in need of thanks are the following women: Tracey Baptiste, Anne Ursu, Laura Ruby, Linda Urban, Laurel Snyder, Martha Brockenbrough, Olugbemisola Rhuday-Perkovich, and Kate Messner, for their keen wit, their sharp tongues, their boundless spirits, and their muscular support. Never underestimate the power and capacity of women to support women. Especially women writers. You ladies are my heart's dear darlings.

And of course I have to thank Steven Malk, my extraordinary agent, who responded to my horrifyingly timid email saying that *maybe* I might have a collection and *probably* no one will want to read it so *maybe we should just forget the whole thing* with his usual deep reading, incisive comments, and grand plans. I'm so lucky to have him in my corner.

And lastly, but dearest to my soul, is Elise Howard, who sees inside the story that I thought had died and finds its hidden, beating heart, and who knows my work better than I do myself. It is my dearest wish that every writer can have an editor with that much intelligence, analysis, wisdom, wit, and kindness. I'm awestruck to have her in my life.

It should be noted that I am, always and forever, in a state of awe and gratitude for the fact that there are readers in the world. There is, at its center, something immutably miraculous about the substance and process of reading stories. We read because we hunger to know, to empathize, to feel, to connect, to laugh, to fear, to wonder, and to become, with each page, more than ourselves. To become creatures with souls. We read because it allows us, through force of mind, to hold hands, touch lives, speak as another speaks, listen as another listens, and feel as another feels. We read because we wish to journey forth together. There is, despite everything, a place for empathy and compassion and rumination, and just knowing that fact, for me, is an occasion for joy. That we still, in this frenetic and bombastic and self-centered age, have legions of people who can and do return to the quietness of the page, opening their minds and hearts, again and again, to the wild world and the stuff of life, pinned into scenes and characters and sharp images and pretty sentences—*well*. It sure feels like a miracle, doesn't it? I thank you, readers, and I salute you. With an open heart and a curious mind, I, too, return to the page. Let us hold hands and journey forth.

BRUCE SILCOX

Kelly Barnhill lives in Minnesota with her husband and three children. She is the author of four novels, most recently *The Witch's Boy* and *The Girl Who Drank the Moon*, winner of the 2017 John Newbery Medal. She is also the winner of the World Fantasy Award and has been a finalist for the Minnesota Book Award, a Nebula Award, and the PEN/USA literary prize. Visit her online at kellybarnhill.com or on Twitter: @kellybarnhill.